AN INCONVENIENT PLAN

KYLIE GILMORE

An Inconvenient Plan: © 2018 by Kylie Gilmore

Cover design by Sweet 'N Spicy Designs

Published by: Extra Fancy Books

ISBN-13: 978-1-942238-43-0

These two really needed each other…

1

───────

The Night That Went Wrong...

Josh Campbell drove an oddly quiet Hailey Adams to his apartment, the tension thick in the air. So, okay, maybe there'd been some bad blood between them over the years, but it was mostly in good fun. At least that was how he'd seen it. But tonight at Garner's Sports Bar & Grill, Hailey had been shaken by the news that their parents—his dad and her mom—were shacking up after only five weeks of dating. He'd never seen his dad in love before, but it was written all over his goofy lovesick face. Hailey's mom, Brandy, had the exact same dopey expression, so they were a good match.

In any case, he'd been enjoying his usual sparring with Hailey when she blew up at him and then got all teary. Her friends had made it clear that he'd hurt her feelings and needed to make things right. It was ladies' night and he'd been way outnumbered. But it wasn't just that. Now that their parents were serious about each other, he figured he should be the bigger person and apologize. Not like she was a complete innocent in all their sparring. Whatever. He'd apologized and offered to right the wrong between them—the wrong that had started it all—him keeping her money for his work as her paid escort. He never should've taken her money and he knew it. Part of their twisted history. Now she was going back to his place to get the money with all the enthusiasm of a prisoner on death row.

Yup, Saint Josh here, taking the high road with Hailey for the sake of their families. If he and Hailey kept fighting, it might cause a rift between their parents. His dad hadn't had a serious relationship since Josh's beauty-queen mom walked out on him and their six kids more than twenty years ago. No visits, no phone calls, not even a card. His dad deserved this happiness with Brandy.

The Josh-Hailey feud must die.

Their one-upmanship had gotten a little out of hand. He took full responsibility for his part in it—calling her princess for her snooty ways, slipping a ghost pepper into her nachos that probably torched her taste buds for a week, refusing to serve her favorite mojito drink for months at a time, tweaking her nose at every opportunity. She was so easy to rile up that he found it impossible to resist.

Hailey's part in their feud had been much worse than his. First off, she'd started a rumor that he was impotent that had tanked his sex life and led to a lot of sympathy from the women who came into the bar. And then she'd "fixed" that terrible rumor by implying the real issue was a tiny dick. Devious brilliant woman knew just where to strike. No guy could prove himself without whipping it out. She was a worthy opponent, he'd give her that.

He parked in front of the old Victorian in Clover Park he called home, at least the first-floor apartment on the right. Hailey stayed frozen in place in the passenger seat of his Miata convertible, staring straight ahead. He got out, walked around, and opened the passenger-side door for her. His dad had drilled gentleman manners into him. Most women were ridiculously grateful for his manners like they were starved for a kind gesture from the opposite sex. He liked being the guy who showed them not all men were scum.

Hailey got out without a word, and he shut the door behind her. She glanced sideways at him like maybe she was nervous. No big deal, just a simple exchange. Sure, he could've brought the stupid shoebox of money to her, but it was the principle of the thing. If she was going to renege on their original agreement, then she could go to his place and get it. Which he'd told her many times, admittedly just to see her blow up at the idea of being alone with him at his place. She hilariously called his place a "den of sin." Even better, she called him beast or cad or, his personal favorite, scoundrel. Her old-fashioned turn of phrase slayed him.

He walked ahead of her to the front door of the house, unlocked it, and held it open. She took her time catching up to him. Once she was in the front foyer, he unlocked his apartment door and held it for her. She cautiously stepped inside, looking all around. Maybe she was looking for the whips and chains in his so-called den of sin. The beige sofa and worn wooden coffee table were probably a shock.

She removed her white wool coat, setting it over the end of the sofa. She wore a blue dress that clung to every perfect tempting curve. Add in her long silky strawberry blond hair, pale blue eyes, and flawless skin and it was easy to see why she'd won so many beauty-queen pageants. He reminded himself of every reason why he shouldn't be with her—they fought nonstop, their parents, his aversion to beauty queens —and turned from temptation. Not only was his crap mom a beauty queen, so was his ex. No more beauty queens for him.

He headed toward his bedroom, where he'd stashed the shoebox in the back of the closet. She followed closely behind, her floral scent strong, her heels clicking on the hardwood floor, her quickened breath audible. He wanted to tell her to calm the fuck down because he wasn't going to do anything to her, but he knew part of his irritation was that he got jumpy with someone being close behind him. Leftover trauma from his old life as a paratrooper in the army, dropped from a plane into enemy territory, often in the dead of night, engaging in hand-to-hand combat.

He recognized the tension for what it was, reminded himself where he was now and why, and kept going. The PTSD was behind him, mostly, after ten years, but it never really went away. There were always reminders—his quick-trigger reflexes if someone grabbed him from behind, occasional insomnia and nightmares. He liked a bar between him and a crowd, wanted his back to the wall in any situation, and preferred a high five or a cheek slap to touching anywhere else. He'd let a woman in close when it suited him, but even then he preferred to have control. No sudden moves, nothing behind his back, and nobody got hurt.

He sped up, leaving more space between them. He just had to give her the money and get out of here before either of them did something they'd regret. Like have another fight or, the flip side, something physical. He got the feeling she wanted him, but didn't want to want him. He got it because he had the exact same problem. Why else would she keep coming back for more? If he really bugged her that much, she'd completely ignore him. Either way—fight or fuck— would be a disaster. It was time to make amends.

"I know what you want," she said from behind him. Not close, but her flowery scent lingered.

He opened the closet door, ignoring her. *Mission Shoebox, get 'er done.*

"You want a clear affirmation of desire and consent," she said.

He stilled, the hair on the back of his neck standing up. *Alert! Danger, danger.* Her odd phrasing did nothing to take away from her intent for something that absolutely could not happen. *Complete the mission!* He moved quickly, shoving some shit out of the way on the high shelf where he'd stashed the box.

Her voice was breathy and sexy as hell. "You told me that once."

He didn't remember saying that. If he did, he'd been messing with her. He grabbed the shoebox and turned to face her.

Her dress dropped, pooling at her feet. His mouth went dry. Sweet Jesus. She was stunning standing there in a light blue lace bra, matching thong, and black heels. Full breasts, toned body with smooth creamy skin, a sweet curve of hip, the lacey revealing thong. Better than any centerfold. *Kill me now.*

"I desire," she said, "and I consent. So let's do this. We both know that's where this has been heading since day one."

"This wasn't the plan," he croaked. He tore his gaze away, forcing his mind back to the mission—high road, ending the feud. No temptation was worth the inevitable crash and burn, and then they'd be stuck together forever because of their love-goggled parents.

He met her eyes, desperately trying to focus on her face. "Princess, that's not how this is going to go." He congratulated himself on the gentlemanly move. He was showing great consideration and restraint.

Hailey blinked a few times like she wasn't comprehending.

He waited for her to catch up.

Finally, she said, "You've been flirting with me for years. Wasn't that your version of flirting? Fighting with me? Why else would you be so surprised you hurt my feelings?"

"That wasn't flirting. I was playing with you. When I flirt —" he leaned close to demonstrate, tucking the shoebox under one arm "—it's much more close up."

Her breath warmed his lips. "Like this?"

He gritted his teeth. "Yeah." He snagged her dress off the floor and handed it to her with the shoebox of money. "You should go."

"You're rejecting me?" she asked in a small voice.

He stroked her hair to soothe the rejection, surprised at how soft it was. He'd thought it was hair-sprayed into perfection. "I'm taking the high road for the sake of our family. I just wanted you to come over, get the money, and, you know, bury the hatchet."

She kicked his shin, and he jumped back. "Go to hell!" she hollered and then hurled the shoebox at him.

He threw an arm up before the box could hit his head. The lid popped off on contact, and money flew everywhere— twenties, tens, fives, and singles—a five-hundred-dollar mess. She'd basically emptied her wallet every time he'd showed up for a wedding. All part of her business plan as a wedding planner. His part in the transaction was not so commercial—he couldn't stay away from her. He either needed to be committed for insanity or commit. Holy shit. Was he ready for a commitment? With her? He swallowed hard. No, it couldn't be. He couldn't possibly *want* to get further entangled with the most high-maintenance difficult woman on the planet. Doomed to fail, he reminded himself. Glued together forever by family. Hailey the beauty queen was off-limits.

She stepped into her dress and pulled it up in jerky motions.

"Hailey—"

"No, call me princess. Make sure you really sneer." Her luscious breasts disappeared from view as she finished getting the sleeveless dress in place, reached back, and worked at the zipper. "I'll call you what you really are—a jackass!" That was much worse than her usual cad, beast, or scoundrel.

She marched to the front door.

He followed. Her dress was only halfway zipped up she was in such a hurry. "Come on. I'm trying to do the right thing." She grabbed the doorknob, and he caught up to her, snagging her by the hips. "Hold up."

She stiffened. "What?"

"Zipper." He pushed her long hair over one satiny soft shoulder, barely resisting sinking his teeth into the exposed skin along the nape of her neck. *No, no, no.* He did the zipper for her. He really should be named a saint for this, except he could never earn sainthood because he did it slowly, greedily taking her in. The curve of her ass, the dip in her lower back, the straight line of her spine, all that skin. Finally he stopped torturing himself, finishing the zipper between her shoulder blades. Definitely Saint Josh here.

She turned. Her pale blue eyes reflected desire, anger, and hurt, all wrapped up together.

His voice came out gruff. "New start tomorrow. Clean slate."

She lifted her chin in her usual haughty way. He

couldn't work up much ire with the memory of her near-naked body burned into his brain. "Maybe I don't want a new start."

"Then I'll have to try extra hard to convince you. We're probably going to be family soon."

She whirled, raced out of the apartment, and slammed the door behind her.

He rubbed the back of his neck, turned, and spotted her coat hanging over the sofa. He snagged it and went out the door, but she was already gone. Geez, she moved fast.

He caught up with her marching down the sidewalk, huddled against the cold. It was the middle of February in Connecticut, dead of winter. "You forgot your coat."

She took it and put it on, never breaking stride. "Thank you."

He kept up. "You're just going to walk back to Garner's? It's a good twenty-minute walk in the cold. I'll drive you."

"No."

"Come on. You're being stubborn to your own detriment."

She stopped suddenly, surprising him. "Has it occurred to you that I don't want to spend even one more minute with you? My pride is in tatters, and I don't want to hear one more stupid thing out of your mouth."

"Would it help if I offered my desire and consent too?" Not that he'd act on it. He was just trying to restore her tattered pride. *Tattered.* Another old-fashioned word that would've made him laugh if it weren't for the grim truth that she'd rather walk home in the bitter cold than drive in a car with him. FUBAR. Mission fail.

She jabbed a finger in his chest. "This is exactly why I don't want to talk to you. You think it's all a game, that I have no feelings whatsoever."

"I don't think that. I was trying to give you back your pride."

"Too late."

"I'm getting my car. I'm driving you."

"Do whatever you want. It's no concern of mine."

He jogged back, got the car, and drove alongside her. "I'll

pay you five hundred dollars to get in this car." That was the shoebox money.

She stopped walking.

He stopped the car.

She walked over to the passenger door and kicked it. "Hey!" he said at the same time as she said "Ouch!"

"Stop beating up my car and get in!" he barked.

She kept walking, limping a little, chin raised. He wanted to grab her and shove her in the car, but he knew she'd fight him tooth and claw. Damn, this woman was a lot of work. She drove him bat-shit crazy, and he was only going to see more of her now that their parents were living together. FUBAR and NWGBFU! (Fucked Up Beyond All Recognition and Now We're Gonna Be Family, Ugh!). Why had he thought it would be an easy thing to right the wrong? Nothing with this woman was easy.

Her limp was more pronounced now, but she never slowed her pace. He had to admire her gumption. She was a trooper with a real fighting spirit, though not a rational one.

"Did you break your toe?" he asked, driving at a snail's pace.

"No."

"What can I say?"

She stared straight ahead. "Nothing."

"I'm sorry."

She held up a palm like *shut it*.

"Hailey, come on."

"Good day, sir!" She sped up.

He bit back a laugh. Swear to God, where did she get this stuff from? He followed her all the way back to her place, an old colonial in Clover Park, much closer to Garner's. He'd passed the old house before, but never knew she lived there. Despite all their fighting, usually at Garner's, the bar he worked at and managed, he didn't actually know her that well. What he did know about her was through his sister, Mad, who was close with Hailey. He watched her go around to the back of the house, probably to get in through a back entrance.

He drove off, parked in the lot behind Garner's, and then just sat there for a few minutes, trying to come up with a game plan for when he walked back into ladies' night and all of Hailey's friends saw him alone. There would be questions. They'd left together and everyone knew it was to settle their dispute over the money. He finally decided to keep his mouth shut. He'd let Hailey tell the story any way she wanted to, even if it sounded like he was in the wrong. He wasn't the one who'd stripped down…*don't think about it.*

He went inside and slipped behind the bar. It didn't take long before her friends let him know they were mad at him, even his own sister.

And he still had Hailey's shoebox of money.

He refused to comment on the situation no matter how much her friends harassed him. One thing was clear—he'd been right to resist temptation. The two of them together were a disaster; even when he tried to make up with her they fought. And there were way too many people—family and friends—ready to butt in on their weird contentious relationship.

He'd let her cool off and they'd put this entire thing behind them. Hopefully soon. Otherwise, Hailey as part of his family would haunt him forever.

2

Six weeks later...

Josh had looked death in the eye more than once as a para-trooper, but nothing had prepared him for this—Hailey, a blubbering mess in his office. Her long strawberry blond hair hung in her face, matching her blotchy skin.

It was like her fighting spirit just broke. And in its place were tears and snot. Damn, she was an ugly crier. He'd had to hide her back here in his office at Garner's before she ruined their parents' engagement party.

He offered her a box of tissues. She grabbed one, blew, and then sobbed some more, the crumpled tissues piling up in her lap.

This was not the Hailey he knew. He wasn't even sure why she was crying. He only knew he was the straw that broke the beauty queen's back. He'd been working behind the bar and she'd been about to have a drink when he'd informed her, "I'm best man, so I'll be your wedding escort again." (She was maid of honor for their parents' wedding.)

She'd looked at him for one horrified moment and burst into tears.

He'd never seen her cry before. She was usually so put together, more prone to anger than a breakdown. His sympathy pain was so great he almost wanted to cry along with her, but he couldn't. He'd been dry-eyed since he was eight years old and his mom had walked out the door never to return. In some ways he'd grown up that day. As the oldest with his identical twin, Jake, he took care of his younger siblings. Still did. And now that Hailey would soon be his "little sister," it was his responsibility to take care of her too.

Hailey shook a crumpled tissue in the air. "I don't know what's wrong with me. I can't stop crying. What's wrong with me?"

Damned if he knew, and he knew better than to hazard a guess in her fragile state. He looked into her red swollen pale blue eyes, at a complete loss as to how to comfort her.

She sniffled and more tears leaked out along with sad little sobs. Like a kitten who'd been abandoned in the rain, all scrappy heartbreak.

His shoulders tensed, creeping up toward his ears as if that would block out the sound.

"I don't want anyone to see my eyes like this," she whispered. The engagement party was still going strong, all of their friends and family having a great time without them. Probably wondering what was taking them so long back here too.

She blew her nose again. "I should go back to the party."

They'd gone this round already. Hailey: *I should go back to the party.* Him: *Let's go.* Hailey: *But how can I? My mom will think I'm not happy for her, but I am! Sob!*

Before she could get going again, he said, "How about we take a walk? The cold air will help clear your head. Maybe we could stop and get your money from my place." He really would like to get that off his hands and know that he'd righted the wrong between them.

The crying abruptly stopped. His shoulders eased away from his ears as the fire returned to her eyes.

"Are you nuts?" she exclaimed.

He completely relaxed. Fighting with her was so much better than feeling helpless watching her fall apart. "Must be."

She huffed, all indignant. "Damn right you are. You think I want a repeat of what happened last time?"

He bit back a smile. Not because what had happened last time was so great, but because she was back in fighting form.

She jabbed a finger at him. "Don't you smirk at me, you scoundrel!"

A-a-a-and she was back.

~

Hailey held the cold compresses made from folded paper towels to her eyes. "Thank you."

"No problem."

Josh was being so nice to her, bringing her cold compresses and hiding her embarrassing tears in the privacy of his office, but she couldn't even work up a smile. Normally she could always work up a smile. Her pageant training had taught her that. Something in her broke today. Her mom had found her forever love, all of her friends had found their forever loves, while she, a diehard romantic—a fucking wedding planner for God's sake!—had shit.

Okay, so maybe she'd been too busy creating a strong foundation for her wedding planning business to make any real effort to find a relationship, but she had made *some* effort. She'd been taking notes for years on what made relationships work, through intensive study of her friends, her clients, and romantic movies and books. And she'd ended a friends-with-benefits arrangement and let everyone know she was open to a relationship. What had it gotten her? Zilch.

So humiliating. She loved love, she'd even added the moniker "Love Junkie" to her business card so clients would know just how much she supported them in the ultimate expression of their love, their wedding. Now she couldn't even muster the effort to check her online dating profile. It was like her whole identity had broken. No, it had *died*. All this time she'd thought she was a Love Junkie when she was really a Love Loser. She couldn't see a way forward. All she saw was a lifetime of bearing witness to other people's happy endings. And she was the leader of the Happy Endings Book Club too, a romance book club she'd started as a singles book club. Now she was the only single woman left. Ugh. The painful irony. She should've been the first to find her happy-ever-after.

Her eyes welled again, and she took the cold compresses off to help them dry.

Josh stared at her from across the desk. Her nemesis and soon-to-be "brother." Barf. He'd deeply hurt her feelings on *the night that went horribly wrong*. In the six weeks since that night, she'd figured out a perfectly reasonable explanation as to why it went wrong. She'd guzzled down a cran-vodka that was mostly vodka on an empty stomach at ladies' night right before she went to Josh's apartment. Normally she only sipped at wine. Naturally, the alcohol had made her horny—hello, six-month dry spell—and Josh's apartment had been way too hot, like a hundred degrees in there, giving her the strong urge to feel cool air on her skin. On top of that, in her woozy state, she'd mistaken the tension she felt with Josh as sexual when it was just the usual irritation. Horny plus hot and irritated equaled a wardrobe malfunction. Embarrassing, yes, but perfectly understandable. It could've happened to anyone in similar circumstances. If Josh brought it up again, she'd explain it in exactly that way. Wardrobe malfunction brought on by too much vodka summed it up nicely. Except—

That was a lie.

Despite their twisted history of one-upmanship, despite all their fighting, she and Josh were cut from the same cloth. They both loved a challenge, they both felt passionately about their chosen professions (he'd been saving for years for his dream bar), and they were both steady and strong. That stability was something she'd worked hard to achieve as an adult after her unstable childhood. So there she was back on that fateful night, sitting at the bar with her friends, reeling from the news that her mom and Josh's dad, Joe, were moving in together after only five weeks of dating. Worlds colliding! Her hard-won stability tipped to the anxiety of her childhood with her flaky mom about to ruin everything.

Hailey was sure her mom would ditch Joe, and then the Campbell family would turn on Hailey by association for hurting their dad. Mad Campbell was her best friend, she was close with many of the Campbell brothers, and Joe had always treated her like part of the family. Poor Joe had already had a wife who ditched him and his six kids. Her mom would just reopen that wound and leave everyone furious.

And then there was Josh behind the bar, being his laid-back rock-steady self. In that emotionally charged moment, she'd realized Josh was *exactly* the kind of man she needed in her life. In fact, he might be the only one who truly understood her (since they were similar in the ways that counted), the only one who could give her comfort just by being his strong stable self. For so long she'd had all these pent-up feelings where Josh was concerned. He excited her, aggravated her, entertained her, and, okay, she could admit he turned her on with his sexy confidence that told her she'd be in good hands.

Despite everything, she'd trusted that he'd catch her when she fell into his arms.

Only she'd fallen face-first into utter humiliation. He wasn't even tempted. She was standing there exposed (literally), and he'd turned her down flat.

She'd scrambled to put some distance between them in any way she could. Drawbridge up, battle lines firmly back in place. A drunken wardrobe malfunction was the only way to save face.

"Come on, Hailey, let's get some fresh air. We'll get your money—"

"No." She tried to add a good glare, but her eyes were too swollen to pull it off. At least he'd called her by her real name instead of princess. Probably because he felt sorry for her. She was an ugly crier and rarely gave in to tears, preferring anger, which was motivating, or sheer grit to get through. The last time she'd cried was when she'd ended her friends-with-benefits relationship. The time before that? Way back when she was a kid and found herself homeless for the second time because her single mom didn't pay the rent. The first time she'd been too shocked to cry. Just another example of her mom's flakiness. She'd regularly skipped out on work and gotten fired, which was why they couldn't make rent and ended up homeless twice. Add to that the fact that her mom fell in and out of love easily and no relationship had ever worked out, and it was easy to see why Hailey craved a stable foundation. No one and nothing had ever stuck for her. Even now she kept waiting for her life to fall apart.

"Let's go, princess."

Back to that, are we? "Listen, you cad, I am never, ever stepping foot in your place again." And he knew very well why.

His lips twitched. "Never ever?"

She seethed. He never stopped giving her a hard time. Like she had no feelings at all, like she was his personal entertainment system or something. Poke her here, see the reaction; poke her there, watch her go nuts. If she wasn't such a mess right now, she'd march right out of his office.

Josh leaned forward. "Can you keep a secret?"

She eyed him suspiciously. There were always layers to what he said, subtle innuendoes and digs just waiting to come out. On the other hand, Josh had never shared anything remotely private with her, and she was intrigued. No. He was just trying to reel her in and then *whammo!* Some twisted joke at her expense. She refused to take the bait.

She crossed her arms, feigning indifference.

His voice dropped to a nearly inaudible whisper that had her leaning in.

"What?" Dammit! He'd reeled her in again!

He didn't smirk like she thought he would. Instead he raised his voice a little. "That shoebox of cash has been nothing but trouble. Not just between us. Clarissa and I had a huge fight over it."

Clarissa was his ex-girlfriend, a beautiful bohemian yoga instructor who always seemed to be underfoot. She'd run into the woman absolutely everywhere for a while there. It was hard not to take it personally that Josh happened to get a serious girlfriend just as Hailey announced to the world that she was newly single and open to a relationship. Kind of like he was thumbing his nose at her: *I have what you want and you have nothing.* Not that she'd wanted to be in a relationship with Josh at the time. Back then she'd been sure they'd kill each other. She hadn't seen past the sparring like she did now to the kind of man he was at a deep level. She almost wished she didn't know the real deal with Josh because here he was helping her through a personal crisis in his irritating but strongly supportive way, and she had to fight to keep her walls up for her own self-preservation. She needed to move on with her life. She couldn't keep letting herself get sucked in by Josh. He'd given her a clear message—not interested.

Josh didn't elaborate further over his and Clarissa's fight, just sat there like there was nothing more that needed to be said. She needed details!

She clamped her mouth shut for a good ten seconds before blurting, "Why did you fight over the money?"

Josh shrugged his big muscular shoulders. He was extremely fit like he'd stuck to his soldier-training regimen, an attractive trait both for the hard work it took and the results, which she'd admit to him only with a knife to the throat. "She found the money and thought I was into strip joints or something crazy like that. I told her the truth. It was yours and I planned to give it back one day."

"You did?" She couldn't hide her surprise. Until very recently, she'd thought he'd lord it over her forever. The truth was he'd earned that money fair and square as her paid escort to the many weddings she planned. She couldn't very well show up alone to weddings when she was supposed to be a Love Junkie. Back when they'd made that arrangement, she'd been a little desperate. The guys her age at the time, early twenties, kept flaking on her or showing up really late to the weddings. Josh lived and worked in town and had been very dependable and punctual. It was a business arrangement— she got a wedding escort; he got money toward his dream bar. But after their falling-out, he forfeited all rights to that money. She'd demanded it back. He'd taunted her for years that she'd have to go to his place to get it in a tone that screamed sexual innuendo. Hmm, in hindsight, her naked offering wasn't so out there. He'd been hinting at exactly that if she ever had the nerve to show up at his place. Clearly he'd been messing with her because he didn't even touch her once she was there. The cad.

Josh gave her a look she couldn't interpret, and she was usually excellent at reading people. It was somewhere between *you're an idiot* and offended.

"Yes, I planned on giving the money back," he said in an aggrieved tone like she was supposed to know better. It was both *you're an idiot* and *I'm offended*. She was good at reading people after all. "I never should've taken it in the first place. You needed it to build a stable foundation for your business. Peace of mind, security, and all that."

She sucked in air. She'd been right about him. He truly understood the value of a stable foundation and understood what it meant to her as well.

Josh went on. "After our fight, she was done with me. She even got a new job and moved to a different town." What an extreme reaction. Hailey would never pick up and move over a man.

Well, that explained why she'd stopped running into Clarissa all over town. They broke up over her money? How strange. And delightful. Damn, Josh had turned her into a terribly petty person. Only he brought out this side of her.

She tried to hide the secret enjoyment from her voice. "That was rash of her. She sounds like an idiot."

Josh regarded her seriously. "She made me a better man."

She tensed, irritated with Clarissa all over again with her laid-back, mellow, la-di-da attitude. Nothing would ever get done in the world with that kind of attitude. "I can't believe you broke up over a shoebox." So stupid. What a stupid couple.

"She said I was hanging onto you."

She shot straight up in her seat. "What? That's ridiculous. We were fighting like cats and dogs at the time." Was it true? Had Josh had feelings for her back then? What happened?

Had their fighting gotten so out of hand that they'd squashed any chance they'd had to connect?

He inclined his head. He'd shaved today for the special occasion, his square jaw pronounced. His dark brown hair was rumpled like always, but he wasn't wearing his usual flannel shirt over a T-shirt, faded jeans, and sneakers. He wore a light blue dress shirt, unbuttoned at the collar and rolled up at the sleeves, revealing corded muscular forearms. Dark blue dress pants with a brown leather belt and dark brown leather shoes too. Dressy but still true to his casual self. She tore her gaze away and stared at his desk. He cleaned up nice.

"I told her that," Josh said. "How could I be hanging onto you when we have no history?"

Her head jerked up. "Well, we have gone on some wedding dates."

"Escort service. You paid me. Exhibit A, the shoebox of cash."

"And we did have one boring dinner at that fancy restaurant in the city." Not like he'd asked her out. She was supposed to be having a business dinner with his identical twin, Jake, and Josh had pulled a switcheroo to teach her a lesson. Jerk. She still couldn't figure out what lesson she was supposed to have learned.

"Boring!" he barked. "I thought you lived for that stuff. Limo, posh restaurant, drooling over Jake's yacht."

"You were a boring braggart. And the portions at that restaurant—"

"Were too small."

"Yes." She quieted for a moment, remembering the event two and a half years ago. She and Josh had a long strange history. "And I didn't appreciate that you tricked me with that twin switcheroo to teach me a lesson. All I learned was not to trust you."

He blew out a breath. "It was stupid, I guess. Sorry."

"You don't sound very sorry."

He groaned long and loud like an obnoxious beast.

She huffed daintily. "Obviously we have a history. We've been fighting for years. Still do."

One corner of his mouth curled up in a classic Josh smirk. "More like razzing each other."

She pursed her lips. "I got very worked up."

"Bah. I told you before I was just playing with you."

She sincerely doubted that. There had definitely been some heated words between them in the past. "I took up yoga because of you…briefly." That was before Clarissa the yoga nut breezed into town. Not that Hailey would've spent the money on classes. She'd watched some YouTube videos. Everything she earned was either saved or funneled back into her business. Her goal was always a stable foundation.

Josh's eyes twinkled with good humor. "That sounds rough."

"I couldn't hack it," she admitted. "I couldn't stay still long enough."

"It's boring as hell."

She stared at him, surprised he thought so. She'd heard he'd gotten way into yoga with Clarissa. "It is!"

He smiled, his brown eyes crinkling at the corners. A genuine smile. "Look at us getting along."

She softened toward him. Maybe she should take that shoebox of money off his hands and let bygones be bygones. Then she remembered the last disastrous time she went through this with him six weeks ago and decided to handle it another way.

"You know what, Josh? You keep the money. Put it toward your bar. I don't care about it anymore."

"Yes, you do."

Back to arguing with her! It was always a fight with this man, even when she was trying to be the bigger person. This was exactly why she kept getting sucked in! He pushed all her buttons all the time!

"It's fine," she assured him through gritted teeth. "Really."

He smirked. "You're just afraid to go back to my place."

"I'm not afraid!"

"I admit last time was a complete disaster."

She looked away. "I don't want to talk about it."

"Me either. This time will be different. Keep your dress on and everything will go fine."

Her lungs constricted. Time seemed to stop. The words hung in the air between them *keep your dress on*. His casual comeback cut deep. After her meltdown today, after his stinging rejection while she stood there naked and vulnerable, after she'd started to warm to him again—it was all too much. How dare he bring up that humiliating night like it meant nothing!

She leapt from her seat. "You beast!"

"What'd I say this time?"

3

———

After the exhausting engagement party for her mom and Joe, Hailey was relieved to be back in her office in Ludbury House on Monday. She made some notes on her online calendar and leaned back in her chair. Work was going well. It was the end of March and she had weddings booked solid every weekend from May through August, including her mom's wedding, her friend Carrie's wedding, and her friend Mad's wedding. Carrie's wedding in May was especially important because it would be featured in the national magazine *Bride Special*, along with a feature on Hailey as the wedding planner. It promised to be a huge article with Carrie's wedding documented in full from proposal to planning the wedding to the ceremony and reception. Zach had proposed to Carrie during the get-together Hailey had arranged at Garner's to show the *Bride Special* people how warm and inviting the Clover Park community was for locals and visitors alike. They'd loved it and asked permission to include the proposal in the article.

She fully expected to be booked solid year-round once the article published in the August issue. She'd be able to bring her part-time employee, her friend Ally, on full-time. It would be everything she'd ever dreamed of when she'd created this job for herself in her beloved hometown of Clover Park, minus her own happy-ever-after. Maybe this was how it was meant to be. Maybe she needed to save all her love and energy for other people's happy endings. Clearly, she was good at it. She'd helped many couples get together among her friends and helped several engaged couples stick together during the sometimes stressful wedding planning process.

Her fur baby, Rose, a white terrier-Chihuahua mix, grumble-barked in her sleep, her little legs pumping in her pink Sherpa-lined bed. Must be one of her chase dreams. Rose had been her comfort ever since her friends gave her the sweet thing three months ago on New Year's Eve. They'd recognized how out of sorts she'd been after saying goodbye to her friends-with-benefits relationship with Liam. Too bad she hadn't been able to bring Rose to last night's engagement party since her mom was allergic. She'd managed to return to the party after her crying jag, where her friends were all sweet concern and support. Her mom hadn't even noticed she'd been crying. She'd thought Hailey's long absence was because she and Josh were doing some wedding planning since they were maid of honor and best man at their parents' wedding.

She sighed. She so dreaded her mom's wedding. She was sure her mom would flake on Joe. The fact that her mom and Joe had gone from dating to engaged so quickly did not inspire confidence.

She clicked over to her email. Ooh! Something from Judith Mayer, the *Bride Special* reporter. She'd been hoping to hear from her soon. The article would come out in a little over four months, and they'd said they'd let her read an advance copy of the feature on her. She quickly read the email and gasped. They'd decided to run her wedding planner feature in the April issue, in print as of today, a copy was in the mail to her, and it had published online a week ago! Carrie's wedding would appear in August as planned. Apparently, a wedding fell through and they'd needed to fill the space in the April issue quickly. She clicked on the link for the article and slapped a hand over her mouth. Omigod, the headline was everything—Queen of the Happy-Ever-After.

The picture of her in a lavender cocktail dress standing on

the front porch of Ludbury House had turned out spectacular. She'd hoped they'd get a lot of the historic mansion in the picture since it was one of the main selling points for brides. Ludbury House was a gorgeous two-and-a-half-story white clapboard mansion with white columns and a wraparound porch. The home and manicured grounds had previously been the summer retreat of a wealthy New York City family back in the late eighteen hundreds. The town of Clover Park owned Ludbury House, and Hailey paid rent for the office space and use of the building for weddings. She also had to share the space occasionally for community events. The town loved that she regularly hired local businesses for the many needs of the weddings she planned. It was a mutually advantageous arrangement, but she dreamed of one day being able to buy the mansion from the town and truly own every part of her business. That would cost upwards of two million, so still just a faraway dream.

She started reading the article, hoping she came across as warm and friendly instead of the bundle of nerves she'd been at the time. So far so good. Judith described Ludbury House in glowing terms and Clover Park as a "quaint New England town centered around Main Street with shops and restaurants." More scenery—Baldwin Park, churches, Victorian homes, modern colonials, etc. They described her as cheerfully incandescent and said all things romantic came naturally to her. Nice!

Whoa, wait. Hold on now. Judith hinted that her romantic side was because of the "palpable love" between her and Josh. She gulped. Hopefully Josh wouldn't see this article. He'd never let her live the love thing down. The truth was, a little over six months ago, she'd asked Josh's brother Logan to join her for part of the interview, playing the part of her devoted boyfriend because she wanted to look like she was part of their close-knit family and not single. Josh had shown up instead, trickster that he was, trying to catch her off guard and then laying it on thick with the reporter. Here we go, a big juicy Josh quote.

Josh: "I come from a large family—four brothers and a

sister—and she's got us all wrapped around her little finger. This is a woman who understands family, community, and how to bring them together. Any couple that looks to her for wedding planning can be assured her heart is invested in their happiness. She's queen of the happy-ever-after."

Heart pounding against her rib cage, she stared at the words, the implications slowly sinking in. He'd given the outstanding headline with his quote, and he actually respected her and her work. At the time she'd thought his smirky smile after everything he said at the interview had meant it was all a game, but reading it now without the smirk, it all sounded so sincere. Did he really mean these things?

She kept reading. More incredibly wonderful Josh quotes described her as "a dynamo building her business from the ground up" and "a smart successful businesswoman." And the best, "Clover Park is lucky to have her." Her throat tightened, her eyes hot.

She hit a quick reply to the reporter, thanking her for the glowing article, and then just sat there, stunned. She should thank Josh. It was Monday afternoon. He was probably at work only a short walk away. He rarely took time off. Neither did she. They were both workaholics in their own way, both working toward a dream. He'd put his dream of owning his own bar on hold to pay his sister, Mad's college tuition. Hailey had only recently learned from Josh's dad that Josh had helped out Mad. Frankly, she'd been shocked to hear it because his billionaire twin, Jake, easily could've afforded it, which she'd said to Josh, and he'd gotten pissed and walked away. Apparently, he had a chip on his shoulder about money since he could've gotten in on the ground floor of his twin's company, but instead chose a less lucrative career path. She could understand that angst. If she had a twin, she'd assume they'd be equally successful. But it was the life Josh chose, so he shouldn't get so bent out of shape about money.

Another email popped into her inbox. Oh, it looked like a potential new client. The email was from phillyabroad. The subject line read Planning an Exclusive Wedding. She clicked on it.

Dear Ms. Adams,

My sister Silvia Rourke has asked (more like begged) me to contact you on her behalf in regards to her upcoming wedding. She read about you in *Bride Special* and insisted she had to have you. She's in her senior year at Yale, hurtling toward final exams, while also out of her mind as a bride-to-be. Obviously I spoil my little sister by indulging her desire to have a "beautifully romantic" stateside wedding with her American fiancé, instead of the planned private legal ceremony. She will have a traditional wedding back home this summer. In any case, if a stateside wedding is to occur, it must be completed before July 1 and it must be done in complete privacy from the press. I will be staying in New York City for a monthlong visit both business and family related. If you're available to meet, please let me know at your earliest convenience.

Regards,
Phillip Rourke,
Prince of Villroy

Ahhh! Hailey jumped from her seat. Was this for real? Her planning a wedding for a princess? Maybe it was a joke. Her friends knew she was a superfan of Prince Phillip. He had dark brown hair on the longish side, sexily rumpled, curling a bit on the ends, piercing aquamarine eyes, stubbled jaw, and a sexy smirk of a smile. His stats were readily available: five feet eleven, age twenty-eight, Norwegian and Irish descent. He was delicious, an A-grade hottie, and frequently photographed doing his prince thing throughout Europe. Villroy was a small island country just off the southwest coast of France, and the pictures she'd seen were mostly stunning scenery—the royal castle at the center, cute white cottages with blue trim, fields of heather, dramatic cliffs, and blue sea.

A Viking tribe known as the Wild Ones originally populated the island. She'd always imagined Phillip was quite the wild stallion.

Double ahhh!!!

Okay, first things first. She texted Mad—the one most likely to pull a prank—and point-blank asked her if she was behind this turn of events. Mad had never heard of Silvia and assured Hailey she'd never mess with her at work. She shivered with excitement and quickly sat at her desk, searching online to see if there really was a Princess Silvia Rourke soon to be married to an American. She didn't keep up with the entire royal family, only the hot one. She sucked in air a moment later. It was true. There was even an official royal announcement! She looked to the ceiling and screamed. Rose startled awake and leapt out of her bed, running in a circle around the room, barking her head off. Probably looking for the intruder. Hailey hurried over and scooped up her little love bug, looking adorable in her spring outfit—a bright yellow bow on a tiny ponytail on top of her head with a matching yellow and white polka-dotted thin sweater.

"It's okay, Rose. I'm just happy." She cuddled her close and stroked behind her ear. Rose quieted, resting her paws on Hailey's shoulders. She danced around with Rose in her arms. Woo. Good thing she didn't have any more client appointments this afternoon. She rushed back to her seat, settling Rose on her lap, and wrote back.

Your Royal Highness,

I would be honored to plan your sister's wedding. I will make time whenever it is convenient for you to meet. Will your sister be joining us? I'm in Clover Park, Connecticut, which is about an hour outside New York City. Just let me know the time and place. Please be assured of my utmost discretion. I previously worked with Claire Jordan and successfully kept the press in the dark for the entirety of her attendance at several mutual friends' weddings.

Sincerely,

Hailey

Claire Jordan was an internationally famous movie star and a good friend of hers. She almost wanted to add a title to her name like Phillip had. Ooh, how about her new title from the article? Hailey Adams, Queen of the Happy-Ever-After. She laughed to herself and left it out. She hit send, stood with Rose in her arms, and did a happy twirl in her office. Rose whimpered, which meant she needed a bathroom break.

She grabbed the leash from her doggie purse, clipped it to Rose's collar, and took her out the back door for some privacy. It suddenly occurred to her she was booked solid this summer for weddings and had no room for a royal wedding. Crap. It wasn't like you could move a wedding after a year or more of planning. No matter. She'd make it work. Maybe she'd use an alternate location for the ceremony and reception, or maybe she'd plan the wedding for a Friday or Sunday night. She did have those nights free, mostly to give her time for prep and cleanup for the usual Saturday and Sunday weddings. She'd temporarily staff up if she had to. How could you say no to this kind of opportunity?

Rose finished her business and attacked a dead leaf. Hailey scooped her up. "Good girl. Back to work."

She headed back to her office. Since no one else was around, she shut the office door and gave Rose free rein to explore the office. She'd hidden small treats inside dog toys in various spots around her office to give Rose a job to do. She changed the spots every morning before she let Rose in from where Hailey tied her leash to a chair in the hallway. All part of their fun routine. Rose got busy sniffing, and Hailey went back to her desk, her mind racing with royal wedding ideas. Time flew by.

Just before she was about to close up shop for the day, she checked her email one last time. Eep! The prince replied! She clicked on it.

. . .

Dear Ms. Adams,

You may dispense with the formal greeting of your highness. That's more my older brother's style. I'm one of many spare heirs to the crown, second in line, which affords me a great deal more freedom than my brother's stuffy duty-filled lifestyle. I will arrive at Ludbury House with my sister on Friday at five p.m. I look forward to meeting you.

Phillip
The Spare

She laughed. He had a sense of humor and sounded very down-to-earth for a prince. Oh, wow, now she really had to go thank Josh. If he hadn't said such nice things about her, calling her Queen of the Happy-Ever-After, none of this would've happened.

She pulled the treat jar from her desk drawer and shook it. Rose came running, sat, and lifted both front paws in her beg position. She fed her a treat. "Good girl. Time for a walk." She put on her tan spring coat and tied the belt. Then she put her pink doggie purse over her shoulder and settled Rose inside.

She practically floated down the sidewalk and across the street to Garner's Sports Bar & Grill. This had turned out to be the most amazing day. And to think it happened the day after she'd hit an all-time low bawling her eyes out at her mom's engagement party. Welp, there was nowhere to go but up when you hit rock bottom like she had. Now she might have an amazing new client. Why, if this went well, maybe she'd plan more weddings for the royal family. According to her brief online search, there were six royal siblings besides the princess, all of them single. How cool would that be?

She shook her head at herself. She never stopped dreaming. This wasn't even a sure thing yet. She opened the front door of Garner's and stepped inside, instantly warming in the familiar space. To the right was the restaurant area with several booths and tables, where a few young families were having dinner. Straight ahead was the long wraparound dark cherrywood bar, which was empty. Josh stood behind it, leaning against the bar and watching the news on one of the TVs perched over the bar.

"Hi, Josh!"

His head swiveled toward her. "You sound cheerful."

"I am." She closed the distance, and Rose set off a warning growl. Rose hated Josh. Hailey had no idea why. Josh had never even touched Rose. Maybe it was because he growled back at Rose. "Settle," she told Rose. And she did. Hailey had gone through an intensive training program with Rose, who was now certified as a therapy dog.

"What's up?" He wore a black T-shirt with ripped jeans that molded to his tall muscular frame. His stubble was back too, a five-o'clock shadow that always made him look a little dangerous, or maybe that was the edge to him hidden under a charming laid-back persona. He was a former soldier, cool and calculating. She'd seen the cool calculation in his eyes the first time they'd met, though as she got to know him over the years, his dark eyes reflected other things too, sometimes sharp intelligence, sometimes a deep soulfulness bordering on sadness, but mostly good humor at her expense.

She pulled out her phone, brought up the article, and showed him. "This."

He took her phone and read the *Bride Special* article, brows drawn together in concentration. Yup, it was all there in black and white. Josh secretly respected her. She wasn't just his personal entertainment system. She was so bowled over by what he'd done, calling her Queen of the Happy-Ever-After, and the subsequent outstanding turn of events, she blurted, "Why didn't you say queen of the happy ending? I did start the Happy Endings Book Club to help single women find their happy endings."

Josh's dark eyes sparked with amusement, and he smirked. "Ah, princess, I hate to be the bearer of bad news, but you do know what a happy ending is, right? You see the double meaning that could maybe leave the wrong impression?"

She tensed. "Only in dirty minds like yours."

"In everyone's mind."

She lifted her chin. "I'm reclaiming it to be a happy thing."

He lifted one corner of his mouth in his smirkiest of smirks. "Sure, it can be real happy."

She huffed. "The joy kind of happy." Rose started growling again.

Josh growled back, and Rose barked ferociously. She shifted away from Josh and soothed Rose, rubbing her cheek against Rose's muzzle. Rose gave her a doggie kiss and settled into her purse for a nap. Hailey took a seat at the bar and carefully tucked Rose by her feet, out of sight of Josh to keep the growling and barking to a minimum. She rarely did that in a crowd at the bar, in case someone accidentally kicked Rose, but the bar area was empty at this time on a Monday.

Josh set her phone on the bar. "I'll ask the editor to run a correction. You can be Queen of the Happy Ending if you want."

She tucked her phone away. "No, it's fine. Just wanted to point that out. Your way is okay too."

"Thanks, that's big of you."

"I actually thought the double entendre of happy ending was more clear than happy ever after."

Josh smiled widely, a genuine smile that lit up his handsome face. *No. You are immune. He respects you, but he does not reciprocate. Boundaries.* "So you saw the double meaning this whole time?"

She tossed her hair over her shoulder. "Of course. But isn't it what everyone wants? The great sex and the forever love?"

He inclined his head. "Some people do."

"Everyone."

He crossed his arms, his black T-shirt pulling tight across wide shoulders and muscular biceps. "Nope."

"Definitely." She tore her gaze away from his bicep, forced her mind from his hot edginess. Would he be aggressive in the bedroom like her favorite erotic romance series, the Fierce trilogy? She'd yet to experience that. *Listen to what he's saying, an extremely unromantic thing. Stop fooling yourself.* She was a warm-and-fuzzy romantic (usually), and he was a cold realist. They weren't compatible, just like she'd thought before.

He lifted one shoulder in a careless shrug that indicated he didn't agree that everyone wanted great sex and the forever love, which was a completely *guy* way of saying he only wanted the sex.

She tensed, irritated beyond reason with his careless shrug. Romance was important. It was the basis of her career, her lifestyle, and all of her friends' happy endings. Maybe he should take note that all of his brothers, his sister, and even his dad had found their loves! Maybe if he wasn't so down on romance, he would find love too. Of course, there was Clarissa. He must've done something right for the woman to stick around for two months.

Take a breath. Josh always seemed to push her buttons. She never even knew she had buttons until he started poking at her.

He placed his palms on the bar and leaned into her personal space, his voice dropping to a husky whisper, "Some people might just want the sex."

A hot throb between her legs alarmed her. It was exactly what she'd suspected he'd say, but the way he said *sex* sounded so…well, it sounded like a hard fuck. The kind she fantasized about. She met his dark heated eyes and swallowed hard. Her voice came out in a croak. "Like you."

He straightened. "Jury's still out on that one."

She stared at him, wanting to know what he meant by that, but knowing if she asked, he'd say something teasing that set her off. She'd come here to thank him not engage in another fighting match. She had to stop getting sucked in. "Anyway, thanks for saying such nice things in that article. If it weren't for you, I wouldn't be meeting with a prince on Friday to maybe plan a wedding for his sister."

"A prince?"

She let out a happy laugh. "Yes. A real prince. Phillip is from Villroy Island, and he's handsome and funny. It's, like, every woman's dream to meet him."

Josh's lip curled. "Well, have fun with your prince. If he really is one. Maybe it's a scam. Who ever heard of Villroy Island?"

"It's real. Look it up. Bye. Thanks again!" She picked up Rose and sailed out, floating once more with dreams of her royal wedding planning future. Not even Josh's muttered, "Princess meets the prince, fucking perfect," could ruin her lovely royal fantasy.

4

———

As soon as Hailey left, Josh pulled out his phone and looked up the prince online. A ton of results popped up, mostly calling Prince Phillip the Royal Hottie. He scrolled through the pictures. Great. The guy looked like a movie star, all tousled dark hair, gleaming white teeth, probably had a personal trainer for that build. In half the pictures he was shirtless on a beach with a supermodel. Yup. Total playboy. And it seemed he exclusively dated models. Unfortunately, Hailey could hold her own with any model, which made her a prime target. Hadn't he seen that up close and personal at his place seven long weeks ago? She haunted his erotic dreams. He'd even started daydreaming about her. *Fuck me.* Why her?

He and Hailey were wrong for each other for reasons he frequently reminded himself of—they fought constantly, their parents, his aversion to beauty queens. But that didn't mean he wouldn't look out for her. As a friend.

He kept searching the internet, looking for damning evidence against the playboy prince. Oh, great, he was wealthy and heavily involved in charity work providing clean water to impoverished countries. *He is the worst.* Josh's gut did a slow roll, which he ignored as he looked up Villroy Island. Sickeningly gorgeous. An island surrounded by deep blue sea with quaint cottages and a fishing port. The royal palace with towers and turrets perched on a hill in the center of it all looked like something out of a damn fairy tale.

The prince would turn Hailey's head, showing off his glamorous lifestyle straight out of one of those romance novels Hailey loved. Hadn't she started a book club based on that kind of fairy-tale life? The woman lived for romantic fantasies, but this one could end very badly for her. It would be so easy for the prince to take advantage and then just throw her away when he was done with her. Hailey deserved better than that.

He closed his eyes, his gut tight, and blew out a breath. Was he actually jealous of a man he'd never met? Or was he doing his usual protective big-brother thing?

He jammed a hand in his hair. What the hell was wrong with him? Ever since that night, that fucking night he could *not* stop thinking about, he'd been on edge. He was losing his mind, all for a woman he didn't want to want.

Off-limits. Forget it! He shoved his phone in his pocket and went back to work.

~

Josh prowled behind the bar on Thursday night, waiting impatiently for Hailey and her friends to arrive. The Happy Endings Book Club met across the street at Something's Brewing Café every other Thursday and always stopped by Garner's afterwards for drinks. He could count on it. Tonight he was really counting on it. He needed to warn Hailey about this prince she was meeting with tomorrow.

He'd spent way too much time this week figuring out the best way to warn her off the playboy prince without risking her ire and decided after drinks with her friends would be the best time. She'd be in a good mood and mellow. Maybe he'd work on getting her to forgive him for his rejection too. They should be friends. He'd invite her to his place and offer her a drink or something, they'd talk things out, and he'd send her home with the shoebox of money that had brought him nothing but trouble. That was the only way they'd ever get a clean slate and end the bad blood between them.

He stilled as she walked in, her hand on Mad's arm, confiding something to his little sister. His chest warmed at the sight. Mad was the youngest and only girl in their family, with five older brothers and a single cop dad. She'd never had women friends before Hailey took her under her wing. Now Mad had a whole posse of women friends and seemed to have come into her own as the confident woman he always knew she could be.

Four years ago, he'd seen the rut Mad was in, working at a bar in a seedy section of the city, living in a crap apartment that was frequently broken into. His sister was smart but lost. He'd helped her move back home, got her a part-time job at Garner's, and helped her get the paperwork and funds together for community college. Later she'd transferred to the University of Connecticut. She'd paid what she could in tuition and he'd paid the rest. He'd paid her last tuition bill in January and had been saving to buy Garner's ever since. He'd tried once before to buy Garner's, but his offer hadn't been high enough to entice the owner Clive Garner to retire. He was hoping to make another offer soon and really hoping Clive was ready to hand over the reins. It wasn't like Clive and his wife, Heather, were involved in the day to day. They trusted him to handle things.

Once Garner's was all his, he planned on building an addition to the back of it with a dance floor, an old-fashioned jukebox, pool tables, and darts. He wanted it to be a night-time destination, not just a place you got a beer and split. He figured it was easier to renovate this place than to build new. He'd seen enough of the world in the army and after—good and bad—and was happy to set down roots in the sleepy town of Clover Park. Everything he needed was right here.

Mad reached the bar first and took a seat. He was so damn proud of his baby sister graduating college soon. He'd dropped out of college, bored and restless, and had joined the army. Her hair looked ridiculous, nearly to her shoulders, dark brown to the tops of her ears, dyed red the rest of the way down. She was growing it out, back to her natural brunette for her wedding in June. He'd offered to chop off the red with some handy kitchen scissors, but she'd declined.

Mad lifted a hand in greeting. "Hey, Josh. Can I get a beer?"

"Shouldn't you be studying for finals?"

She rolled her eyes. "They're four weeks away. I'm still learning new stuff."

He poured her favorite beer on tap and set it in front of her. "Don't be slacking at the end. I need a good marketing plan out of you." She was a marketing major and that was their deal. She'd help him out with his dream bar with great marketing ideas.

Mad grinned. "You'll get it."

Hailey appeared at Mad's side, her pink dog purse over one shoulder. Thankfully Rose was asleep in there; otherwise she'd be barking at him. "I'll hire you for a marketing plan too," she told Mad. "Maybe you could be a marketing consultant for local businesses."

Hailey didn't look at him. Normally that wouldn't faze him. Hailey had a lot going on at all times, but tonight it bugged him. Probably because he had urgent matters to discuss with her. He waited impatiently for them to finish their conversation.

Mad took a sip of beer. "Maybe. I might just do that on the side. I want to get some experience first at a larger shop." She turned to him. "Did ya hear about Hailey's prince?"

Mouthy smartass. *Hailey's prince.* He grunted at Mad and turned to the rest of their friends. "What can I get you, ladies?" He took everyone's orders, committing them to memory, and even agreed to Hailey's favored mojito, which used to be a battle between them. As in, she ordered a mojito and he claimed to be missing a key ingredient to make it. See how he'd grown? He really was trying to make amends.

He served up the drinks in his usual quiet way, listening to the women talk. This time the talk was all about Prince Phillip. The women were in a heated debate over the proper protocol for proposing a fling with a prince, which he did *not* need to hear. Obviously Hailey was the only one available for a fling, and he'd be damned if he'd let her be taken in by a player looking for his next lay. What Hailey said next alarmed him.

"He's so-o-o handsome. You ladies know he's been my go-to fantasy forever. I always picture him when I read a swoony romance."

Mad elbowed her. "Perfect fantasy for other vibratingly good moments too."

The women roared with laughter, Hailey too *and* she blushed like it was true. Fuck, this was worse than he'd thought. She was meeting her fantasy lover in real life.

He made her mojito, his brain cranking for how to best broach the subject in light of this new information.

Hailey fanned herself with one hand. "It's going to be so hard to keep my cool when I finally meet him. And he's done so much great charity work too, very involved in clean water for countries that desperately need it. He's the total package."

"And you want his package," Mad quipped and then she looked right at him, practically taunting him with this prince.

The women tittered.

"I wouldn't kick him out of bed," Hailey said.

The women laughed and teased her good-naturedly.

Enough!

"Hailey, drink's up." He set her mojito in front of her, keeping his hand on the glass when she tried to take it.

Her pale blue eyes flashed at him. His pulse quickened; something about the fiery fighting spirit in her excited him. He was much more aware of the effect she had on him now that he'd seen her near naked. Before he would've just moved right to battle engagement. Now he suffered for the good of their family. Why was he torturing himself by staying away from her? All of the important reasons to stay away wavered when he saw her up close again. He was done fighting it—

He wanted her.

The tension in his shoulders eased. It was a relief to finally admit what had been staring him in the face this whole time. And it was more than just his natural competitiveness with another man encroaching on his territory. She was beautiful and sexy and smart, and she was his to protect.

And that prince, that damn fantasy prince who'd easily lure her to his bed given the opportunity. Hell. He couldn't let her fall prey to a user guy like that.

"Thank you, Josh," she said, baring her teeth in a fake smile. That smile popped up when she was agitated, like someone had told her frowning wasn't pretty or something.

He leaned close and whispered, "I get off at ten. Come over after. We'll have a drink and talk."

"Ha!" she exclaimed loud enough to draw all eight of her friends' attention. "If you think I'm ever going to your place again, you are *sorely* mistaken." Rose popped her purple bowed head out of Hailey's purse, took one look at him, and barked. And barked and barked and barked.

"Quiet," he commanded Rose.

Bark! Bark! Bark!

He kept his voice low, leaning across the bar. "I want a clean slate between us, and I have something important to talk to you about. Give me a chance to make things right. I'm sorry about last time."

Hailey spoke above the noise of her stupid barky dog. "Last time I was drunk on vodka. That will never happen again."

He stiffened, straightening to his full six feet. She had not been drunk. Her eyes were clear that night, and she'd only had one drink, although she had gulped her drink down quick. Maybe she hadn't eaten before. Shit. He'd actually thought she'd wanted him. He'd even felt a little self-right-eous by sticking to the friend plan in light of mutual wanting. Hell, he'd always wanted her. He'd just resisted it because he'd thought they weren't right for each other for reasons that now seemed insignificant. *Fuck me.* He retreated to the other side of the bar to regroup, and Rose instantly quieted.

He worked, he stewed, he grumbled at his sister and sisters-in-law, who just wouldn't shut up about how cool it was that Hailey would be meeting her dream prince tomor-row. It was like they had to rub it in, trying to get a reaction out of him. What was the big deal about being a prince? The guy was born into it. Not like he had any choice in the matter.

Finally, Mad asked Hailey if she could take Rose on a walk before they all left for the night. Now he could speak privately to Hailey without all the barking. He crooked his finger at her to join him at the far end of the bar away from her friends.

She looked away, pretending not to notice his request.

He stifled a groan of pure aggravation and made his way over to her. Now he had to whisper or her friends would add in their two cents. He didn't want to put on a show. This was too damn important.

"Enjoy your mojito?" he asked.

She eyed him suspiciously. "Yes. Why? Did you do something to it?"

She always thought the worst. Maybe he deserved it. He had given her a hard time before—teasing her, trying to best her in competitive one-upmanship, rejecting her sexy drunken invitation. She'd even said she'd learned not to trust him after he'd pulled that switcheroo date with Jake. Josh had figured financial security was important to her because she was way into her work and had shown such an interest in his billionaire twin and his company. It had gotten his back up because the one thing Josh didn't have was financial security, and there was Jake, looking just like him and offering what Josh couldn't. So he'd taken Jake's place, tortured himself over her enthusiasm for every braggy luxury thing he could think of, and then pulled the plug on the date, unable to stomach her interest in his twin. Of course, now he knew she thought he'd been a boring braggart as Jake, but at the time it had felt like she preferred Jake. He'd been an idiot, trying to compete with his twin over a woman he wanted but didn't want to want. His visceral repulsion for the beauty-queen thing in battle with his primal lust made him do really stupid things. It was him, after all, that she'd paraded around as her date at weddings, so he must've passed muster right from the beginning. He ground his teeth. All he could do was try to earn back her trust.

"It was just a regular mojito." He lowered his voice. "Maybe you could stick around after closing. Just to talk."

"We can talk now," she said in her normal voice.

Her friends were listening. None of them were looking this way, but they'd stopped talking to each other.

"Privately," he whispered.

She did not whisper back. "Anything you have to say, you can say in front of my friends. I have no secrets."

His temper flared. She was making this too hard, being completely unreasonable. Unless…she wasn't getting what he was trying to do here. He'd thought he'd explained how important it was that they talk, how they needed to get on better footing. Why wasn't she getting it? She was smart and genius-level diabolical with her cheery battle tactics. Was she completely done with him?

He dropped his voice to a guttural growl that was more demand than request. "I want you *alone*. Tonight."

Her lashes fluttered down, her fingers rubbing the side of her neck. A good sign—almost flirty and definitely less confrontational. "Oh."

His fingers tingled with the urge to touch her, stroke her soft hair, her cheek, her neck. He glanced over at her friends, who immediately turned away. *Nothing like an audience when you're trying to connect with a woman.* "So?"

She looked into his eyes for a long tense moment, taking his measure, he figured. Trust him, not trust him. He remained perfectly still, gazing back at her steadily. Finally she spoke in a soft voice. "I don't want to keep rehashing things, and I've got a lot to do with the prince arriving tomorrow—"

"Yup."

He started cleanup, tucking glasses under the bar, avoiding the curious eyes of the women. This sucked. She was closed against him. The prince would surely take advantage with Hailey fangirling all over him. Hailey's words tormented him in an endless loop. *He's been my go-to fantasy forever. He's the total package. I wouldn't kick him out of bed.*

Mad returned with Rose, and the women left, telling him

goodbye. Hailey nodded once at him, gave him a small smile, and left. She was at least a little warmer toward him since the article had come out with his praise in it. He'd told her at the time he'd meant it, but she hadn't believed him. That was how much she mistrusted him. How was he ever going to regain her trust if she wouldn't spend time with him?

He scrubbed the bar top with a rag. He'd grown since his relationship with Clarissa. She'd made him more self-aware, showing him how his subconscious manifested in his real-world decisions. And she'd given him some relaxation techniques for his occasional rough night. Unfortunately, Clarissa hadn't been right for him in the long haul. She was too good—angelic level of good. He'd tried to meet her where she was at, in her enlightened hippy lifestyle, knowing all along it just wasn't him. Worse, his newfound self-awareness made him realize what he really needed in a partner wasn't an angelic enlightened woman like Clarissa, but someone with sharp teeth that took a bite out of life. Someone with claws and fire and a warrior's spirit.

He needed his equal.

It hit him like a slap. He'd just described Hailey. *She* was his equal.

That meant she was supposed to be with him. They belonged together. Dammit. If he hadn't been so hardheaded about Hailey for so long, he would've seen what was right under his nose. And now he had a prince to work around and a lot of bad blood to wade through to get her to even consider him. There were so many ways it could go wrong between him and Hailey, but the idea of ceding the battlefield now that the smoke had cleared was an impossibility.

All he needed was a strategic plan to win the war, victory to them both. The flip side, a loss, would damage him, Hailey, their parents, everyone they considered family. The stakes could not have been higher. All of his warrior instincts fired up, ready to charge ahead.

5

———————

Hailey was beside herself preparing for the royal visit. She'd managed to get through two morning appointments with clients, nearly jumping out of her skin while waiting for them to make their choices on menus and tableware. All she could think was *Get out of here! I need to polish Ludbury House until it shines! The prince arrives at five!* As soon as she finished her last appointment, she wolfed down a late lunch and inspected every room of Ludbury House, even the upstairs rooms, where the bride and groom had dressing areas. She felt like a butterfly bouncing off the walls. Rose must've picked up on her nervous energy because she was on edge too, barking at every little sound all day long.

At four thirty, she stopped fluttering around the mansion and rushed to the bathroom to touch up her hair and makeup. She wore a new-to-her pale green silk and organza dress with white shoulder straps and a white band across her mostly bare back. The dress had been a steal from the consignment shop in Greenport, where most of her wardrobe came from. The dress ended at her knees, and she'd paired it with nude suede strappy heels. Sophisticated and sexy.

Not that she was prepping for seduction. She just *really* wanted this job. Planning a wedding for a princess would be fantastic. Not to mention how wonderful it would be to mention Princess Silvia Rourke as a client in her marketing down the line. Anyway, it wasn't like the prince would be interested in a scrappy businesswoman clawing out a living. She might fantasize about him based on his pictures, but she had no delusions in that regard.

She headed back to her office, sat at her antique replica mahogany desk, and then just admired the saved picture of Prince Phillip on her laptop. Dark brown rumpled hair, stunning blue-green eyes, chiseled cheekbones to die for, stubbled jaw, magnificent muscular body in a casual white T-shirt and black jeans. Swoon!

Her phone chimed with a text. She didn't recognize the number. *We're here.* Her heart jumped. Royalty on my doorstep!

She texted back: *On my way.*

She'd arranged for the royal siblings to come to the back door of Ludbury House, out of sight of Main Street. There was a parking lot back there. She rushed out of her office and through the long hallway that led to the back of the house. Rose raced ahead of her, nearly tripping her on the way as she barked her sweet little head off at the visitors. Rose normally only let out one short bark at clients who came in through the front door. Her fur baby was smart enough to know it was an unusual occurrence for someone to go to the back door.

Hailey arrived in the kitchen, glimpsing her visitors through the window of the back door. Six people stood there, four burly men wearing black blazers along with the prince and princess. She recognized the royal siblings from their online pictures. Princess Silvia Rourke, looking much more girl-next-door than her glamorous pictures online, with her dark brown hair up in a high ponytail, peeked her head around a large man's shoulder to beam at her.

Hailey smiled and waved. Then she scooped up Rose and pulled the door open. "Welcome to Ludbury House! So nice to meet you all." She stepped back and one of the burly men stepped forward.

"Security," the man said. "May we look around?"

"Of course. It's just me and Rose here." She held up Rose a

little, who'd stopped barking to check everyone out. "We'll be meeting in the ballroom."

The guard left to scout the mansion, and two more men followed, fanning out in different directions.

Silvia went right to Rose. "Aren't you a cutie? Hello, Rose. I'm Silvia." She met Hailey's eyes, her hazel eyes warm. "Nice to meet you too, Hailey. May I hold her? I've so missed having a dog at university." Her accent held hints of French and something Hailey couldn't quite place. It was unique and pretty.

"Of course." She handed Rose over. And then *he* walked in. Prince Phillip, the hot one, even more stunning in person. Tall and fit, his wide shoulders filled out a crisp white button-down shirt that complemented the tanned tone of his skin with charcoal gray tailored pants and Italian leather loafers. His dark brown hair was thick and tousled like he'd run his fingers through it, his blue-green eyes twinkled with good humor, and he had high cheekbones she'd kill for, and that devastatingly sexy smile. She flushed hot from head to toe. Oh my God. What if they hit it off? What if she married him and became a real princess? Not just the sarcastic kind that Josh called her.

"Hailey," he said in the same charming accent as his sister, "it's wonderful to meet the Queen of the Happy-Ever-After in person."

She beamed. "You're wonderful too! I mean it's so wonderful to meet you too." She offered her hand to shake, and he lifted her hand to his lips, his stunning eyes the color of the sea locked on hers. Her belly dipped. *Ahhhh!* The hand kiss was so old-fashioned, so gentlemanly romantic. Her secret desire for a man straight out of a romance novel—equal parts dashing and romantic—was actually coming true.

He slowly released her hand, his eyes never leaving hers. Her lips parted, her pulse thrumming through her veins.

"Knock off the romance routine, Philly," Silvia said. "We're here for me, not you."

Reality intruded, and Hailey stifled a sigh. This was just standard routine for Phillip.

Phillip shot a dark look at his sister. "And we're here because I set it up, so cool it." They sounded just like normal siblings.

The last security guy came in and locked the door behind them. "I'll escort you to your meeting place."

"Sorry about the security," Silvia said. "My big brother is overprotective. Two of them are for me; the other two for Phillip."

"No problem," Hailey assured Silvia. "No problem" was her go-to phrase for most anything the bride said. Some things were easier to accommodate than others.

"She means a different big brother, Gabriel, the heir, not me." Phillip gave Hailey a charming sexy smirk. "I'm much more freewheeling."

She got a flutter in her belly, seeing his sexy smirk in real life after admiring it online for so long. She could see why women threw themselves at him. "Can I get you a drink or snack?"

"No, thanks," Phillip said.

Silvia handed Rose back to Hailey. "Actually, I'm going to dinner after this with my fiancé's family."

Hailey quickly picked some Rose fur off Silvia's pale peach short-sleeve sweater. At least Silvia's pants and heels were white, so any lingering Rose fur would blend.

Silvia looked down at herself and laughed. "No worries, I've got it." She brushed the remaining shed fur off her chest. "My fiancé has handed the reins of our wedding over to me." She crinkled her nose. "He's such a *guy* guy, you know?"

"A little rough around the edges," Phillip put in.

"Says Mr. Sophistication," Silvia replied. "Cade is more into mountain climbing and kayaking than picking out a color theme for our wedding. We're a classic opposites-attract kind of couple."

Hailey wasn't so sure about the opposites-attract thing. She'd always thought compatibility with similar interests and outlooks would make for a smoother path. Though that wasn't the most important thing. After observing so many successful relationships, she'd concluded the key was finding someone who accepted you just for who you are (and vice versa). A perfect match was someone you really clicked with and experienced very little friction because of your mutual acceptance. Only that hadn't worked for her. Her friends-with-benefits arrangement with Liam had met all those requirements—they never fought, the sex was outstanding, and they genuinely liked each other. Problem was, several years later, it never did turn into love. What the hell did she know about relationships? Her breakdown five days ago at her mom's engagement party had been a humbling wake-up call.

She moved right past Silvia's remark to the business at hand. "I'm sure the three of us will come up with something wonderful. Right this way." She gestured for them to follow and made her way over to the large empty ballroom. Once in the ballroom, she set Rose down to find a sunbeam to nap in. Hailey always met for a first appointment with clients in here because this was where the reception would be held. A glossy white enameled table along with red velvet cushioned chairs stood in the center of the room under an elaborate gold and crystal chandelier. The table was already set with a vase of cheerful red tulips (Silvia's favorite flower), three white binders, a pen and notepad, her business cards, and a rose corsage for the bride.

"Please have a seat," Hailey said, indicating the cushioned guest chairs.

Silvia sat down. "Phillip is just here to make sure I don't do anything too crazy."

Phillip chuckled and took the seat next to his sister. "Must keep up appearances."

"Welcome to modern times, *Dad*," Silvia said.

Hailey took the rose corsage with baby's breath out of its plastic container and crossed to Silvia. "For the bride. May I pin it to your sweater?"

"Sure, thanks!"

Hailey attached it. Silvia fingered a rose petal, smiling just like every bride Hailey had ever given a rose. Most brides liked feeling special right from the start.

She walked around the table to her seat. Phillip unexpectedly joined her, holding her chair out for her in a gallant gesture that made her giddy. "Thank you," she murmured, taking her seat.

"My pleasure," he said in a husky voice.

Silvia rolled her eyes and smacked his arm as he walked back to his seat.

The security guards returned. Three of them stood along the wall of floor-to-ceiling windows and the fourth by the entrance to the room. Rose went over to sniff one of the guards' shoes.

Silvia looked around the ballroom. "This is gorgeous! I love the parquet flooring and the white crown molding." She looked up. "And the chandelier. So romantic!"

Hailey beamed. She loved this room too. "It really is romantic, especially when we have an evening reception with candlelight."

Silvia squealed, and Phillip gave her an indulgent smile. So sweet the way he looked out for his little sister!

Hailey handed them each a business card and started with her standard spiel. "We're meeting in the center of the ballroom so you'll feel what it'll be like when you're the center of attention." She shook her head at herself. "I suppose you already know what that feels like, Silvia."

"I do, but I hope you can make it feel like a romantic intimate event."

"Absolutely," Hailey said.

Phillip picked up her business card, reading it, and then looked at her, a hint of amusement in his eyes. Her cheeks heated. The card was embossed with silver bells and read Hailey Adams, Love Junkie, Wedding Planner. She should probably take out Love Junkie. It didn't fit her outlook so much now.

She turned to Silvia. "Tell me how you imagined your big day."

Phillip spoke up. "Her big day is the wedding back home. This is a smaller affair meant to take care of legalities."

Silvia rolled her eyes. "So romantic, Philly." She turned to

Hailey. "I just can't bear for my first wedding ceremony to be some boring legal matter in a judge's chambers. When I read your feature article in *Bride Special* online, I just knew you'd understand how to make it special. I have the dress, a gorgeous silk sheath with beading on the bodice, but I'd also like something that's really us. Cade and I adore live music, especially jazz."

"Oh! We have one of the best jazz singers in the world right here in Clover Park. Zoe Reynolds. She recently won a Grammy."

"Are you serious?" Silvia exclaimed. "I love her! Do you think she'd do it?"

Hailey grabbed her pen and made a note of it. "She performs in town on occasion. Once we set a date, I'll ask her."

"That would be amazing! Wait until I tell Cade."

Hailey smiled. "What else would make it your dream wedding?"

Silvia warmed to the topic. "I'd love tulips." She gestured to the bouquet on the table. "Nice touch. Also, beautiful satin ribbons and bows, everything pastel and soft, glowing under candlelight. Dreamy and romantic."

Just like Hailey used to imagine for herself when she'd thought a happy-ever-after was just around the corner. "I'm getting the picture. It sounds lovely. Indoors or outdoors? We do have beautiful grounds with a large patio."

"Has to be indoors for privacy," Phillip said with a wink.

Hailey felt herself flush as if Phillip had invited her someplace private. *Focus!*

Silvia nodded. "I love this ballroom. Indoors is fine."

Hailey wrote that down. "We'll often have the ceremony in the front foyer with the bride walking down the grand staircase to her groom. There's room for seating up front and extra seating in the adjacent parlor. Would you like to take a look?"

"Absolutely!" Silvia stood, all smiles.

Everything went smoothly from there despite Hailey being a little flustered. She could swear Phillip was sending her heated glances, but every time she checked, he looked to his sister. Silvia loved absolutely everything. It wasn't hard for Hailey to guide her to the dreamy romantic options for her wedding. It was nearly identical to what Hailey would've chosen for herself.

Finally, they'd worked their way through the binder options for catering, flowers, cake, all the little details that made a wedding special, and Hailey circled back to the most important thing she needed to know and the most difficult to accommodate. "Now we just need a date," she said brightly. "I understand it needs to be before July first. My Saturday and Sunday daytime weddings are fully booked through August. How would you feel about a Friday night or Sunday night wedding?" She held her breath, hoping Silvia was invested enough in the possibility of a wedding here that she'd be agreeable.

"I'd like a Friday night," Silvia said. "Then we'll have the weekend for a mini-honeymoon."

Hailey beamed. "Wonderful!"

"After finals," her brother put in sternly.

"No kidding," Silvia snapped. "Careful, you're starting to sound like Gabriel."

Phillip winced. "Duly noted."

Hailey and Silvia checked their calendars on their phones and thankfully found a date that worked, the last Friday in May. Hailey was especially happy it was after Carrie and Zach's wedding, which would be featured in *Bride Special.*

Silvia offered her hand to Hailey, and Hailey shook it. "Thank you so much for this, Hailey. You've exceeded my expectations. My wedding in Villroy is dictated mostly by tradition. This one is just for me."

"I'm thrilled to be a part of it. Oh, one last thing. Will you need me to add extra security, or will you be using your people?"

"Our people are fine," Phillip answered for her. "A total of twelve for outside and inside. And I cannot stress this enough, no paparazzi, no pictures leaked, no advance notice anywhere of the event."

"No problem," Hailey said. "We've had similar circumstances when Claire Jordan attended weddings here, and there's never been an issue."

Silvia stood and the security guards moved toward her. Hailey stood and called over to Rose, who was happily trotting behind one of the guards.

Phillip appeared by her side. "Would you like to have a cup of coffee? We passed a café that looked promising on our ride in. I have my own car back to the city since we knew Silvia was meeting her fiancé."

Hailey sucked in air. "Sure, that would be lovely." Her voice squeaked a bit, and she prayed he didn't notice.

Silvia went up on tiptoe and kissed Phillip's cheek. "Thanks for your help and for running interference with you-know-who. You're a saint for sitting through all this wedding talk."

Phillip winked. "Anything for my little sister."

Silvia smiled and patted his cheek before sailing out of the room, two security guards in tow.

The moment Silvia left the room, Phillip leaned down to confide, "Keeping her stateside wedding in line with royal expectations is half the reason for my visit. Shh, don't tell her. She hates to feel like we're babysitting her."

Hailey smiled. "I think she's lucky to have family looking out for her."

"Agreed." He bent his arm and offered it to Hailey in a gentlemanly gesture. "Shall we?"

6

Josh waited in the shadows of the church rectory across the street from Ludbury House on a reconnaissance mission. He knew Hailey was meeting at five o'clock with the playboy prince, thanks to Mad. He hadn't told Mad of his new strategic plan regarding Hailey, but his sister had always wanted him to make a move on Hailey and gave him ample information to make that possible. Not like he was going to barge in on them. He was gathering intel. Would Hailey walk the prince out after their meeting, all smiles and flirty body language? Would they get into one of those black Mercedes with the tinted windows parked behind Ludbury House and drive off together? Was the playboy prince a rival or a nonstarter?

The answer arrived a few minutes later when a large man in a black blazer stepped through the front door of Ludbury House and scanned his surroundings. Security. Josh shrank back against the wall. A moment later, he looked again. The security guy stood to the side. Hailey appeared first in a light green dress with white straps over her bare shoulders. The dress emphasized her narrow waist. High heels, of course. She looked fresh, young, and as glamorous as his movie star sister-in-law, Claire Jordan. Clearly Hailey was swinging for the fences with the prince. She had her pink dog purse over one shoulder and he didn't hear a peep out of Rose when the prince appeared at Hailey's side. The prince took Hailey's hand and tucked it into the crook of his arm, a gentlemanly move. Damn, this guy played hardball. Another security guard appeared, and the group left the porch, walked down the sidewalk, and headed down Main Street.

He waited. They went into Something's Brewing Café. Okay, he'd gotten the intel. Conclusive evidence the playboy prince was a rival. Hailey wasn't just walking him out, she was spending time with the guy, which she would never do unless she was interested. Now what? He needed to prove he was a better option than a goddamn prince.

But was he?

Sure, he could pull out the gentleman manners, but the prince had that too. There was no way Josh could ever offer the kind of glamorous jet-setting lifestyle that Prince Phillip could. The kind of lifestyle Hailey would probably love. She'd even told him how much she'd love to travel to exotic places when they'd had that switcheroo date way back when. All he could offer was a life rooted in Clover Park, a suburban community where not much exciting happened. He liked that about Clover Park. It was steady and safe—filled with families and a few colorful characters like that kooky grandmother Maggie O'Hare, who looked out for him and everybody in town, it seemed—but it wasn't glamorous.

His shoulders drooped. Maybe he'd missed his chance with Hailey.

He headed over to Garner's, even though he wasn't supposed to be working tonight due to his clandestine mission. Mad had taken a shift behind the bar for him. He had a ridiculous amount of vacation time racked up. He never took a day off and he rarely got sick. He lived clean, ate healthy, mostly because he was a foodie, and didn't get close enough to anyone to pick up an illness. Only his twin ever dared invade his personal space, which felt fine, they were like two halves of a whole, being identical. The guys understood his need for a perimeter of personal space after his time in combat.

It was a little after six when he walked into Garner's. The dining area was full and people were waiting for a table. Always good to see on a Friday night. He greeted a few regulars as he moved through to the bar. Several people sat at the bar, where Mad was chopping some limes.

"I'm back," he told her, heading around behind the bar.

Her head whipped toward him. "Aww, man. I was hoping to keep all the tips from tonight for my honeymoon."

"Tips are all yours." What did he need the money for anyway? Tips could never add up to a princely sum. Ha. Royal humor. He glanced out the window of the dining area over to Something's Brewing Café and spotted Hailey's familiar strawberry blond hair, her back to him as she stood in line for coffee. He used to think of her hair as light red, but she called it strawberry blond, and the luscious-sounding words stuck in his mind.

Mad appeared at his side. "Thanks, Josh. You're the best."

He grunted, his gaze still riveted on the action across the street.

"Hey, there's Hailey. I wonder how it went with the prince."

He didn't respond.

"Wow. She just texted he asked her out for coffee. I don't see him, do you?"

He ignored her. He saw him all right, his profile turned toward Hailey. There was a security guard behind him and one standing by the door.

Mad elbowed him. "You think coffee's like a first date?"

He shifted away. "Coffee's like coffee."

"I don't know," Mad said, going back to slicing limes. "I think the order is beverage, dinner, and then some of the ol' in and out."

He glared at her, but she didn't notice, her gaze fixed on her task. Hailey wasn't the kind of woman who rushed to bed. Was she? Hmm…she had stripped down to her bra and thong and offered herself the first moment she'd ever been alone with him. Why? Did she just want him for sex? Because now that he knew they belonged together, that was a very bad thing. Maybe she didn't see him as relationship material. His gut churned, an all too familiar acid feeling when he got thinking about Hailey.

Maybe she'd been drunk on vodka like she'd said. So it was good that he'd been a gentleman, even though it sucked right now. He never wanted to take advantage. He wanted her willing and begging for it. An image of a flushed pink Hailey in all her naked glory, panting, begging him to give it to her flashed through his mind. Fuck. He forced his mind back to the hideous prince, his new nemesis. The battle lines were drawn.

Mad finished with the limes, wiped her hands on a paper towel, and checked her phone. "Mind if I take a break? Hailey wants me to stop by the café to check out the prince."

He stared at her. Women did that? Ran potential lovers past their friends first? "Check him out for what?"

Mad grinned. "It's a girl thing. I'll just casually show up like, oh, hey, nice running into you. Then later I'll tell her what I thought of him and any potential between them." She looked proud of herself for knowing about girl things. He was proud too. It had taken a while, but Mad was finally up on the intricacies of women's relationships. No easy feat. He didn't know any guy, him included, who'd cracked that code.

Still, he wasn't ready to yield the battlefield just yet. He tugged a lock of her half brown, half red hair. "Sorry. I need you here. I'm going to take the night off after all."

He stepped out from behind the bar and headed toward the door.

"Tell the prince I said hi," Mad called from behind him with a laugh.

He flipped her the bird over his shoulder. Brat.

He headed across the street and decided he'd play it exactly like Mad had planned, all casual, like he'd just happened to run into them. He walked into the café with its deep red walls, glowing golden sconces, and dark wood tables and chairs, his gaze quickly narrowing to the table where the prince sat with his arm around the top of Hailey's chair, his fingers mere millimeters away from her bare shoulder. Another few minutes and that hand would be on her bare shoulder or in her soft hair or worse.

He closed the distance between them, careful to keep to his usual amble so as not to alert the security guard standing a few feet away. "Hey, Hailey, nice running into you." Smooth was his middle name.

She straightened. "Josh! What're you doing here?" Rose popped her head up from Hailey's purse under the table and growled at him.

He lifted one shoulder. "Stopped by for a coffee. Mind if I join you with…"

"Phillip," the prince supplied, offering his hand.

Josh gave him a firm handshake. "Nice to meet you. I'll be back in a minute after I put in my order."

"No." Hailey pasted on one of her fake smiles. "Sorry. Phillip is only in town for a short time. I'll see you another time. Enjoy your coffee!"

He ignored her brush-off. The stakes were too damn high for that. Instead he pulled out a chair, set it on Hailey's other side, and took a seat. Rose started up her *I hate Josh* barking spree. He spoke above the racket. "How long are you in town for, Bill?"

"It's Phillip," Hailey said through her teeth. She dug into her purse and fed Rose a treat under the table. Rose quieted as she chewed.

"That's what I said," Josh replied.

Phillip scratched the side of his neck, eyeing him and then Hailey. "Would you prefer I leave you two alone?"

Smart man. "Yes."

"No!" Hailey turned to Josh. He smiled pleasantly. She fake smiled back. "May I speak to you for a moment in private?" she whisper-shouted.

"Sure." He turned to the interloper. "Could you watch Rose? Thanks."

Hailey marched to the back of the café to an empty children's section. Her back was bare—the dress open all the way to the sweet dip in her lower back just above her curvy ass. Only a narrow white band across the middle of her back held the sides of the dress in place. He clenched his jaw. This was how she dressed for the prince?

He leaned against the wall in a casual slouch by a short kids' table, hiding the intensity of all he was feeling. It was worse now that he saw the prince up close, looking all pretty, the perfect match for beauty queen Hailey. Jealousy took a gleeful ride on top of missed opportunity and unsatisfied lust. "What's up?"

She stood in front of him, her pale blue eyes flashing fire. The jolt it gave him was more than lust; it was a primal recognition of a warrior's spirit. She was magnificent. "What is up?" she half-shouted. "I'll tell you what is up. Just because our parents are getting married, that doesn't give you the right to show up here acting like an overprotective big brother."

"Sorry, little sis. Mad was concerned, so I stepped up."

She huffed. "Mad was happy for me. You came here because of some twisted sense of honor. News flash, I can handle myself."

He straightened out of his slouch, keeping his voice low. "I see a player moving in for the kill, I can't just stand by."

She leaned in, whisper-shouting at him, "I have plenty of experience handling men, even players, so back off! I do *not* want a scene here like when you had a throwdown with Blake Grenier over me. Phillip has security here." Blake Grenier was the costar in his sister-in-law Claire's Fierce trilogy movies.

"Blake was an asshole. You knew that and you still wanted to go upstairs with him." That still pissed him off. They'd been at the Fierce trilogy movie wrap party with Claire and crew. Josh knew the real deal about Blake from Claire, and he also knew Claire had warned all of her friends, including Hailey, to stay away from Blake. So when Hailey hadn't listened to Josh's request not to go upstairs with Blake, he'd been forced to warn Blake away from Hailey. The man came at him and he'd neutralized the threat.

Hailey's cheeks and neck flushed pink, her voice loud

now. "He was giving me a tour of where they filmed the Fierce trilogy!"

He went nose to nose with her. "He wanted your panties as a fucking trophy."

Her breath quickened, lips parted, eyes locked on his. The air vibrated between them for a tense electrifying moment. His gaze dropped to her luscious pink lips, the urge to stake his claim so powerful he held back for a second more, needing to be sure he was under control.

She shifted back a step. "Look, I get that you're protective, but I don't need it. Now go before I sic Mad on your ass."

He crossed his arms. "Mad would back me up. She'd look out for you just the same as me."

She looked over to the prince, who now held Rose in his lap. *Asshole kissing up to her dog.* She turned back to him. "Goodbye, Josh."

"I know his type. He uses women and throws them away. Look him up. He dates models from all over the world."

She flicked her long hair over one smooth shoulder. "So you think he wouldn't be interested in me because I'm not a model?"

He lowered his voice to a husky tone. "Not in the way you'd want." *Not like me.*

She lifted her chin, proud and haughty and beautiful. "You have no idea what I want."

"Try me," he drawled.

She stiffened, but her eyes never left his. She was at least curious what he might offer.

"Is there a problem?" a masculine voice asked.

They both turned to see Phillip standing there.

"Where's Rose?" Hailey asked.

"Back in your purse," Phillip said.

"You left her alone?" Hailey cried. "She could run away." She rushed back to Rose.

Josh spoke under his breath to the playboy prince. "I'll be keeping an eye on you."

Phillip laughed. "I'm not too worried. If she actually

wanted you, you'd be the one sitting with her, not me. I get the feeling you've known each other a while."

Josh wanted to punch him so badly, but he knew security would close in and there'd be a scene, as Josh would have to neutralize the threat of three men. Hailey would be furious after she'd just told him no more throwdowns.

"Asshole," he spat and stalked toward the door.

Rose barked at him as he passed by Hailey. What did he ever do to that little rat? Geez, he had to win over a beauty-queen wannabe princess *and* a rat-dog? Why couldn't he just have it easy and be born a prince?

But that had never been the way life rolled for him. He had to work hard for everything he'd ever gotten. No one handed anything to him. He opened the café door and headed outside, not bothering with the coffee. Fine. He'd have to be smarter and work harder to get what he wanted, just like always. No choice in the matter now that his eyes had been opened. He'd start with the dog. If he couldn't even win over Rose, what chance did he have with her owner? Surely he could outsmart a dog. All he had to do was carry a treat in his pocket.

The owner required more finesse. He headed across the street to Garner's, stepped inside, and caught his sister's questioning look. Why hadn't he thought of this before? His sister had the inside track with Hailey. He wasn't above using that kind of intel. A frigging gold mine.

7

Hailey welcomed her mom and Joe Campbell to Ludbury House for a Wednesday five-o'clock appointment and walked them to the ballroom. She was the maid of honor and had agreed to be their wedding planner. She was still waiting for the other shoe to drop, as it always did with her mom. At some point her mom would flake on this relationship and leave Hailey desperately trying to pick up the pieces. She'd never had a stable foundation—not with family or a home— and the Campbells were the closest she'd gotten to experiencing that. Her recent group of friends through the Happy Endings Book Club was also entangled with the Campbells through marriage and engagements. Everything in her life tied back to them, and she didn't want anything or anyone to screw that up. *Mom.*

Hailey took a seat, and the happy couple sat across the table from her, holding hands, their fingers entwined. She had to admit they looked totally in love. Her mom had come straight from work, wearing a sophisticated robin's egg blue dress with cutout lace panels at the bodice and her sides. Joe wore a black long-sleeved cotton shirt with faded jeans. They were an odd pairing of dressy and casual, but maybe when you were old (her mom had turned fifty last week) the pickings were slim and you just went with anyone your age who happened to be single.

Geez, she was becoming downright cynical now that she was staring down thirty. In three years anyway. But there it was, the big three-oh taunting her like a big ol' deadline for what was rapidly becoming a delusional fantasy of happy-ever-after. Sadly, Phillip had left the moment he finished his coffee last Friday at the café, saying he had to get back to the city. Obviously Phillip wasn't interested in her. He'd probably just wanted a friendly coffee, being a stranger in a strange land.

She handed the rose corsage to her mom. "For the bride. You can just hold it if you don't want to pin it to your beautiful dress."

Her mom beamed and removed the rose from its plastic casing. "I'll put it in my hair." She smoothed her long strawberry blond hair back—dyed to match Hailey's hair—and tucked it behind her ear. Her mom's hair was naturally blond and white. She was a former model and clung to her looks with a death grip. She regularly got Botox too.

Her mom turned to Joe. "What do you think?"

Joe smiled, his brown eyes warm and tender. "Beautiful. And the rose is nice too."

Her mom sighed dreamily. "Oh, you. Such a sweetheart."

Joe cupped her mom's cheek, and her mom closed her eyes, leaning into his hand.

Hailey's stomach rolled, the ninth circle of hell in all its ironic glory—a love junkie revolted by romance. It was probably partly due to the fact her mom treated her more like a friend than a daughter and overshared the details of her sex life. Needless to say, Hailey knew way too much about Joe and his animal instincts. Also, his use of handcuffs. As her mom had said in her giddy state, what could you expect from a former cop?

Hailey cleared her throat loudly, hoping to break what was now a goggle-eyed staring contest between the nauseatingly happy couple. Finally they returned their attention to her. "Why don't we get started? Mom, tell me how you envision your perfect wedding."

Her mom's first marriage to Hailey's father had been a courthouse wedding brought on by the fact that her mom was pregnant with Hailey. Her dad had been a rock star lead singer. He'd died while flying his prop plane in bad weather when Hailey was three. She had only a vague memory of him since she was so young when he died, and her mom said he wasn't around much anyway. Hailey took no pleasure in his music and disassociated herself with her rock royalty lineage, declining to attend his band's induction into the Rock and Roll Hall of Fame. As far as she was concerned, her dad was a sperm donor and didn't deserve the honor of being called dad.

Joe Campbell, on the other hand, was the dad she'd always wished she had. Mad had no idea how lucky she was to have him. The man had showed up at a designer women's boutique during their girls' day out to help Mad pick out her wedding shoes. He was probably the only man who had ever stepped foot in the ultrafeminine shop, which was how he met her mother, who worked there as a salesclerk. Fate or bad luck? Hailey fervently hoped her mom didn't flake and dump him. The man had already been dumped by his first wife.

Hailey's gut clenched. She so wanted to believe her mom had changed and matured into a responsible person. Different than the mom she knew as a kid, who couldn't hang onto a job, which was why they'd been evicted from their apartment more than once, not having the money for rent. Though her mom had been at the same job at the boutique for years now. It was just that Hailey loved the close-knit Campbell family. They were the kind of family she'd always longed for, the way they all got along, hung out even as adults, and had each other's backs. Josh Campbell was the irritating exception to their wonderful family. Where did he get off playing overprotective big brother with her? Twice! An unsettling thought occurred. Did he actually see her like a little sister? Because she'd thought there'd been some chemistry there. Unless it was completely one-sided, which would explain why he'd turned her down flat. How embarrassing. *Deny, deny, deny. I am a fortress of Josh resistance.*

"Hailey?" her mom asked.

She jolted, alarmed that she'd lost focus. She never lost focus with a client. "Yes?"

Her mom and Joe exchanged a concerned look.

Hailey pasted on her pageant smile. It had seen her through many a difficult situation. Besides, she didn't want frown lines. "Sorry, I'm a little tired. Could you repeat that last part?"

"Sure," her mom said. "We want to get married at St. Joseph's here in Clover Park and have the reception at Garner's. Something small and intimate."

Joe chimed in. "We want to throw business Josh's way. He put in an offer on Garner's and it was accepted today."

Hailey's jaw dropped. Josh could afford to buy Garner's after paying Mad's tuition these past four years? He lived so modestly she never would've guessed. He must be really savvy with his money, a man who understood the importance of saving. Like her. That stable foundation was so important. "Wow. Good for him."

Joe smiled proudly. "He'll take full ownership on May first. We thought we'd get married the Saturday after that." That was three and a half weeks away.

Hailey checked her online calendar. Since they didn't need Ludbury House for the wedding, they were easier to accommodate. She'd ask Ally, her friend and part-time employee, to take over for the wedding already booked for Ludbury House that day so Hailey could attend her mom and Joe's wedding. "Would an afternoon wedding ceremony and reception work for you?" That way she could make sure things were running smoothly with Ally before she stepped out for their wedding.

"Works for me," Joe said.

"Me too," her mom said. They smiled and cooed at each other. *Hurl.*

Hailey made a note in her calendar. "I'll check in with the church and Garner's first thing in the morning, though I'm fairly certain the church is available. Let's call it a go, unless I tell you otherwise. Just a few more questions for you."

"Whatever the bride wants," Joe said.

"Smart man," her mom said.

Hailey's teeth hurt from the sweetness. She cracked open a binder and got down to business. Half an hour later, they finished. It would be a small wedding with only their immediate family and closest friends invited. Nothing fancy or elaborate. Simple and easy.

Joe reached across the table to Hailey, offering his hand. She went to shake his hand, but Joe's big hand enveloped hers and he gave her a squeeze instead. "I'm thrilled you'll be part of my family soon, Hailey. I couldn't ask for a better daughter. You've done so much for Mad. I mean, with all the girl stuff she missed out on in our family. We're damn lucky to have you on board."

Hailey's eyes stung unexpectedly, and she swallowed over the lump in her throat. "Thank you. I'm happy to be a part of things. Mad's been—" Her voice choked. *Do not cry.* Mad was the first friend she'd ever had who really saw the person Hailey was on the inside. Never catty or judgmental, Mad— just by being the tough kickass woman she was—had helped Hailey claim her own strength as a woman. Mad had also taught her self-defense and had attempted to share her love of basketball by inviting Hailey to her Saturday game with her brothers, opening a whole new world to Hailey with big brothers and feeling like part of a team. Not that she was any good at sports, but it had been so nice to be included. She was used to working solo. "You have a lovely family," she croaked.

Swear to God, if her mom flaked and ruined this thing with Joe, Hailey would wreak vengeance.

Her mom smiled brightly. "Why don't we all head over to Garner's to congratulate Josh on his new bar? Then we can find out right away if the reception date works for him."

Hailey froze. She hadn't seen Josh since their confrontation at the café five days ago. She'd been so rattled after that, she'd had trouble focusing on her conversation with Phillip.

Maybe that was why he'd rushed back to the city. She'd bored him away. "You two go. I, uh, have to take Rose for her nightly walk."

Rose heard her name and woke from her nap under a sunbeam by one of the large floor-to-ceiling windows. She stood and stretched, blinking her big dark eyes.

"We'll have dinner," Joe said. "My treat. And don't worry about Rose. Her legs are so little she'll get plenty of exercise walking to Garner's."

"But my mom's allergic," Hailey said, grasping at straws.

"I took some allergy medicine before I came here," her mom said. "I knew Rose would be nearby for our meeting."

The happy couple stood, smiling and looking at her expectantly.

There was no easy way to say no. Unless…

"It's probably crowded over at Garner's," she said. "I'm not sure they'd have a table. Maybe somewhere with a larger dining room?"

Her mom frowned. "It's Wednesday night. How busy could they be?"

"I got this." Joe pulled out his phone and tapped it a few times. "Hey, Josh, it's Dad. You got a table for four free? Great! Be there in five." He hung up and met Hailey's eyes, his dark eyes gleaming with triumph. She was starting to see where Josh got his devious side from.

"I'll get my purse," she said.

Josh tucked his phone back in his jeans pocket. Party of four. Probably his dad, Brandy, and another couple. His dad had become more social since he got together with Brandy. It was great to see. At fifty-five, his dad was enjoying a new carefree phase in his life after years as a single dad raising six kids and mentoring so many more through the Police Athletic League. It took a certain strength of character and a huge heart to be the kind of hands-on dad he'd been for all of them. Josh hadn't appreciated it as a kid. He'd taken it for granted, but now watching the hard work of being a dad up close through his brothers Ty and Alex, he finally understood. Truth was, the results of his dad's efforts were an integral part of Josh's life. Now that everyone was grown up, their family, including his honorary brothers from the Police Athletic League, remained close.

He heard her musical laugh first, all of his senses on high alert as he turned toward the door. Hailey walked in with Rose in her purse, laughing at something his dad said. She looked stunning as usual in a pale pink dress that clung to her gorgeous body. Brandy followed close behind. This was the party of four? Did they think Rose was going to sit in a chair like a person? Then he remembered he was supposed to be winning over Rose. He dropped to his haunches, pulled out the stick of butter he'd stashed in the mini-fridge under the bar, and quickly rubbed some butter on the inside of his wrists and then added a dab behind his ear for good measure. It didn't show, had only a slight scent, but Rose would lap it up. He hoped.

He stashed the butter and straightened to his full height, quickly grabbing a rag to wipe the bar like it was his intention all along.

"Josh!" his dad boomed, striding toward him. "Congrats on the bar!"

He smiled so big he felt his eyes crinkle at the corners. "Thanks, Dad." The owner, Clive Garner, had accepted his offer—the same offer he'd given a little over a year ago—with enthusiasm. Josh had figured he'd start there and raise the offer if Clive was on the fence, even if he had to take out a huge loan. He needed this to happen that badly. It was part of his strategic plan. He wanted to show Hailey that he had a stable foundation, owning his own business. He knew she'd respect that since it was what she worked so hard at with her business. Fortunately he didn't have to go bankrupt in the effort. As Clive had said, the timing was right and he'd rest easy, knowing Garner's was in good hands.

"Yes, congratulations!" Brandy said, hurrying to the bar, all smiles.

Hailey took her time walking over, her expression completely neutral. He'd hoped she'd be excited for him. No time for wallowing in disappointment because his dad reached across the bar top, shaking his hand and pulling him in for a hug.

His dad pulled away and met his eyes directly. "Damn proud of you, son."

Josh pressed his lips tightly together, the words hitting deep inside. Of course he knew his dad was proud of him, of all of them, really, but something about hearing the words spoken out loud got to him. "Thanks," he managed.

Brandy beamed at him. "We'd love for you to join us for dinner. Our treat as congratulations, plus there's a few wedding things we want to run by you."

It wasn't too busy on a Wednesday, only two guys nursing beers at the bar, watching the game.

He checked in with Hailey, who stood very still, looking extremely uncomfortable. Their squabble last Friday was probably still on her mind. He hadn't seen her since because he'd been working hard to get this bar deal done. In fact, he'd planned on telling her his big news tonight, but their parents had beaten him to it. He suddenly got the feeling this was a setup, a parent-arranged date to get him and Hailey together. Was it possible he'd been trying to protect their parents from the Josh-Hailey fallout when they were actually all for it?

He looked over to his dad, who jerked his chin at Josh and moved a few feet away from the women.

Josh joined him. "Yeah?"

His dad kept his voice low. "Brandy and I think it's time you and Hailey stop fighting. We want you to be friends, or at least civil to each other. There's going to be a lot of family events—birthdays, holidays, parties, all that good stuff—and the last thing we need is to be taking sides in a war."

"No war. I'm making amends. I like her."

His dad did a double take that said he knew *exactly* what Josh meant by that. "Don't even go there. That's even worse. Be civil, but keep your distance, okay? For the sake of the family. The last thing I want in my new marriage is drama."

Josh clenched his jaw and looked away. Turned out his first instinct had been right. Stay away from Hailey for the sake of their family. What had made him think they'd work out anyway when they fought so much? Just because he wanted her? Just because he'd gotten jealous of the stupid prince?

"Okay?" his dad prompted.

"Yeah, I got it. Civil." He called over to the women, "I'll get someone to sub for me and join you for dinner."

"Wonderful," Brandy said with a big smile.

Hailey pasted on her fake smile. Rose popped her little white furred head out of Hailey's purse and growled at him. Her fur was clipped in a ponytail on top of her head with a dark pink bow that matched her thin doggie sweater. The color coordinated with Hailey's dress. *Whatever floats your boat.*

He headed back to the kitchen to see who could sub. Well, this sucked. At least Mad had been on his side, giving him some inside info on Hailey, which had resulted in one extremely embarrassing purchase. He hadn't decided yet if he had the nerve to give it to her, and now that would never happen.

By the time he got to the dining area, his dad and Brandy were sitting next to each other on one side of a booth. Hailey had wedged herself into the corner of the other bench seat with Rose sitting on the bench next to her. The woman knew how much Rose hated him. Well, the joke was on her. The Rose barrier was going to crumble tonight in a butter-induced fall. This should count toward making amends and keeping the family peace. He was sure Rose would accompany Hailey to all of their family functions.

He slid his hand close to Rose's nose, letting her sniff the butter on his wrist before taking a seat. "So how's the wedding planning going?" he asked, fighting to keep his expression neutral as Rose's raspy tongue licked his wrist, tickling him. Hailey hadn't noticed Rose's licking yet. She stared straight ahead.

"Great!" Brandy exclaimed. "Hailey has made everything

so easy for us. We were hoping to have the reception here at Garner's the Saturday after you take over as full owner."

"Late afternoon," his dad said.

"Sure, no problem," he said, trying not to laugh. Rose held his wrist in both paws and was lapping at it like he was a juicy bone. "Construction starts the following Monday, so the timing is perfect."

"Excellent," his dad said.

"Construction?" Hailey asked.

"Yup. I'm having an addition built on the back with room for a dance floor and a couple of pool tables."

"Ambitious," Hailey said softly.

He lifted one shoulder up and down. "It was always my plan. My dream bar."

"I remember," she murmured. "Congratulations. It must feel great to realize your life's dream."

He inclined his head. It did and it didn't. Because his dream wasn't complete without Hailey on board, and now she never would be. There was no way to hide the energy between him and Hailey—both good and bad—if they got involved. He had to back off to the civil-acquaintances corner. He didn't kid himself he could spend time with her as friends. He wanted her too much.

Brandy smiled. "Hailey, maybe you and Josh could work out some of the logistics for the wedding reception."

"I'll take care of everything, Mom," Hailey said in a bland tone. "You just enjoy being a bride." Clearly Hailey didn't want to plan with him. No problem. He was happy to leave it all up to her.

His dad and Brandy exchanged a look that said, *Well, we tried.* Like he and Hailey were a hopeless case.

The waitress stopped by to take their order, one of his new employees. She did a good job, though he was a little distracted by Rose's paws marching across his lap to sniff out his other wrist. She went to town on it, stretching across his lap, her little tongue tickling his wrist.

"Oh my God!" Hailey exclaimed. "Rose is sitting in your lap!"

Rose didn't even react, just dug in further, holding his wrist with both paws and licking like crazy. He shifted his wrist so it was less obvious, and Rose rolled to her back, trying to get her head under his arm again.

"I guess she likes me," he said casually. The butter had to be gone by now, but Rose wouldn't stop licking.

Hailey stared at Rose, who was now sniffing up his bare arm in a T-shirt, probably looking for more delicious butter. *Just call me dognip.* He scratched Rose behind the ear and she licked his wrist enthusiastically.

"She's giving you kisses," Hailey whispered in an astonished voice. "She must trust you."

Rose went up on her hind legs, rested her front paws on his shoulder, and licked the dab of butter behind his ear.

"She's hugging you just like she hugs me!" Hailey exclaimed.

"She likes me." He turned to Hailey. "Maybe she knows I got her a present."

Hailey's jaw dropped, her eyes wide. "You did?"

He held onto Rose with one hand as he shifted to pull the small collar from his back jeans pocket. It was pink with rhinestones. Just the kind of sissy dog-wear Hailey put on Rose on a regular basis. He handed the collar to Hailey. "For when she attends weddings."

Hailey snatched it from his fingers. "It's darling! She'll love it. Thanks so much!"

"No problem. I know she's a big part of your business." Rose's tongue wandered, licking his neck. He must be covered in dog slobber at this point. He handed Rose to Hailey. "Here. Try it on her."

She took Rose, cooing over her as she switched out the collar.

His dad gave him a smile and knowing look across the table.

Yeah, that's right, I kissed up to her dog. Sue me.

Hailey held up Rose proudly, wearing her new collar.

"Beautiful!" Brandy exclaimed.

"Very nice," his dad said.

Hailey turned to him and flashed a smile that grabbed him by the balls. She was pure incandescent happiness shining in his direction for the first time ever. It took his breath away. Why hadn't he thought of kissing up to her dog sooner?

She settled Rose back into her dog purse on the bench seat between them. Rose scrambled out to climb on his lap and promptly fell asleep. If only Hailey were that easy to get into his lap. Ha! Not for sex, that door was closed. More of a trust thing. He wanted to earn back her trust most of all.

Dinner was…interesting. Brandy kept up a steady stream of conversation, his dad chimed in on a regular basis, and Hailey was quiet, sneaking glances over at Rose curled up on his lap, and glancing up at him like she still couldn't believe it. He'd put his napkin over Rose so he wouldn't spill on her, and it looked like a little blanket.

As soon as the check arrived, his dad snatched it up. "My treat as congratulations for Garner's. You going to keep the name?"

"Thanks, Dad. I'll keep the name for now since everyone knows it."

"Thanks for dinner, Joe," Hailey said.

"Of course," his dad said with a smile.

"Yes, thanks," Brandy said.

His dad smoothed a lock of Brandy's hair behind her ear. "What's mine is yours, sweetheart."

Brandy smiled at his dad, her eyes watering. They kissed.

He looked away and caught Hailey's eye, who looked revolted. It *was* weird to watch your parent all mushy and romantic with someone in front of you. He crossed his eyes and stuck out his tongue. She giggled.

His dad set the check down. "Actually, we're going to stay and get some coffee too." He turned to him. "Josh, could you do me a favor and take a bookcase over to Hailey's place?"

Josh shot him a look. First his dad told him to keep his distance, and then he sends him to be alone with Hailey at her place? What the hell? "Right now?"

His dad stared back and spoke in a tone that brooked no

argument. "It's a nice gesture to help out your new stepsister. The bookcase is in my truck parked out back."

Josh seethed, not liking the heavy-handedness of his dad's plan to end the war. Josh was doing just fine with his own better plan to make amends and move things forward with Hailey, until his dad had to squash it.

Brandy wiggled her fingers at Hailey. "You remember that bookcase you always liked of mine? The distressed wood, pale blue—"

"I love that bookcase!" Hailey exclaimed. "You're giving it to me?"

Brandy smiled and nodded. "The antique look doesn't go with Joe's place. I know you've always admired it." She turned to him. "Josh, would you be a dear and move it to Hailey's apartment? I'd so appreciate it."

Family was overrated.

8

———

Josh stifled a sigh as Hailey turned to him expectantly. There were so many holes in this stupid move-the-bookcase setup he couldn't believe Hailey didn't see it. First of all, his dad was just as big as Josh and kept fit. He could easily move the bookcase himself. How did he get it into the truck in the first place, huh? Second, the bookcase just happened to be in the truck parked in back of Garner's? Obviously Brandy and his dad parked here ahead of time with their plan in mind and then walked to get Hailey. They easily could've driven a few more blocks and delivered the bookcase to Hailey's place.

"It's too heavy for us to move," Brandy said in a chirpy voice. "Your dad hurt his back just getting it into the truck."

His dad shot him a look that said, *End the war, son. Here's how you do it.*

Fucking A. He didn't need help ending the war. He could do things his way.

"I'd really appreciate it," Hailey said to him. "If you're not too busy."

"Sure." Like he could deny her anything. Okay, at one point he'd denied her drinks at the bar, but she'd tanked his sex life with that impotence rumor, so they were even. Sort of. She might be a little up on him with that devious move.

Hailey wiggled a bit in her excitement. "It's so gorgeous!

The front was made from an antique picture frame carved with these curlicue swirls all along the top and sides. Truly unique."

He held out his palm to his dad, who dropped the pickup truck's keys in his hand. "Be back soon."

"No hurry," Brandy said. "We're going to just enjoy our coffee."

"Leave Rose with us," his dad said. "We'll take her for a walk around the block after coffee."

"Are you sure?" Hailey asked, oblivious to their parents' maneuvering.

"Absolutely," his dad declared.

Josh got out of the booth and waited for Hailey to hand over Rose to his dad and scoot out. She was so classy that she managed to get out of the booth while keeping her dress anchored down, not giving him even a glimpse of what was underneath. Probably a thong. Not that he was looking or thinking about her thong. Much.

He led the way around the bar to the back exit, Hailey's heels clicking along next to him, her floral scent washing over him.

"I can't get over how Rose curled up in your lap," Hailey said.

"Warm spot, I guess."

"She only sleeps on someone she trusts."

He met her eyes. "So I finally earned her trust. How about yours?" He kept his voice light, knowing she wasn't there yet, but wanting her to know he hoped for that.

She pursed her lips. "I'm not a dog."

He chuckled to himself. Nope, she was no dog. He headed through the parking lot and stopped at the truck, opening the passenger-side door for her.

She looked up at him, fire in her pale blue eyes. "Let me guess, you're doing that devious little laugh because you're thinking I'm a bitch, like Rose is a female dog."

"So suspicious."

She cocked her head. "Were you baking today? You smell like cookies."

Heat crept up his neck. "Nope. Get in."

She went up on tiptoe to sniff him, and he remained very still, really hoping she didn't notice any lingering butter scent on him. "Actually, you smell like Rose. I thought I smelled cookies."

He bit back a smile. She eyed him for a moment and finally climbed in the truck. He shut the door behind her and headed over to the other side. The bookcase was tied down with crisscrossing bungee cords in the truck's flatbed. Five shelves, a little over three feet wide. His dad easily could've handled it.

He climbed into the driver's seat and pulled out of the lot. "So how's your prince?"

"He's not my prince."

"What did you guys do after coffee?" Mad had told him nothing big had happened. Just coffee. He had to check with Hailey, though, because Mad could've been holding out on him through some twisted girl code that prevented her from revealing Hailey's private info. It had happened before. Mad knew about the impotence rumor Hailey started long before Josh got wind of it and had claimed girl code prevented her from sharing with him. Mad was an unreliable informant, but she was all he had.

"Nothing. Just coffee."

He couldn't tell if she was disappointed or if it didn't bother her. Her tone was subdued. "You into him?"

She laughed.

"Are you?" he pressed.

"He's not interested in me like that. He's a client."

"That doesn't answer my question."

She smoothed nonexistent wrinkles out of her dress. "Why do you care?"

"Looking out for you, princess."

"Don't," she snapped.

Dammit, he was screwing up this golden opportunity to make amends. It was the first time he'd been alone with her since that disastrous night at his place.

"Sorry about calling you princess," he said. "I meant

Hailey. Our parents want us to make amends, and I want that too."

She sniffed. "Old habits die hard, I guess." She turned to him. "Wait, did our parents say something?"

"My dad told me to end the war between us for the sake of our families. So what would it take?" He left out the part where he was warned not to cross the line with her. What was the point? He'd do the right thing, and it was unlikely she'd attempt to seduce him again after his rejection. Besides, she had the playboy prince turning her head. Her fantasy man.

She took a deep breath, looking thoughtful. "It would help a lot if you were nice to me."

"Nice," he bit out. "And what am I now?"

"Confrontational."

Pot calling kettle, please pick up the phone. "Maybe it would help if you were nice to me."

"I'm always nice!"

He shut his mouth before they started fighting again. But guess what? She wasn't always nice and he *liked* that about her. He liked her fighting spirit, liked that she had sharp teeth and claws. She matched him like no woman ever had before. Hell.

A few minutes later, he pulled up in front of the old colonial where she lived. He'd never been invited in before. He'd always met her at Ludbury House for their wedding-escort dates.

"You can back into the driveway," she said. "The owner is away on business. I have the basement apartment, and the entrance is in back."

Hailey lived in a crap basement apartment? He never would've expected it, given how great her wedding planning business was going. A horrifying thought struck him. It must've cost her dearly to pay him to be her wedding escort. He barely resisted slapping his forehead at his complete miscalculation. Shit, shit, shit.

"You got it," he said, forcing his tone to sound normal. He backed the truck into the driveway and turned it off. She hopped out of the truck before he could open her door for her.

He went to the bookcase, untied everything, and slid the thick quilted movers' blanket under the bookcase to the end of the flatbed. He set the bookcase on the driveway. It wasn't light, but it wasn't all that heavy either. "Lead the way."

She went around the back of the house and down some concrete steps. He waited for her to unlock the door and then followed her down, setting the bookcase inside the living room of her apartment. Then he just gaped at girly nirvana. The sofa was floral, the lamps on the end tables had shades with white fringes, the bookcase was filled with romance novels, and the coffee table held a fanned-out display of bridal magazines. This was a woman who lived and breathed romance. So why was she so prickly with him? She should be softer, more open to his new attempts at reconciliation. Just because he'd turned her down once when she'd dropped her dress to the floor…nope. Do *not* go there.

He rubbed the back of his neck, avoiding looking at her sexy body, trying to get the image of her in only a bra and thong out of his head. Again. He glanced around. The living room was open to a small dining area and a kitchen separated by a half wall. A short hallway led to what he assumed was her bedroom and a bathroom.

He met her eyes, back under control. Mostly. "So, uh, where do you want it?" *Now why did that sound dirty?*

"My bedroom. I'll show you."

Now that really did sound dirty, though she said it real casual-like. He followed her into her bedroom—an explosion of pink, lace, and flowers. Had any man ever breached this girly territory? The bed had a brass headboard, a rose-patterned comforter, and white lacy covers on two large pillows with a bunch of satin pillows in various shades of pink piled in front of them. The dresser and nightstand were white with rose decals she'd probably put on herself. A border of roses along the top of the walls added to the flowery effect.

"Are the roses in honor of Rose?" he asked.

She glanced around. "No, they were here first. She was already named Rose when I got her. Guess it was fate."

He moved the bookcase to the wall by the bed's headboard. She had a nightstand on the other side. It was the only place the bookcase could possibly go.

"Perfect!" she exclaimed. "Or should we move it next to the dresser?"

"It won't fit there."

"Sideways?"

"Half of it will be inaccessible."

She planted her hands on her hips as she studied the space. "I guess you're right." She turned to him with a smile. "Now I have to move to a bigger place that goes with my bookcase."

He smiled back. "Looks that way."

She left the bedroom, and he followed, his gaze involuntarily dropping to her curvy ass. She stopped at the entrance to her kitchen and turned to him. He jerked his gaze up to her eyes.

"Snickerdoodle?" she asked.

The simple act of hospitality warmed him. She was letting him in, sort of. "No, thanks. I don't like sweets." He did like her fudgy brownies, they were incredible, and he still hadn't figured out the secret ingredient. She wouldn't share the recipe because he was the enemy. In any case, she hadn't offered brownies.

She tossed her hair over her shoulder. "How can you not like sweets?"

He stepped closer. "I just don't."

She threw her hands up. "But that's the only thing I can cook!"

He closed the distance between them, still keeping a gentlemanly space so he could resist hauling her into his arms. *Off-limits.* "I can cook. My boss made me take a bunch of cooking classes for Garner's."

Her cheeks flushed pink. "Mad says you took those classes because you're a foodie."

"What else did Mad say about me?"

She pursed her lips. "Only good things. She's president of the Josh fan club."

He grinned. At least Mad had come through for him.

She eased back a step into her kitchen and flicked on the light. "This must be why you're so cranky all the time." She turned and helped herself to a glass of water. Guess her hospitality vanished, since she didn't offer him any water.

"I'm not cranky. What, you think the kind of food you eat affects your personality?"

She set her glass down on the counter with a thunk. "Yes."

He crossed his arms. "You're not very sweet."

She slammed her hands on her hips. "I am so."

He slowly shook his head, smiling.

She dropped her hands and smiled a little back. "Well, I don't eat many sweets either. Usually I give them away."

"Hypocrite."

She gestured for him to move back since he was blocking her exit from the kitchen. He shifted, and she rushed past him like he was about to pounce on her. Did she sense the raging lust coursing through his veins? Maybe. But she had no idea how strong-willed he was. He could control himself—keep his distance for everyone's sake. *But what about you?* a voice whispered in his head. *What about what you want?*

"I guess we should go," she chirped, standing much too far away from him.

They stared at each other. Seconds ticked by in charged silence. Every nerve ending crackled to life; his pulse thrummed, all of him tuned into her, hungry for her.

She let out a shaky breath, smoothed her hair and looked away.

"Lead the way," he said.

She went to the door and held it open for him. He strode over and then stopped in front of her, gazing into her eyes with all the lust he'd bottled up for way too long. In that moment all he cared about was her, connecting with her in every way possible.

The door slammed shut—her doing. And that was a go. His gaze never left her eyes as he rested one palm above her head and leaned close, almost but not quite touching, their bodies so close he felt her heat.

Her voice was breathy. "Josh?"

"Yeah."

"If we cross this line, it could backfire really badly. We fight so much. And our parents are getting married in three and a half weeks."

He pushed his guilt away, too far gone to dwell on it. "Maybe if we stop battling our lust, we'll stop fighting, and it will all work out."

She swallowed. His gaze caught on the pulse point beating rapidly in her throat.

He ran his fingers down her throat. "You star in my erotic dreams."

She licked her lips and stared at his mouth. "Are you going *Fierce Longing* on me?" There was a note of hopefulness in her voice. That was part of the erotic romance series her book club was into. He'd seen the movies since his sister-in-law had produced and starred in them. They were *hot*. And the guy, man, he did *not* hold back in staking his claim on his woman.

He spoke close enough he could feel her breath against his lips. "Do you want me to go *Fierce Longing* on you?"

Her breath hitched. "Of course not. I'm—"

He shut her up, his mouth claiming hers, his fingers spearing into her hair, holding her in place, taking what he'd wanted for so long. Everything in him ratcheted up, hot and urgent. He deepened the kiss, and she opened immediately, soft and yielding. *Fuck yes.* The kiss turned wild, urgent, and he fought for control. She made a mewling sound in the back of her throat, her nails digging into his shoulders. He bunched the fabric of her dress with both hands, ready to rip it off her. *Slow down.*

He broke the kiss, trying to catch his breath. "You enjoying my fierce kiss?"

"Stop gloating." She closed her eyes and waited for more.

He gave it to her. Her hands were on his ass now, pulling him closer, her hips lifting to meet him. His cock surged, his need out of control, his hand sliding up the inside of her thigh, reaching a damp scrap of panties. Jesus. He tore his mouth away, breathing hard.

"What?" she asked.

He dropped his hands from her and shifted away. "I don't want to rush with you."

"But I'm into it."

Reality crept in. Their parents were waiting back at Garner's for them, expecting him to end the war in a civil friendly way, not return looking like he'd just gotten laid. He wanted to do a lot more than kiss her, and he suspected she did too. Any way he figured it, the timing sucked. Not only that, he'd left his post at work. He was supposed to be on break.

He jammed a hand in his hair. "I should get back to work."

"You're the boss now." She stepped close again, her hands roaming his chest, revving him further. "Can't you give your-self the night off?"

He stilled her hands on his chest and held them. "The timing is bad, nothing personal, okay? I'm into it too, but they need me to cover my shift. Plus I have to get the truck back to my dad. Your mom and my dad are waiting for us." He left out the fact that crossing this line now while their parents waited was like a big fuck you to his dad after their agree-ment for Josh to keep his distance. In his defense, he'd always been hardheaded with a mind of his own, and his dad knew that. Still, it would not go over well. This was exactly the drama they were supposed to avoid.

She yanked her hands from his. Then she left without a word, heading up the stairs that led outside.

He blew out a breath, adjusted himself, and caught up with her on the driveway. "You get that it's just the timing, right?"

Her eyes flashed. "I'm tired of you rejecting me. You-you tease!"

His lips twitched. "I'm not saying no, I'm saying later."

She glared at him, her mouth forming a snarl that was too

damn sexy. "You go back to Garner's with our parents. I'm staying here."

He held her by the chin. "Are you really mad at me?"

Her lips parted like she wanted him to kiss her again, and her pale blue eyes went soft. So frigging sexy. "No. I'm just very horny, you beast."

He smiled and slid his hand to cup her cheek. "Okay, then."

"Do you really think we could work out? I used to always think we'd kill each other, but then, I don't know…when you kissed me, it felt different."

"Maybe the solution is to kiss more." He stroked her soft cheek with his thumb and gave her a quick kiss. "I'll have my dad drop off Rose, and I'll text you later with the plan."

She slapped a hand over her mouth. "Omigod, I forgot Rose."

He smirked. He'd kissed her senseless. *Nice.* He turned and headed for the truck, not willing to risk another kiss. It made him senseless too.

"Maybe I'll reject *you* next time," she called from behind him.

He turned, grinning. "Sure. Unless I go *Fierce Longing* on you. Turns out it makes you forget everything but me."

She whirled and went back inside.

Some mysterious force drew him in, retracing her steps and standing on the other side of the door. Maybe he wasn't quite done with her tonight.

He heard the snick of the lock and a chain deadbolt. Then a distinct *bonk*. Like she'd kicked the door or smacked it with her head in frustration. Either way, he liked that she wanted him that badly after just one kiss. She must be just as crazy in lust with him as he was with her.

He jogged back up the stairs and over to the truck. This was the second time he'd had to go back to Garner's without her. The first was on that disaster of a night when he'd tried to give her the paid escort money back. There would be questions from his dad and Brandy. Geez, Hailey was really making him look bad by staying behind. Like he'd failed to make things right between them. He couldn't tell them how far he'd gone in the other direction.

He smiled to himself. That kiss told him everything he needed to know. This thing between them was real. Drunk on vodka, my ass. *Nice try, sweetheart, you're mine.*

And screw everyone else. He was determined to make this work so no one could ever say shit about their relationship. The alternative—all-out war within family lines—was too big a disaster to contemplate.

9

———

Two days. The cad. He'd kissed her, worked her up something fierce, and then she hadn't heard from him in two frigging days! She jumped every time she got a text, only to be disappointed. She'd thought after years of fighting that they'd finally moved forward. That kiss had been amazing, like *take me now* amazing, and now…nothing. She needed a serious guy—a man, not a boy who wanted to play games. She blew out a breath of frustration. Now it was Friday, and for some stupid reason she'd thought she'd spend it in bed after…God, how long had it been since she'd had sex? More than six months. Brutal for a woman of her passionate needs. Fuck Josh, the fucker.

Did he think she was at his beck and call? No, sir. Not her. She clicked over to her email. Oh, she had an email from Prince Phillip. A small tingle of excitement ran through her, but then she remembered he hadn't shown much interest in her. He was probably just following up on some details on his sister's behalf. He was taking the lead on the stateside wedding mostly because he wanted his sister to focus on her final exams. Yup. He'd sent the final guest list and made a few requests she could easily handle. She downloaded the guest list, which included a good number of the Rourke family. She was a little surprised so many family members would travel for the stateside wedding when the official royal wedding in Villroy Island would happen only a couple of months later.

She hit reply on the email, assuring Phillip everything would be taken care of. Her phone dinged with a text a few minutes later.

Phillip: Thanks, Hailey, you've made this wedding planning thing so easy. I just got back to my hotel and had to deal with my sister's annoying requests after an exhausting day of business meetings. You understand what that's like, I'm sure. I don't know how you do it, dealing with clients all the time.

His tone felt less formal than usual, like he needed someone to talk to. She quickly texted back: No problem. I enjoy working with clients, but I know what you mean. Sometimes you need downtime. :) I was surprised how many Rourke family members are making the trip to Connecticut. You must have a very close-knit family to attend both weddings.

Phillip: Bah. Those are the riffraff with diluted bloodlines, my Brooklyn cousins. They're not invited to the Villroy wedding because their dad married a commoner against the wishes of the family and abdicated the throne. Silvia's such a bleeding heart she invited them. Apparently, she's spent a lot of time with them since starting Yale. She likes gruff and grumbly men, says they're charming.

Can I call you? I'm too tired to visit with you, but I sure would like a friendly ear.

Eep! She typed back a cheery *Of course!* Her phone rang a moment later. "Hello," she said warmly.

"Ah, that sweet voice just made my day. I've had nothing but rejections all day from stuffy suits."

"What kind of business are you working on, if you don't mind my asking?"

He blew out a breath she heard loud and clear through the phone. "I'm not supposed to talk about it, but if you swear to keep it in confidence…"

"Absolutely. I'm the queen of discretion."

He laughed. "Queen Hailey of Discretion, I love it. So I've been in talks with the top brass of hotel chains because we're considering building a resort back on Villroy. We're losing the young people, who're heading off for more exciting jobs in England and France. The hope is that we'll bring in tourism money and keep some of our young workforce. We can't be an island made up of just the older generation. That's the beginning of the end. Of course Gabriel, the heir, doesn't agree. That's my older brother stick-in-the-mud. He thinks we should keep on as we have been, the traditional way with fishing, but I had to put some feelers out. Someone has to think modern around here. I want to put together a resort proposal with hard numbers and convince him."

She thought for a moment about a resort and what people might do there. "You could have a resort that included taking tourists on fishing expeditions. It would be a unique experience and allow you to keep your traditional way of life."

"Thank you! This is what I've been saying to Gabriel."

"Though if I was on vacation to a nice resort on an island kingdom, not that I've ever travelled that far, but if I did, I would most like to tour the royal castle. Ooh! You could have destination weddings at the castle. Give brides the total fairy-tale experience."

Silence.

"Just an idea," she quickly added.

"No, I see the appeal. It's just that it's a private residence. Quite a few of us live there still. It's so big we don't get in each other's way."

"Completely understand the need for privacy."

"Tell me more about your business. I'm curious how you've built it up so quickly in such a short time. Silvia tells me your feature article in *Bride Special* puts you in an elite league of wedding planners."

She smiled so big her cheeks hurt. Pride warmed her through and through. She'd worked so hard for everything she had, and she rarely got any compliments on her hard work. Most clients took her for granted, as she stayed in the background making sure everything with their wedding went smoothly. Clients expected the wedding to be perfect—that was what they paid a wedding planner for—but it took a lot of work to take it to that level. "Thank you, Phillip. That means a lot to me. You really want to know the nitty-gritty of my wedding planning career?"

"I really do. Maybe it'll help me think up some good business ideas for back home. Maybe a resort isn't the answer."

"It's not a bad idea at all," she assured him.

"So how does it work? You own that mansion? Do you live there too?"

It seemed like he really did want to know how things worked, and it pleased her to talk shop. She talked and talked and talked. Phillip kept up a steady stream of questions and was such a good listener that it was easy to do.

"You're incredible," Phillip said when she'd finished.

She flushed and sat a little straighter in her seat. "Thank you."

"I know this might sound completely out there, but I'd like to make you an offer."

"What do you mean?"

"You said you rent Ludbury House from the town. For the stability of your future business, you should own it. I'd like to buy it for you."

She gasped. She'd looked into buying it last year, and the cost was way out of her league—two million plus hefty property taxes. Even figuring out a scenario where she lived upstairs to save on rent and rented the mansion back to the town for community events didn't bring it close to her budget. *What a princely offer!* "It's much too expensive. I could never ask that of you."

"In return you could consult with me on the resort or any other ideas you conjure to help Villroy. I'm truly impressed with all you've accomplished single-handedly."

She was speechless.

He went on. "Would a ten-year loan with two percent interest work for you?"

She blinked as it occurred to her he was negotiating a business investment and not making a princely gesture toward her. "I'm afraid it's still out of my budget." She'd already done the math, and even a thirty-year loan would be tough.

"Work up some numbers and we'll see if we can work something out."

"It would have to be a much longer loan to bring it within range."

"Email me the details when you get a chance. Now there's something I'd like to ask you."

"Anything," she replied immediately. The man was trying to help her make her dreams come true.

He chuckled. "Ah, Hailey, a woman after my own capitalistic nature. I like that we see eye to eye. Just between you and me, I've been in a rut. Literally. I broke up with someone after five years, and then I rutted my way through Europe. That's the other reason I'm here; besides babysitting my sister and putting out some business feelers, I'm supposed to be lying low. Then I met you, accomplished, beautiful Hailey. All of that to say, would you be my date for my sister's wedding? You're the kind of classy woman who could restore my reputation."

She *was* a classy lady and didn't mind helping him out. "Sure. You mean Silvia's wedding here, right?" Silvia had already invited her as a courtesy, but this would be a little different, going as his date. She'd need to get Ally to help cover some of the background details on the wedding day so Hailey could focus on helping Phillip restore his image in front of his closest family and friends.

"Here and back home," he replied. "All expenses paid, of course."

Ahh! The prince wants to bring me as his date to the royal wedding on Villroy Island!

"They wouldn't mind that I'm a commoner?" she blurted. He'd said before his Brooklyn cousins weren't invited to the Villroy wedding because their dad abdicated the throne by marrying a commoner.

"My cousins are only excluded because their dad was the

heir. I'm the spare and get more leeway. You will be treated royally, I promise."

"That would be lovely," she replied in what she hoped was a calm composed voice. She'd always wanted to travel, but never had the money. She'd never even flown in a plane before. The furthest she'd been was an eighth-grade field trip to Washington, DC, by bus.

"Wonderful," Phillip said. "I'll send you the details. There will be quite a bit of press back home, and this will really help me out. Thanks again."

"Thank *you*! I'm really looking forward to it."

"Talk soon."

"Any time."

He hung up. She disconnected and just sat there for a long moment in shock. Was she really going to Villroy Island as the guest of a freaking prince in a royal wedding? What did this mean? Was she just a prop to restore his reputation, or was he interested in her? He was very appealing—handsome, surprisingly down-to-earth, and an actual prince. She shouldn't get hung up on the prince thing, but it was hard not to. It was like every fairy-tale movie she'd ever seen. The royal thing was impossible to resist.

She needed to talk to Mad, her best friend and the only woman she knew who spoke "guy" fluently on account of her slew of big brothers. She texted her first: *Desperately need to talk. Is this a good time to call?*

She knew Mad had a busy schedule between working shifts at Garner's as bartender and waitress and finishing up college with her bachelor's degree. Plus she lived with her fiancé and half the time they were going at it.

Mad texted back: *Come over. Park's grilling burgers. We'll throw one on for you.*

Hailey: *On my way!*

She quickly closed up shop, took care of Rose, and got them both into her car. Mad lived in an apartment in Eastman, the town next to Clover Park. She was so relieved Mad was available. This kind of news couldn't be delayed.

When she got to Mad and Parker's first-floor apartment,

Mad answered the door in her usual worn T-shirt, cargo shorts, and black work boots. She was petite and fit, her body swimming in her "comfortable" clothes. Her hair was up in a high ponytail, which gave it a very interesting look since she was growing out the dyed fire-engine red. Now just the ponytail was red and the rest dark brown.

"Your hair almost looks normal," Hailey said, flicking the ponytail.

"Right? I'm starting to remember what I used to look like." She scooped Rose out of Hailey's purse and cuddled her close. "Hello, puppy."

Hailey stepped inside to a comfortable space with a black leather sectional, ottoman, and glass coffee table. A big-screen TV hung on the wall across from the sofa.

"Stick around after dinner," Mad said. "We're watching this cool car show where they restore classic cars." Parker worked at a classic-car restoration shop. It wasn't Hailey's speed, but she appreciated the way Mad always included her.

"Maybe. Depends on how tired I am. It's been quite a week!"

"I hear that. Beer?" She set Rose on the floor, who followed Mad to the kitchen, sniffing for crumbs.

"I'll just get some water." Hailey went to the kitchen too and got herself some water. She knew where everything was.

Mad took two bottles of beer from the refrigerator, popped the tops, and took one to the small concrete patio, where Parker was grilling. He was tall with an athletic grace, his short dark brown hair emphasizing sharp cheekbones and an angular jaw. Hailey waved to him through the glass patio door. He lifted a hand in greeting with a smile. Parker was such a good match for Mad, both of them athletic, strong, and tough. He was reserved whereas Mad was outgoing, but they balanced each other out.

Mad returned with a tennis ball that she bounced over to Rose in the kitchen. Rose couldn't get her mouth around it, so she just kept chasing it as it rolled all over the kitchen.

"All right," Mad said, taking a seat on the sofa. "Spill. For someone who's desperate to talk, you sure take your time."

Hailey joined her, setting her water on the coffee table. "It's called being polite."

"Ha! It's called stalling." She took a pull on her beer. "What did Josh do this time?" She knew their rocky history. She'd witnessed most of it.

"It's not him. Okay, remember Prince Phillip?"

"Ah, yeah. Hard to forget the guy you wouldn't shut up about. What happened? He ask you out?"

She squirmed a bit in her seat and then crossed her legs, folding her hands on top in a composed pose. "Even better, I think, I'm not sure. I can't figure out where I stand. First off, he offered to buy Ludbury House for me."

"What?" Mad screeched. She set her beer on the coffee table and leaned forward. "No fucking way!"

Hailey nodded, pleased Mad saw the enormity of this event. "I know it sounds outrageous, right? But it might be just an investment for him. He offered me a loan with low interest."

"Did he ask for a percentage of your business?"

"No."

Mad sliced a hand through the air. "He's trying to buy your love. He probably doesn't have the cash for an outright gift, so he's offering what he can. Total prince move. He's into you."

Hailey smoothed her hair with a shaky hand. This was beyond exciting. Mad was usually spot-on with guy speak, except when she teased Hailey that Josh was into her. Josh might have kissed her recently after *she* took the initiative, practically begging him to go *Fierce Longing* on her, but there was a long stretch of time where she knew he hated her. Maybe not hate, more strong dislike. Whatever. Why was she thinking about Josh now? He'd completely blown her off. Games. She didn't have time for that shit.

Mad eyed her. "You into the prince thing?"

"Who wouldn't be? It's like every fairy-tale fantasy every girl grows up with."

"Not me."

"Well, I did. And not only did he make that nice offer to

help me with my business, he invited me to be his date at the royal weddings for Princess Silvia, both here and on Villroy Island this summer!" Her voice cracked on a high note of excitement. She could hardly believe she'd be traveling in that elite circle. Imagine the people she'd meet!

Mad grunted and grabbed her beer, tipping it up to her mouth and speaking around it. "He wants you."

She wiggled a little in her seat. What if she became a princess?

Or she could just be one of the many women Phillip rutted and threw away. Hadn't he said he'd rutted his way through Europe? Maybe now he was rutting his way through America. Hailey was of an age where she needed to know there was at least a *possibility* of a relationship to go with the sex. She'd thought maybe Josh—no. *Stop thinking about that jerk.* She wanted a relationship. Otherwise, she would've stayed in her friends-with-benefits arrangement. All of her physical needs had been met that way for years, but, in the end, she'd longed for love.

She slumped into the sofa. It pained her to admit, being a huge fan of love, but she'd never experienced love herself. It was kinda embarrassing given her job and her marketing angle as a love junkie.

"What about Josh?" Mad asked.

"What about him?"

"Don't play dumb. I know something's going on there. Josh is different now."

"He is?"

"Yeah, he's whistling and shit."

Heat spread through her, half-embarrassed, half-turned on at the memory of their kiss. "I don't know why."

"Liar. What happened? And don't tell me nothing."

Hailey blew out a breath of exasperation. She couldn't talk to Mad about Josh. Mad would take Josh's side. He was her big brother and she owed him for helping her pay for college. "Look, I just wanted you to translate Phillip's guy speak. I don't want to talk about your brother."

"Fine. I'll ask him."

Josh would never share the details. He was much too private for that, and everyone knew Mad had no filter. She worried her lower lip. She knew Josh so well in some ways, and in other ways he was a complete mystery. She never should've crossed the line with him. He'd sounded so sincere when he'd said they could stop fighting and make it work. Then nothing. Her throat tightened. She was tired of Josh stomping on her feelings. Now she was stuck with him forever thanks to their parents. Talk about awkward around the holidays. She'd have to see him with whatever girlfriend he brought around, like when he was gaga for Clarissa. Dammit.

"Whatever," Hailey said. "Thanks for the translation. Are you going to the book club meeting at Claire's on Sunday night?" The Happy Endings Book Club meeting had been moved to Claire's place instead of their usual meeting at Something's Brewing Café. Claire was too famous a movie star to appear in public without causing a stir, so they sometimes met at her home in Connecticut.

"Yeah, I'll give you a ride." Mad liked to share rides so they could talk, and she also liked to be in the driver's seat.

"Thanks."

Parker slid the patio door open. "Burger time."

She joined Mad getting out the condiments and chips. Then they settled at the small breakfast bar that divided the kitchen from the living room and dug in. Park sat on a bar stool on the end, then Mad, then Hailey. Rose lay down under the breakfast bar, prepared to pounce on any burger that might fall her way.

Mad told them about her classes and a big group project she was working on, launching a new product. The great thing about Mad and Parker was that Hailey never felt like a third wheel; she just felt like part of the gang. That was how Mad had made her feel right from the beginning with her family too, casually including her like she was actually part of the family. Of course, that made her worry about her flaky mom ruining the good thing Hailey had going with the Campbell clan. Everyone would turn on her because her mom hurt their dad. And that made her think of Josh, the one part of the Campbells she couldn't seem to make peace with. Did Josh have any intentions toward her? Did Phillip?

Had Josh already forgotten about their passionate kiss?

Men and their stupid games. Fuck them all. After this she'd go home to the best kind of man—the fictional one in her latest steamy read. Book boyfriend for the win.

She glanced over as Mad laughed and Parker smiled back, love in his eyes. Hailey's heart squeezed painfully hard. Was love ever going to happen for her?

10

———

Josh played the worst basketball game of his life with the guys on Saturday afternoon. His limbs were like lead, his focus shit. He'd intended to get in touch with Hailey on Friday—once he knew she was off work—for dinner on Sunday night. He was needed at work on Friday and Saturday nights, the busiest time for Garner's, so it had to be Sunday. He'd spent most of Thursday thinking up the best date ideas that would show his serious intentions, and settled on dinner at his place. Then he spent most of Friday thinking up the best menu. He'd planned on making her dinner, slipping the money he owed her into her purse when she wasn't looking, and giving her the gift that he'd special ordered for her. They'd kiss, for sure, but he was determined to take it slow. He wanted her to know this was for real, not just him acting on lust like most men probably did with her. And then the whole thing came to a crashing halt when Mad called to tell him the stupid prince had offered to buy Ludbury House for Hailey. Talk about a big gesture. Obviously the guy was into her. Not only that, Hailey had agreed to be the prince's date at a wedding on Villroy Island. What the hell was she doing accepting dates from another guy after they'd shared that intense kiss?

What if she went to Villroy and never came back?

The prince offered glamour and glitz, the fairy-tale kind of life that he knew Hailey dreamed about. Hadn't she said she fantasized about the prince whenever she read one of her romantic stories?

He stalked off the basketball court and grabbed his water bottle.

Jake, his twin, appeared at his side, grabbed his own water bottle, and drank. Josh knew from a lifetime of twin connection that Jake knew he was playing like shit because he was upset. He probably also knew it was because of Hailey. Most things rolled off his back, but Hailey's pink claws were into him good.

"Hey," Jake said.

Josh grunted and drank more water. He didn't want to talk about it.

Jake wiped his mouth on his T-shirt sleeve. "You free this afternoon? I got something back at the house I want to show you."

He went for a neutral expression, lowering his lashes, his poker face that worked with everyone but Jake. Still he had to try, his mood too shitty to inflict on anyone. "What is it?"

Jake hip-checked him. "Come over and find out."

He eyed him. Jake grinned.

Josh stated the obvious as a warning. "I'm in a shitty mood."

"This'll cheer you up." Jake exhaled sharply. "It's a present, okay? Too big to give to you here. Would you just come over?"

A present? A big one? It wasn't their birthday. He'd be lying if he said he wasn't curious. And it sounded a helluva lot better than having a heart-to-heart talk with Jake about woman problems. Ever since Jake had married Claire, he acted like he was an expert on relationships.

Josh inclined his head. "Sure, thanks. Let me shower and I'll meet you there."

"Later," Jake said and headed for his BMW.

Josh headed for his Miata convertible, his mind turning over why he was getting a present and what it could be. The new focus helped the dark cloud lift, his mind clearing. He never should've touched Hailey in the first place. He'd known it was wrong, and for some stupid reason he'd thought it would just work itself out. His fingers gripped the steering wheel tight. He had his dream bar, family, friends that were like brothers to him, and…lots of good stuff going on.

Jake had *amazing* stuff going on. Josh pulled through the security gate of Jake and Claire's horse farm that was more of an estate. Claire was wealthy from her work as a movie star and her film production company, and Jake was wealthy from his tech company Dat Cloud. Josh could've gotten in on the ground floor of Dat Cloud, but he'd taken a different path. He had no regrets. Just an occasional twinge of what might've been. He passed a couple of historic houses on the property before pulling up the circular drive of the main house. Jake and Claire had moved in a few months ago in January, so he'd been here before, but he still hadn't gotten used to it. The place screamed money at the top of its lungs.

He got out of his car and just took in the gorgeous property for a minute. Acres of rolling hills with woodlands just beyond, all of it in the bloom of spring—flowering trees, bright green new leaves and grass, landscaped beds of bright yellow daffodils. Horses grazed in a large paddock by the pond. More barns and stables off in the distance. *Must be nice.*

He turned to the large stone and stucco mansion, with arts-and-crafts-style post and beams on the upper levels and the large porch, and headed for the door. He lifted the metal knocker on the door, and the door popped open a moment later. Jake probably knew he was here from the security guard who'd let Josh in at the gate.

"Von't you come in?" Jake drawled in a deep Dracula voice.

Josh snorted and followed him in.

"To the man cave," Jake said and headed in that direction.

Josh followed him through the foyer to the kitchen and the stairs just beyond to the basement man cave. It was basically Josh's dream bar in Jake's house. There were not one but *two* bars down there, one for regular drinks and one for wine tasting complete with a wine cellar of extraordinary wines. The regular bar was in a large room surrounded with all the best stuff—big-screen TV, pool table, Ping-Pong, pinball, old-school arcade games.

Jake bypassed the wine-tasting room and headed for the main bar area, stopping at the far end of the room. Josh stopped next to him, where they both stared at a new addition to the man cave—a gorgeous vintage jukebox. Shiny chrome with lilac trim, the forty-five record player visible through the glass. Another addition to Josh's dream bar in his twin's house.

"Nice," Josh muttered, trying to keep the envy from his voice.

"It's yours," Jake said.

Josh's head whipped toward Jake in surprise. "This is my present? For what?"

"It's a congratulations-on-your-new-bar gift. Whenever you get the addition finished, I'll have it delivered. What do you think?"

Josh's throat closed with emotion. Here he'd been envious, when his brother, as usual, was being generous. He swallowed hard, turning back to the jukebox. "It's really cool. Thank you so much."

"Sure. It's an antique. Nineteen sixty-two, fully restored. One hundred twenty selection for forty-five RPM records. You can see the whole thing set and play, stereo sound."

"It's amazing." He turned to Jake. "I really appreciate it."

Jake nodded, smiling and looking at the jukebox. "Can't wait to see it in your place. Wanna play pool?"

"Sure." A weight lifted off him. An awesome present and a game of pool were exactly what he needed to relax after two long days planning and then ditching his stupid date idea for Hailey. He was not a prince by any stretch of the imagination, by deed or title. He was just a guy who owned the local bar.

Somehow his big accomplishment—taking ownership of Garner's—felt too little, too late.

Jake racked up the balls and broke. Josh went into deep-focus mode, some part of him needing the win. Time passed quickly as he kicked his twin's ass. The weird thing was, Jake didn't seem to care. Was he letting him win?

Jake set up an impossible shot, aimed, and missed.

Josh finished up, claiming the win.

Jake smiled. "Good game."

"What're you so damn happy about?" Josh barked. "I crushed you."

Jake smiled even wider. "Claire's pregnant. Nine weeks along. We're due October thirtieth." He barked out a laugh. "I'm going to be a dad!"

His chest ached as he stared at his twin's brilliant smile, pure happiness written all over his face. A wave of intense longing momentarily prevented speech. Jake was leaving him in the dust.

"Josh?"

He snapped to attention. "Congratulations! Wow, that's big news." He went over, shook his hand, and gave him a bro hug with a slap on the back for good measure.

Not that life was a contest, but if it was, Jake was winning. His twin had beat him out of the womb by two minutes and had been in the lead ever since—personally and profession-ally. Thirty-five years old and Jake had it all—hugely successful business, a beautiful home, gorgeous loving wife, and now a baby. Soon Jake would be wrapped up in his new family. They'd probably have a slew of kids. Meanwhile Josh had a crappy one-bedroom apartment and had just drained his savings and gone into debt with a loan to buy the bar. Even owning the bar, finally, didn't seem enough. No wife, not even a girlfriend. His mood plummeted from shitty to dark despair. If he could've cried, he'd be a blubbering mess just like Hailey was in his office two weeks ago. Of course, that was before the playboy prince. Now her life was all sunshine and mansions.

Rock-bottom suckage. *Wallow is me.*

A stab of guilt hit him as Jake enthusiastically pulled him into a full-on hug before leaning back, holding Josh by the arms. "You're the first person I told."

Josh swallowed over the lump in his throat. "Really happy for you and Claire." He pulled away and turned toward the stairs. "I'm going to go up and tell Claire congrats."

"Hold up." Jake went to the wall and pressed on the intercom system. "Paging Claire Jordan. Please report to the man cave."

Claire's husky voice came through loud and clear. "Whadda ya need?"

Jake winked at Josh. "I need your pretty ass down here, pronto."

"Bite me."

Jake leaned close to the intercom. "Josh is here."

Claire's loud sigh echoed. "Why didn't you say so? Be right down to see your better half."

"You're my better half," Jake cooed.

Claire made a kissy noise, and Jake smiled like an idiot. *Somebody slap me if I ever look like that over a woman.*

Josh stuffed his hands in his jeans pockets. "When're you going to tell Dad?"

"He and Brandy are coming for dinner tonight, so I'll tell him then. After that, I'll tell everyone else."

"I'm honored you told me first."

"Of course. I'm surprised you couldn't twin sense it. I could barely keep the secret this long."

He forced a smile. "Guess we were overdue for a twin refuel." That had been an elaborate high-five, low-five routine with a revving engine of twin fuel they'd done when they were kids.

"Yeah, ha!"

"Who did Claire tell?" *Does Hailey know?* Dammit. Why did everything circle back to her?

"Claire told her parents weeks ago, who told her brother. Tomorrow night, her friends are meeting here for their book club meeting, and she'll tell them the big news then. Everyone else is on a need-to-know basis. She doesn't want paparazzi showing up to get pictures of her pregnant."

"Understandable."

Jake broke into a wide smile, looking over Josh's shoulder. "There's my beautiful pregnant wife."

"My gorgeous husband and his equally gorgeous twin," Claire returned with her throaty husky laugh.

"Hey," Jake protested. "I'm the prize stallion here."

Josh smiled and crossed to Claire. "Congratulations!" His gaze dropped to her stomach, still flat under a black silk short-sleeve shirt. He met her hazel eyes, her blond shoulder-length hair up in a twist. Even dressed casually, Claire's beauty and presence were mesmerizing. No wonder the cameras loved her.

"Thank you!" Claire hugged him. She pulled back suddenly, her eyes direct. "What's wrong?"

Josh went for a neutral expression. "Nothing."

Claire was having none of it. "You're so tense it's making me tense. And I know this face. Jake has the same expression when something goes south and he doesn't know how to fix it." Damn, the woman was intuitive. "Are you having difficulties with Garner's? Something holding you up with the construction? Trouble getting permits or something?"

Claire was all up in his business because she loved him, loved all of their family, which was the only reason he wasn't irritated that she was harping on his perfectly acceptable need to pretend everything was A-OK during this shitty time. Besides, he didn't want to rain on their happy baby parade.

"Garner's is fine," he assured her.

She narrowed her eyes.

"And so am I," he added.

Jake and Claire exchanged a meaningful look before turning back to him.

He shrugged one shoulder. "I'm just tired. I didn't sleep well last night."

"Insomnia?" Jake asked sympathetically. He knew that was usually related to some lingering PTSD.

"No, just thinking. Tossing, turning."

"That's insomnia," Jake said.

Josh avoided Claire's sharp assessing gaze and focused on Jake. "It wasn't like that. Usually I'm wired with insomnia like I need to get out of bed and do stuff. This time, I felt tired, but my mind kept whirling." He hoped that was enough information to move back to happy baby land.

"Who's on your mind?" Claire asked. She'd been after him to close the deal with Hailey, claiming their fighting was a front. So she turned out to be right. It sure didn't help anything.

"You guys pick names for the baby?" he asked.

Claire put a hand on his arm. "I only want to help, Josh. I love you."

His throat thick, he could only jerk his chin at her. Hearing *I love you* did something to him. He didn't feel very lovable most of the time. Damn, he was turning into a crusty old bachelor at thirty-five.

"I have some sparkling cider to celebrate this occasion," Jake said. "Let's have a toast."

"Aww, Jake," Claire said, going up on tiptoe to kiss him.

Glad for the distraction, Josh took a seat at the bar. A moment later, Claire took the seat next to him. Jake went behind the bar, opened the cider, and poured them all a glass.

Jake lifted his glass. "To a healthy baby!"

"Hear, hear," Josh chimed in.

"Cheers!" Claire said. They all clinked glasses. Claire took a sip, and they followed suit.

Josh hid a wince at the too sweet drink.

"So what's the latest with Hailey's prince?" Claire asked brightly, rubbing it in. *Hailey's prince.* That right there said it all. Everyone saw the writing on the wall. Hailey was a princess who belonged with a prince. "I heard they had coffee," Claire added. "Nice, but I thought a prince might offer something a little more exciting."

Josh slapped his hand on the bar top. "He offered to buy Ludbury House for her! A fucking mansion! Exciting enough for you?"

"Josh," Jake said sharply.

"Sorry, Claire," Josh mumbled. "Didn't mean to snap at you."

Claire nudged him with her shoulder. "I'd much rather hear you say what's on your mind than have you hold it all inside looking so miserable. So the prince offered her a mansion. What have you offered her?"

Josh glared at the bar top. He had one embarrassing gift and a date idea he'd thrown out the window. He couldn't offer her the glitzy fairy-tale life she deserved. The prince was probably like a dream come true for her.

"Offer her what she'll get with you," Jake said. "Don't even try to compete with buying her a mansion."

Josh's lip curled. "Thank you, Mr. Relationship Expert."

Jake kept on doling out advice. "Offer to cook for her—you're like a gourmet chef—invite her to basketball with the guys—"

"She's terrible at basketball," Josh said. They'd all witnessed her unathletic skills on the court back when she'd first become friends with Mad. And he'd abandoned the cooking plan. The prince probably had a chef on staff trained at some fancy French culinary school.

Jake went on like Josh hadn't spoken. "Take her on a picnic at a park. Remember you were going to do that with Claire on the date we switched up? They've got paddle-boarding too at the place we went. That's fun and the weather's warming up."

Josh sent him a *shut the fuck up* look. He was this close to smacking him.

Claire put in her two cents. "Hailey wants an old-fashioned romance. She wants to be courted, wooed, won over."

He stilled. Now that he thought about it, Claire might be right about the romance thing. Hailey's apartment was filled with romance novels and bridal magazines. Maybe he had to prove he was relationship material by doing something romantic. He'd thought the dinner-date idea should qualify, but maybe Claire knew something he didn't. Maybe what Hailey wanted was something even more old-fashioned. He wasn't sure what.

He gave Claire a sideways look, heat creeping up his neck as he mumbled, "You mean like flowers?"

"That could be part of it," Claire conceded.

Jake butted in again. "Old-fashioned? Maybe you should get advice from the old guy. Dad got Brandy to shack up with him within five weeks, and now they're getting married."

Josh met Jake's eyes, and they cracked up.

"Can you imagine taking woman advice from Dad?" Jake asked.

"He's been single for years!" Josh said, still laughing. His dad was much worse than he was in the crusty bachelor department.

"Not anymore," Claire said firmly. "Jake, you told me how your dad appreciated his stepdad treating his mom like a queen. That's how he treated your mom—"

"Fat lot of good it did him," Jake said. This was true. Their mom had walked out on them the day after Christmas when Mad was only one, and never looked back.

Claire went on. "And that's why he took the time to teach you guys gentleman manners. Didn't he say how important it was to treat women like your little sister with care and respect?"

They got quiet.

"Josh? Jake?"

Josh mumbled, "Yeah," in unison with Jake. Twin thing.

Claire turned to him. "Josh, is that how you treat Hailey? With care and respect?"

*Err…*He'd offered his arm to her for an escort more than once. Usually she ignored it though, so he wasn't sure if that counted. Somehow opening a car door didn't sound like enough.

Claire spoke in a gentle voice. "Teasing and razzing each other only goes so far."

He said nothing. It was too damn late to fix this, and it was fast becoming apparent the blame lay at his feet.

"Does she know you care?" Claire asked gently. "Does she know you respect her?" When he remained silent, she added, "Do you care for and respect her?"

Josh pulled his phone from his pocket and tapped it a few times before showing Claire the screen. "Look at the nice things I said about her and her business in the *Bride Special* interview."

Claire's hazel eyes were sympathetic, her voice so soothing he was beginning to think he'd missed something important with Hailey. "That's really nice, but have you ever said anything like what you said in this article directly to her?"

"I said it in front of her during the interview." He turned to Jake, desperate for backup. He couldn't have completely screwed up everything. "Is that the kind of thing you did with Claire?"

"No."

Claire sighed loudly. "I didn't need that. I'm not Hailey. Josh, I know this woman. She wants old-fashioned romance, a courtship."

Josh shoved his phone back in his pocket and then pulled his T-shirt collar away from his overheated neck. "What is this, the eighteenth century?"

Jake laughed.

Claire shot Jake a quelling look and his twin shut up. She turned back to Josh. "I mean like thoughtfulness. Show up at the Happy Endings Book Club meeting here tomorrow night. Read the book and participate meaningfully. Meet her where she's at. If you can't hack the estrogen, you can take breaks to hang with Jake. She needs to know you respect and care about her enough to take an interest in what she loves."

Jake snorted.

"Honey," Claire said sweetly, her smile lethal, "could you bring the fruit salad down here for me? And slice some of the Monterey jack cheese too. I need more protein now that I'm eating for two."

"On it." Jake bolted from the room.

Josh thought about Claire's suggestion. Unfortunately for his manly self, everything she'd just said about taking an interest in the girly stuff Hailey loved made a lot of sense, and it was something he hadn't tried. He'd run out of good ideas, and Claire was presenting a golden one with the insider woman-friend track. Also, it tied in with the embarrassing gift he'd gotten her. Maybe he could slip it into her purse when she wasn't looking. Shit. This was going to be much harder than his dinner plan, but he was just that desperate.

"How long is the book?" he asked, hoping it wouldn't take too much time. He had to work tonight and didn't want to spend an entire Sunday reading a sappy romance.

"Read the fucking book and find out," Claire snapped. "You have to show effort with her. You want easy, keep flirting with random women who walk into your bar. How's that working for you?"

He blinked, taken aback by her tone. Tough love from Claire.

She sipped her sparkling cider. "Sorry, I'm hepped up on hormones and just a smidge more aggressive than usual." Her lips formed a flat line, her hazel eyes sharp. "Of course, I meant every word of what I just said."

"No problem." Damn, Jake had his hands full over here. He pushed his wineglass away. "So, uh, what's the book about?"

"Love."

He'd skim it if he had to. "The whole thing's about love?"

"Yes, it's a journey, much like the one you're on."

His gaze snapped to her knowing look. He was on a love journey, and he hadn't even known it. Maybe things weren't as bleak as they seemed.

11

Things were looking damn bleak.

Josh knew it the moment he showed up for book club right on time at Jake and Claire's house, accidentally intruding on estrogen central. The women were already there, seated in a circle of white sofas and floral-patterned chairs in the formal living room, chattering away. Had Claire told him the wrong time, or had everyone showed up early? One by one they spotted him.

Conversation ground to a dead halt.

His gift for Hailey was in the inside pocket of his black fleece jacket, which he desperately wanted to take off because he was on fire with embarrassment, but he didn't dare risk the additional embarrassment of the gift tipping out onto the floor where everyone could see it. He hadn't wrapped it.

All eyes went from him to Hailey. It seemed like everyone knew he had a purpose here tonight with her. The fire ignited to an inferno of embarrassment as Hailey's brows drew together in confusion. "Josh, what're you doing here?"

He cleared his throat. "You invited me."

"No, I didn't."

He waved a hand lazily in the air, wishing he could rewind back to NEVER TAKING CLAIRE'S ADVICE. "Yeah, you did. Back when you first started book club, you invited me, so I figured the offer still stands."

Hailey's pink lips formed an O of surprise. "That was two and a half years ago."

"You're most welcome, Josh," Claire declared. "Please, take a seat." She stood and dragged a floral-patterned chair over to the circle of women for him.

Man up. You read the book. You're on a mission.

He took the offered seat. The women stared at him. He was dying in this fleece. Why had he worn a flannel shirt over his T-shirt today? A bead of sweat ran down his forehead. He wiped it away and worked on blending in.

Claire took the lead. "I loved this story with the sweet baby niece, didn't you guys?"

Dead silence. The women shot curious looks at him.

Josh spoke up, desperate to get the conversation going. "It was touch and go, but everything turned out great." The ending had been unexpectedly touching despite being a historical story set in long-ago England.

"It wasn't that easy," Mad said. "Remember when—dammit." She gestured across the circle toward him. "I can't talk about hot scenes with my brother listening."

He turned to Claire. *Fix this.*

"I'm pregnant!" Claire announced.

The women exploded in excited congratulations, everyone leaving their seats to hug Claire and exclaim over her. He took the opportunity to remove his fleece jacket and flannel shirt, draping them over his lap.

"Josh!" Mad exclaimed. "Get over here! This is big news."

"I congratulated her yesterday."

"You knew before we did?" Mad asked.

The women turned to Claire in question. Claire smiled. "Jake told him. Twin thing. You know you're all like sisters to me. I had to wait to tell you in person. Please keep it to yourselves though. We're not going public with this at all."

The women quickly settled down, murmuring their understanding of Claire's need for privacy. Soon everyone was seated back in the circle.

Hailey sat next to Mad, across the circle from him. She pulled an e-reader from her purse, glancing over at him. "I usually read aloud a favorite passage for discussion, but before I do, I'm just wondering, Josh, if you're here as a fan of the book or to make fun of it."

He could feel Claire's eyes burning into him, urging him to say the right thing. Claire's words echoed in his head: *She needs to know you respect and care about her enough to take an interest in what she loves.*

He cleared his throat. "I respect the author's work and respect you, I mean, everyone here who enjoyed it."

Hailey's lips curved slowly into a gentle smile, her lashes fluttering down. "That's nice, thank you. So you really read the book?"

"Yup."

Mad pointed at his jacket, which he now saw had a bulky outline from the gift. "Looks like he brought it with him. So old school, Josh, getting the paperback."

"Is it signed?" Hailey asked. "I missed the limited stock of signed copies at Book It."

"It's signed," he replied and then clamped his mouth shut. Signed by the author, yes, but it wasn't the book club's selection. It was her gift book.

"Can I see what she wrote?" Hailey asked. "I heard she writes something different in each one."

"Yeah, pass it around," Mad urged, standing and crossing over to him. She held out her hand. "Lemme see."

He gave his sister his best intimidating stare. "No."

"Why not?" Mad demanded.

"It's private." He glared at his little sister. "Take a seat," he growled.

Mad's brown eyes danced with amusement. "Whatcha hiding, Joshie?"

"Nothing," he snapped.

She lifted a hand to muss his hair. He pulled out of her reach, and she snagged his jacket, racing back to her seat. Damn, he'd fallen for the head fake out.

He could forcibly take it back, but no doubt Mad would

give him a fight. She was a blackbelt, well used to battling her big brothers. He didn't want a brawl with his sister. On the other hand, he didn't want to be publicly humiliated.

Mad fished out the gift.

"Put it back," he growled. "It's not for you."

She stared at it. "Oh, wow." She snort-laughed. "You actually got it?" She flipped open the front cover. "Signed and everything. That's special." She handed it to Hailey, saying solemnly, "It's for you."

The women all spoke at the same time:

"What book is it?"

"Who's the author?"

"Why did Josh get it for you?"

He slouched in his seat, his eyes going to half-mast. Bleakness warred with embarrassment. He'd wanted to give it to her in private while he made the case for why he was relationship material. Now everyone would chime in on it. Hell.

Hailey sounded surprised, her voice high. "I, uh, don't know why, but it's *Accidentally Pregnant by the Cowboy*, signed to me by T.L. Frieze. It says, Hailey, Ride On! Enjoy your very own cowboy. She put a little cowboy hat and then her name."

The hair on the back of his neck stood on end, and he straightened in his seat. Why did Hailey sound so surprised? Mad had told him this was Hailey's favorite book of all time and she'd always wanted a signed copy. He'd special ordered it from the author's website and paid extra for express shipping.

He sent Mad a death glare.

She stuck out her tongue.

He jabbed a finger at her that promised retribution. One of Mad's pranks. Now that he'd finished paying her tuition, she was up to her old tricks. For a while there she was kissing his ass. He should've known.

The women passed around the book. A low buzz of whispering ensued, probably speculating what the hidden meaning was. Like maybe he wanted to knock Hailey up, or maybe she was already accidentally pregnant. *Fuck me.* This was not the old-fashioned kind of romance he was supposed to be presenting to Hailey. Now he looked like a lech.

Hailey stood in her red short-sleeved designer dress that displayed every last curve, looking glossy and perfectly made-up as usual, but it didn't bug him like it used to. She wasn't snooty and above it all. She was passionate, fiery, and he'd seen what lay underneath her designer clothes. He shoved that memory down as she approached him. He glanced toward her side, suddenly realizing she wasn't carrying her dog purse.

"Where's Rose?" He'd even come prepared with a little butter on his wrists and a slice of pepperoni in a small Ziploc bag in his flannel shirt pocket.

She closed the distance between them, her flowery sexy scent washing over him. "Jake took her out to meet the horses in the stable. It's good for her to have a variety of experiences."

He couldn't think of a single thing more to say, despite the emotion bubbling up in him, his heart thudding hard. Suddenly it felt like so much was at stake. His gift had turned out to be a joke, but his intention was very, very real.

Hailey's pale blue eyes studied him for a moment, looking slightly puzzled. He tried not to squirm. "Thank you for the gift, Josh."

He grunted. "Mad said it was your favorite."

Hailey's head whipped toward Mad, who burst out laughing. Hailey huffed and turned back to him. "I appreciate the gesture. Thank you."

"Mad was fucking with me, obviously. Have you, uh, read that one?"

She leaned down to whisper in his ear, and he went stock-still. "Actually, I avoid accidental pregnancy stories because I was one. Mad doesn't know that about me, no one does. I just can't romanticize the single-mom situation, having lived through it."

His gaze met hers as she straightened. She trusted him with something she hadn't even told Mad. "I know what it's like when a parent bails."

She swallowed visibly. "Yes, well, my dad died when I was little, but…he wasn't much of a dad before that."

"Sorry to hear it. And real sorry the book reminded you of it. Just toss it."

She lifted her chin. "I will not. It's the first gift you ever gave me."

"Not like a mansion." Where had that come from? Here they were practically getting along and he had to bring up what's-his-name.

She stared at him, and he saw the moment she understood that he knew what the prince had offered her. She'd probably share with Mad a lot less now that she knew she'd confided in a snitch.

"I suppose you're right," she said softly.

Desperate to salvage the situation, he leaned close and spoke from the heart. "Listen, the book was supposed to show I'm relationship material. I don't care what our parents say. We deserve a chance. Your mom's not gonna bail on my dad just because we might screw up a few times, right?"

Her eyes widened. "I thought our parents wanted us to make amends." She leaned down and whispered, "Are you saying they don't want us to be together?"

He hesitated before admitting, "My dad told me to keep my distance. Be civil and that's it. He thought we'd bring too much drama to the family, destroy the peace for all the family functions, holidays, birthdays, you know, but I say fuck that."

She straightened, her fingers covering her mouth, her eyes shiny.

Shit. He'd said the wrong thing. He was supposed to be making a romantic gesture and he'd upset her.

"Don't worry about my dad," he said urgently. "It's not gonna destroy their marriage. Your mom loves him."

She nodded woodenly and returned to her seat. Then she just sat there, staring at the floor.

His chest ached, throat tight, gut churning. *Now what?*

Claire took charge like a general. "Ladies! Back to our read. And hand Mad that cowboy book. Turns out it's her favorite because her and Park do a lot of cowboy role-play. She plays the horse."

Everyone laughed.

"I do not!" Mad protested hotly.

The women jumped on that, teasing Mad relentlessly. It was absurd to picture them doing the cowboy rodeo game, both of them raised in the suburbs of Connecticut. But he couldn't even muster a smile. Not when Hailey looked so stricken.

Romantic prince of her dreams he was not.

Hailey sat at book club, shaken by the turn of events. All this time she'd feared her mom flaking on Joe would turn the Campbells against her when it sounded like Joe was already against her. She couldn't even assure Josh her mom would stick around if there was a real issue in keeping the family peace. Her mom flaked whenever things got stressful. She swallowed hard, really hurt over Joe's decree. Sure, he didn't mind her being friends with Mad, and he'd said she'd be like a daughter since he was marrying her mom, but he didn't want her for his son. Josh should've told her that before he'd kissed her. She'd been worried about the family consequences, and he'd only said their parents wanted them to make amends. Joe must've thought she and Josh would never work out because of the way they fought all the time. She'd worried about that too, right up until Josh had kissed her. She'd never felt that kind of passion with anyone else. It had made her think maybe they were meant to be together. Then he blew her off and she'd cooled toward him. Now here he was being sweet to her. So where did that leave them now?

She stared at the cowboy book sticking out of her purse. He'd brought her a gift, and he'd braved book club with all of her best girl friends and his sister, who was sure to tease him. And he'd taken it seriously, reading the book and contributing intelligently to the discussion. It was clear he wasn't there to make fun of romance, or of her. And even though Mad, the tricky bitch, had set him up with that cowboy book, the fact that Josh had asked what she might like as a gift must mean he cared for her. He respected what she loved. That went a long way, given their rocky history. For too long she'd felt he was secretly—or not so secretly—laughing at her. Tonight he'd been dead serious. He wanted her to know he was relationship material.

She stroked Rose's wiry fur. Maybe dropping her dress the first time she was alone with Josh had given him the idea she was using him for his gorgeous body. She was a woman of passions, but at the time she'd thought it would bring them closer together. With all those pent-up feelings she'd had for him and, believing she needed his rock-steady self in her life, she'd gone for it. Admittedly, not one of her finer moments, she'd been a little tipsy and a lot worked up over her mom and Joe moving in together. Her clumsy attempt at seduction should've been a red flag that her breakdown was coming six weeks down the line when her mom and Joe got engaged.

She cared about Josh. And when they weren't fighting, like tonight, she was drawn to him. He was the kind of man she could count on. She'd seen him in action, the way his younger siblings and friends turned to him. He'd been there for her during her sobfest at their parents' engagement party. So why couldn't they seem to get in synch?

Now Josh was in the kitchen with Jake while the women talked to Claire about her pregnancy and how she was feeling. She kept tuning into the twin deep rumbles, working out who was who. They were identical, but Jake was much more open and expressive, Josh always reserved. They laughed at similar stuff, though, finished each other's sentences, and occasionally spoke in unison. It must've been great growing up with a twin. Like having a best friend with you all the time.

Claire squeezed her arm. "Could you help me carry some pitchers of water? I put fruit in them so they're tasty. My version of nonalcoholic fun."

"Of course." She handed Rose over to Mad so she'd have both hands free. Mad didn't even interrupt her conversation, still talking as she cuddled Rose. Mad was like Rose's second mom since she'd taken care of her for a couple of weeks before giving her to Hailey as a gift from all of their friends.

The moment they arrived in the kitchen, Claire announced, "Time for the fruity drinks."

Jake and Josh turned at the same time. She could tell them apart because Jake kept his dark brown hair neatly trimmed, his jaw clean-shaven, and his clothes were designer. He also moved much faster than his twin. Josh ambled, like nothing was worth rushing for, really laid-back. His dark hair was long enough to curl at the nape of his neck, always a little rumpled, his jaw stubbled, and his clothes well worn and casual.

Jake smiled at Claire like she was the best woman on earth.

Hailey swallowed down a pang of jealousy and turned to find Josh staring at her with a question in his eyes that she didn't know how to answer. All she knew was she felt something strong for him, yet she feared the consequences of getting tangled up with him. Going against the family that she'd wanted to be a real part of for so long, sneaking around, probably fighting some more with him, which would be so much more hurtful once her heart was deeply involved. And, if it didn't work out, the damage would affect more than just the two of them. The risk felt too high.

She headed to the refrigerator, feeling Josh's eyes on her.

"How're you?" he asked when she passed by.

She stopped and turned back to him, falling back on good manners. "I'm fine. How're you?"

He shoved his hands in his jeans pockets. "Good." His dark eyes were full of question again.

"Good," she echoed.

"I can see why you like book club," he said. "It's cool to talk with your friends about something you love. It's like a, uh, bonding experience."

Her jaw dropped at the unexpectedly insightful observation. "Very true. I had originally intended it to be more of a vehicle to get single people together. That's when I first invited you to it. You know, a singles book club, but we never did get an influx of men, so it turned into a sisterhood focused on romance."

He gazed into her eyes, his voice low and husky. "I should've accepted your invitation back then."

"Oh." Her cheeks flushed. "Well, that was a long time ago. Water under the bridge." Water. She was supposed to be helping Claire with the water.

"We got it!" Claire sang as she walked by with two pitchers of fruity water. Jake followed with another pitcher and a stack of red plastic cups.

Suddenly it was just her and Josh in the kitchen. She gulped, holding her hands behind her back and then dropping them to her sides. Why was this so awkward?

He closed the distance between them and leaned down to her ear. "I didn't come here because I wanted to dish about a book."

She licked her lips, her heart thumping unnaturally hard. "Okay."

He took her hand, raised it to his lips, and kissed the back of it. Just like in the historical romance they'd just read! "Hailey…" He took both her hands in his.

"Yes," she breathed.

"I want a courtship, a slow burn between you and me. This is either going to be for real—make it worth both our time—or not at all. I should've said that the moment I realized we belong together."

Her breath caught. "When did you realize that?"

"When you were giving me hell at Garner's for trying to get you alone to talk right before the prince showed up. You refused to spend any time with me because you were hurt over my rejection, which was only because I was trying to do the right thing, by the way, nothing personal. Now I think the right thing is to be with you, not keep my distance."

Her brows furrowed, thinking on that. "Why would you think we belong together when I'm giving you hell? Do you like when I get mad at you?"

He squeezed her hands. "I like when you're real with me."

"Oh. That was after my embarrassing breakdown in your office." She shook her head. "I've had too many embarrassing moments with you."

One corner of his mouth lifted. "I admit it was hard to watch you cry because of the sympathy I had for you, but I was glad to help in any way I could."

Her heart squeezed at the sweet sentiment. She hadn't known he'd felt especially sympathetic at the time, but she'd been such a mess she wasn't sure she would've caught it. She gazed into his eyes, trying to figure out next steps—closer or away. His gaze back was serious, sincere.

She gulped. "I don't know. I'm really worried. Our family is against us and maybe they have a point. We fight so much and, if it didn't work out, there would be hurt feelings all around."

His big hand slid under her hair, cupping the back of her neck and pulling her in close. Her breath hitched, her stomach dipping, throbbing between her legs. His words ran hot over her lips. "Give us a chance."

His head slowly lowered as his fingers tangled in her hair, tipping her face up for his kiss. She closed her eyes and waited, practically vibrating in anticipation. Finally his lips brushed over hers gently, and then again. She'd never felt gentleness from him. She wasn't sure if she wanted that. It felt too tame, not Josh-like at all.

He straightened, dropping his hand from her hair. She nearly cried in disappointment. That was it? Two tiny kisses she barely felt?

His voice sounded gravelly. "I'm off tomorrow night. Come over to my place for our first official date. I'll make you dinner."

"So we're just going to go behind your dad's back?"

"This is about us, not anyone else." He smoothed her hair behind her ear and placed a warm kiss on the sensitive spot just below her ear, giving her a shiver. "I want to cook you an amazing dinner. It's my one good thing among many flaws."

She laughed a little, though she was still worried. "Well, if it's your only good thing."

He grinned. "I do have another good thing, a great thing, but we're not going to do that tomorrow night, so don't even worry about it."

She looked away, embarrassed because she'd been the one to throw herself at him like some desperate nympho. "I wasn't worried about it."

"I mean, after your dress hit the ground—"

"I got it! Okay, Josh!"

He cradled her face with both hands. "You're so easy to rile up. I'm teasing you, not fighting with you."

She calmed down. It was hard to be irritated when he was holding her like she was special, his gaze tender. "I'll have to think of some good stuff to tease you back with."

"You could try." His hands dropped to her shoulders. "Now before this goes any further, I gotta know you like me for me, not just my pretty face and hunky bod. I'm relationship material."

She smiled, tickled by his turn of phrase. "I like you for more than just your pretty face and hunky bod. Definitely relationship material."

"Excellent." He pulled her into his arms and kissed her like he meant it. Yes! This was the kind of kiss she loved from him. He had this way of holding her, one hand in her hair, the other on her lower back, keeping them in full body contact as his mouth sealed over hers. Not gentle, thank God. He was aggressive, hungry, devouring her. She'd just reached desperately horny level, arching her hips into him in a silent demand for more, when he set her a foot away from him.

"Go back with your friends," he said gruffly. "I'll be there in a few minutes."

"No. Why?" Her gaze dropped to the bulge in his jeans and she smiled, thrilled she'd gotten to him as much as he'd gotten to her. Slow burn would never work between them and she was glad. This kind of passion was rare and something she'd always dreamed of.

She walked back to her friends on shaky legs, praying that she'd done the right thing in taking this next step with him.

12

Josh was tense. She felt it the moment he answered the door for their first official date. Was it because the stakes were high in making this work? Because he was out of his mind with lust he could barely control? She'd spent a little too much time last night imagining what it would be like to be with him naked—wild, out-of-her-mind levels of passion—which was not-so-coincidentally why she wore an off-the-shoulder white jersey knit dress that fit her like a second skin, ending mid-thigh, with black stilettos. But first—a civilized date that would set the tone for the rest of their relationship. No pressure. Geez, now she was tense.

He gestured toward the sofa, keeping his distance. "Make yourself comfortable. Hope you like steak."

He'd made an effort to look nice, from his clean-shaven jaw to the scent of spicy woodsy cologne to his clothes—a pale blue button-down shirt with gray pants and leather dress shoes.

"Steak sounds good." She set Rose on the floor with her wubby, a ratty green bear, and set her purse by the sofa. Then she turned and walked over to Josh. Probably more of a strut, boobs forward, hips swaying. Why wear the dress if she wasn't going to work it? "You look very handsome tonight."

"Thanks. You look nice too. You could wear a sack and still be stunning, but you know that, don't you?"

She was momentarily speechless. It was the first time Josh had commented on her appearance, and it was quite the compliment.

He turned back to the kitchen. "How do you like your steak cooked?"

"Medium well."

"Got it." He stopped and turned back to her. "How about Rose?"

She beamed, loving the way he looked out for her fur baby. "She's never had steak. I'd imagine medium well would be just fine with her."

He flashed a smile that warmed her like sunshine. She'd so rarely seen Josh smiling at her. He was pure masculine beauty.

He went into the kitchen and she followed him. It smelled wonderful. The appliances were white and on the newer side. Various cooking utensils, measuring cups, and bowls sat on the one long laminate counter. A small square table with a white tablecloth in the corner was set for two with a glass vase of roses with baby's breath and unlit long white candles in silver candlesticks. A nice romantic touch.

He gestured toward the vase of roses. "Those are for you. I had to put them in water so they'd bloom in time for dinner."

"Aww, thank you." She bent low and breathed them in. "They're lovely."

He walked over to the counter and reached into a plastic bag. "I got Rose a chew toy. It's made from recycled fire hose." He ripped the tag off and placed the toy in her hand. It was an orange rectangular toy that made a crinkle sound.

"Omigod, we love it. How cute is this?" She went to the living room and knelt next to her fur baby, offering the toy. "Rose, what do you think?" Rose sniffed it and then licked it. Hailey dropped the toy on the floor and Rose leaped on top of it, rolling all over it and licking with great enthusiasm.

Hailey looked back over her shoulder at Josh, standing in the kitchen doorway, smiling at Rose's antics. He was irresistibly sexy, doting on her dog, cooking for her, but she was determined not to throw herself at him. He wanted a slow burn, something real. She wanted something real too. It was just hard to wait now that she'd gotten a taste of passion.

She stood and smoothed her hair. "You have any wine?"

"Yeah, a nice merlot. I'm letting it breathe. I'll pour us both a glass. The steaks have been marinating all night. I've got twice-baked potatoes in the oven. Spinach with mushrooms too. And for dessert—"

"You bake too?"

"It's strawberry shortcake from Garner's. Not too sweet."

She crossed to him. "Yum. So is this your typical first date?"

"No." He went back to the kitchen and checked on the potatoes in the oven. "I usually don't invite women here."

She flushed, thrilled to be one of the few women invited in. Hard to believe she'd once thought his place was a den of sin. "Why not? Is it your private sanctuary?"

He straightened and closed the oven door. "Because most women wouldn't find my place impressive, but you've seen it before so…" He pulled two wineglasses from a cabinet and poured them both some merlot. He handed her a glass.

She deflated at his casual remark. "Thanks." She took a sip. "Anything I can do to help?"

"I got it. Just relax."

She took a seat at the table, watching him get out a large pan, adding butter, and then the mushrooms. It was strange to be with Josh like this, such a domestic scene, so peaceful. "Why do you think we fight so much?"

He glanced over his shoulder at her. "You're so easy to rile up I couldn't resist. I mostly thought it was fun." He went back to cooking, pushing the mushrooms around with a wooden spatula. "Why did you keep coming back for more?"

She stared at his broad back. Why did she keep tangling with him? Half the time she'd been so furious she'd wanted to strangle him. And now…she just longed to touch him, kiss him, taste him. Oh, boy, she really had to stop thinking about getting him naked.

He looked at her. "You don't know?"

She snapped back to attention. "I couldn't seem to stop once we got started. It's kinda sick, though. I mean, I got really upset sometimes."

He inclined his head. "We might've let it get out of hand. I tried to make amends when I realized I hurt your feelings. Anyway, in hindsight, me giving you a hard time was because I was drawn to you when I didn't want to be. I wasn't being clear about my intentions. Clarissa helped me look more deeply at myself. You know, become more aware of my subconscious and how it manifests in real life."

She tsked. *Clarissa.* "Don't you know not to talk about your ex when you're on a date with someone else?"

He went back to cooking, muttering, "Didn't know there were rules."

"Of course there's rules. Your focus should be on the present moment with the person you're with. Did you cook for her?"

He glanced at her. "I thought you just said—"

"Forget it. I don't want to know."

Feeling unreasonably irritated, she left her wine on the table and walked over to the living room to check on Rose. She was curled up on Josh's sofa, hugging her new fire hose toy, sound asleep. Didn't take much for Rose to be content, and hadn't she warmed to Josh quickly after all that growling and barking? She still didn't know what had changed Rose's mind about Josh. It started at that dinner they'd had with their parents. Maybe Rose picked up on Hailey's moods, and when she was cross with Josh, Rose was too. And when she was calm, Rose was calm too. Huh. What a smart empathetic dog.

She returned to the kitchen and took a seat. Josh was fussing with the steaks. She sipped her wine, watching him cook, going through great effort for her, more than any man ever had. Not that she had a ton of experience after letting her friends-with-benefits situation take the place of any real relationships for so long. Being here like this with Josh, she almost felt like she'd stepped into an alternate universe. Nice

Josh, romantic Josh, someone who actually tried to connect with her instead of antagonize her. It made her feel unbalanced like she wasn't sure who she was dealing with anymore. How much did she know about him anyway?

A short while later, Josh lit the candles and set their plates of food down. "Bon appétit." He seemed relaxed now that he was done cooking. Maybe it wasn't pent-up lust that had made him seem tense. Dammit.

"This is amazing. Thank you."

"Yup. Let me know if your steak's cooked the way you like."

She sliced into it, perfectly medium well with just a touch of pink. "It's great."

They ate in silence for a few minutes. She couldn't bring herself to make small talk about the weather or the food, they were past small talk with their history, but she couldn't think of any common ground besides their mutual friends and their parents, which was a minefield all in itself.

She sighed. "Josh?"

"Yeah."

"Tell me something about yourself. Now that we're not fighting, I realize I don't actually know you that well."

"Sure you do. You know my family, my honorary brothers, you know where I work, and you know I'm a foodie. Nothing else to know."

She was sure there was more to him. He was complex and didn't like to show his hand. Mad had said more than once that Josh was a long-term strategist. But what exactly was he strategizing about? Her mind quickly wound through her history with him, looking to fill in gaps in her knowledge. "Remember when you took out women platonically as part of my business plan?" That was another of their arrangements. First he'd been her wedding escort, and then, when she'd seen what a gentleman he was (during his paid hours anyway), she'd farmed him out to single women she hoped to find happy endings. He was just supposed to take them on one date to restore their faith in men by being his gentleman self. Hailey took it from there. Part of her business plan was to bring people together. The more happy couples there were, the more weddings she could plan. In retrospect, she wasn't sure why he'd gone along with it.

He sliced off a piece of steak. "Yup."

"Why did you agree to that?"

"The money." He went back to eating.

"But if you could afford Mad's tuition and you still had enough to buy Garner's and do new construction, I find it hard to believe you needed the small amount I paid you."

"It was fun."

Curiosity got the better of her. "Where did you take the women I sent your way? What did you do?" Honestly, some of the women she'd helped were so shell-shocked by the wretched men they'd dated, they'd about given up hope. After Josh, they were ready to get back in the dating game.

He chewed and swallowed. "Simple cheap stuff like a walking tour of Clover Park, window-shopping, got them an ice cream, took a walk on the boardwalk down by the shore and won a prize at one of those games."

"Why did you really do it?"

He set his fork down and met her eyes. "Honestly, to make you jealous."

Her eyes widened. "Why would I be jealous of a platonic date?"

"I hoped you'd worry it would be more. Admittedly, a real sideways way to go about it. That was before I was in tune to my subconscious stuff."

She pursed her lips. "Before Clarissa."

"Yeah."

"What subconscious stuff?"

"Part of me wanted you and at the same time didn't want to want you."

She sucked in air, her heart thumping hard. He wanted her way back then? That was more than two years ago! She kinda wanted him this whole time too—he was hot—but she didn't want to want him because he fought with her so much. "Why didn't you want to want me? Because of all of our fighting?"

He shook his head. "It doesn't matter. I know better now."

"Because you thought I was a princess?" she guessed.

He stared at her. "Is there any way we can not talk about this and just eat?"

"No."

He stabbed a potato. "You're going to take it the wrong way. Then you're gonna be pissed at me, and all the work I did for a perfect first date will fly out the window."

"Just tell me. I can handle it."

He blew out a breath. "I hated that you were a beauty queen. You seemed haughty, nose in the air with all your designer clothes and your perfect hair and makeup."

"Judgmental, got it."

"It was more like a visceral repulsion for everything I thought you were." She gaped at him, and he rushed on. "Like I said, I was wrong. I hated that pageant stuff and that's on me. I judged you based on my own bad experiences with my mom and ex."

"Your ex? You mean Clarissa?"

"No." He ate some more steak, so she did too. "I'm sure a psychologist would have a field day with this one, but I dated Miss Massachusetts in college. I was in love with her. She was in love with herself. Anyway she ran off and married some rich guy she met at a charity ball. She didn't invite me to the ball; I didn't even know about it. I found out much later from someone else who read about it in the society pages of the paper."

"She just never came back to campus?"

"Nope. Someone on her sugar daddy's staff emptied her dorm room for her a month later."

She gave him a sympathetic look. "You're right. That's a psychologist's session in the making." His beauty-queen mom had also run off with a sugar daddy.

"Thanks. Glad I shared."

She smiled to herself and went back to her meal, thinking over what he'd told her. He had beauty-queen baggage and she'd unwittingly played into that. "I only did pageants to earn scholarship money to college. It was the only way for me to go."

He reached across the table and gave her hand a squeeze. "You did what you needed to do, and you know what? I respect that."

She swallowed over the lump in her throat. Serious heart-felt Josh was more intense than she was used to in a man. "Thanks."

"Now tell me all your dirty secrets. College, love life, psychologist's dream experiences."

They laughed.

She wasn't keen to share just yet, enjoying hearing him open up for the first time. "So after Miss Massachusetts, anyone serious?"

He shot her a look for the deflection, but he still answered. "Mostly I dated and moved along. But, ya know, I was in the army for a while. Too many tours to stick with anyone, not that I wanted to. Came back home, recovered for a while, and finally settled in at Garner's, where it was easy to meet women who walked into the bar."

"Until the magnificent Clarissa, who made you a better man." She couldn't keep the sarcasm from her voice. He talked about his ex way too much.

His dark eyes sparked with amusement, but he said nothing.

"Did you really break up over a shoebox of money?"

He took a sip of wine, his dark gaze locked on hers. "We broke up because she knew I really wanted you, even though I hadn't admitted it to myself yet."

Mind blown. She flushed hot and couldn't think of a single thing to say. Maybe she should be thanking Clarissa for opening Josh's eyes.

He jerked his chin at her. "Your turn. Spill your secrets."

She pushed some potatoes around on her plate. "I don't have any secrets. You make it sound so sinister."

"Don't wimp out."

She scowled. "I'm not a wimp." She tossed her hair over her shoulder. "What do you want to know?"

"Everything."

"There's nothing to tell, really. My love life..." She finished her wine in one long swallow. "I, uh, dated, nothing serious. In high school, guys wanted bragging rights they'd been with me and, once I was made aware of this by a friend, I was careful to keep my distance for my own safety."

He sat ramrod straight, his brows furrowed in concern. "Hailey, that's terrible. Did you tell anyone? Wasn't there anyone looking out for you?"

"Well, I didn't have an overprotective big brother around, if that's what you mean. My mom said that was how men were and she advised me to flirt and be the unobtainable one. She wasn't wrong. I was definitely better off for it. No one wants to be used or abused like that."

"What about your friends?"

"Looking back, hindsight, right? They weren't true friends. I was the most popular girl in school, homecoming queen, prom queen, head cheerleader, that whole deal, a lot of pretty friends, but I think my girl friends all secretly wanted to bring me down a peg. They were jealous of my clothes—most of which my mom got at a steep discount from the boutique she worked at—my beauty-pageant wins, and the attention I got from the news."

His lips formed a flat line, his expression grim. "Were things better in college?"

She nodded. "That's when I met Liam, late in my freshman year. I had decided college was when I'd start dating for real, figuring guys were more mature then and I wouldn't be part of some macho contest, you know, who nailed the beauty queen. So I dated a bit and I got disappointed a lot, thinking something might be developing only to find once they got to know me better, they weren't all that interested. Probably didn't help that I wasn't comfortable getting physical right away. It wasn't that I wasn't interested or curious, it was just that I needed some emotion to go with it. I guess I just wanted to feel loved."

"So Liam gave you that."

She exhaled sharply. "Liam was a nice guy. He was up

front that he liked my looks and only wanted something casual. He felt familiar, safe, probably because we resembled each other in looks—same color hair, blue eyes, fair skin—there's your psychologist dream session right there. Ha! My standards for men were low and I was tired of being a virgin. So…we hooked up. It wasn't love, but it was a relationship of sorts. We were on and off again for years through college and until very recently. We get along really well, he's very cultured and sophisticated, and part of me thought one day it would turn to love, but…it didn't. I finally ended it a little over six months ago because I realized I wanted something more."

He took a sip of wine, his eyes never leaving hers. "You've only slept with one man?"

"That's what you got out of my story?" *Hello? I want a real relationship. Something more is where you come in.*

"One man?"

"Yes."

Josh stared at her for a very long time. She fidgeted with her cloth napkin, folding it in neat creases one way and then refolding it in the opposite direction. He knew she was twenty-seven and he was judging her for her inexperience. He'd probably been with thirty women, no, forty, hundreds! He was a pig.

She crumpled her napkin in a tight fist. "How many women have you been with?"

He glanced at her fist and back to her eyes. "Are you telling me the romance-obsessed, self-proclaimed love junkie, matchmaking wedding planner has never been in love?"

Damn his sharp mind. Look at how quickly he put the pieces together from friends-with-benefits to her embarrassing flaw. She set her napkin in her lap and smoothed it out. He remained quietly judging her.

She lifted her head and tapped the table with both hands. "Let's talk about something else."

He took her hand and held it. "How was I so wrong about you?"

She let out a breath of quiet relief. Maybe he wasn't judging her. "You saw what you wanted to see, I guess."

"I saw what you *let* me see. And now you're letting me in. I like this version of you."

She let out a small nervous laugh. It felt like he was gazing at her soft underbelly, an uncomfortably vulnerable feeling.

He grinned. "And it's sweet that you want me to be the second man you sleep with."

Her lips parted in surprise. "I thought this was going to be slow burn."

"It is. I just like knowing it."

They finished dinner in charged silence. All she could think about was what came next. How slow was slow burn? Was she going to have to be satisfied with a chaste goodnight kiss, or could she tempt him for more without setting herself up for yet another rejection?

She pushed her plate away and blurted, "So now what?"

"You want dessert?"

"No, I'm stuffed. Dinner was great."

"Glad you liked it. Now you can help me wash dishes."

She hid her disappointment, pasting on a smile. "Sure."

He shook his head. "Don't do that."

"What?"

"Don't fake smile at me. Just be yourself. Frown if you want. Do nothing. Just don't be fake."

"I was being polite."

"Don't do that either."

She huffed. "Any more orders you'd like to send my way?"

He rubbed his jaw, his eyes glinting with mischief. "I'll let you know."

~

Later that night, Hailey was faced with the grim proposition of returning home having failed her mission to tempt Josh with her body-hugging dress, which she'd showed off to every advantage. She refused to make a blatant move after he'd turned her down, but she was getting very tense. It almost felt like they were an old married couple. Somehow they'd gone from frenemies to friends and skipped the lover part. After they'd washed dishes—she washed, he dried and put away—they took Rose for a walk, and then they'd watched a movie on TV. Okay, yes, he'd held her hand, but that was it. And he let her pick the movie. Of course, she had to introduce him to one of the most romantic movies in history, an oldie but a goodie, *While You Were Sleeping*.

She should've known the movie didn't give him any great romantic ideas because when it ended, he said, "I don't get it. How was that romantic? She loved a guy she didn't know and then she went with his brother."

"She followed her heart."

"The guy was in a coma."

"She saved him."

He grabbed the remote and turned off the TV. Rose lifted her head from where she was asleep on Josh's lap and then settled back down. "You ever think you'd want to be with my brother?"

She gave him a wicked smile. "Which one?"

"Jake," he bit out. "He's just like me but with money."

She blinked, surprised he was actually serious. He did have a chip on his shoulder about money. "You shouldn't get worked up about his money. You just chose a less lucrative career path."

He clenched his jaw. "I'm not worked up."

She didn't argue the point. So far they'd done really well getting along and she didn't want to end on a bad note. On the other hand, it was clear he had a real, completely irrational concern over his twin. "Jake is…"

He leaned in. "What?"

"Don't tell him I said this and don't tell Claire."

He gestured her on.

"Boring."

Josh grinned. "Why is he boring?"

"I don't know why. He just is."

"And I'm exciting? Me working in a small-town bar living a quiet life is more exciting than a billionaire?"

"I didn't say you were exciting just that he's boring."

He barked out a laugh, startling Rose, who stalked off his lap, jumped off the sofa, and walked over to Hailey's doggie purse. "That's honest. Looks like Rose is ready to go home."

She stood, knowing a hint when she heard one. "Then we'll go." She grabbed her regular purse and tucked Rose into her doggie purse. "Thank you for dinner. Goodnight."

One corner of his mouth lifted in a classic Josh smirk. She tensed, irritated beyond belief. Like he knew how much she wanted him and was teasing her by not doing anything about it.

"Night," he said all casual-like.

She turned on her heel and headed for the door, trying not to show her irritation. She should focus on the positive—he'd cooked her dinner, watched a romantic movie not of his choosing, and treated her fur baby well.

He followed behind her, saying, "I'll get the door for you."

She let out a small sigh of disappointment, reached the door, and turned to him. Her goodnight kiss would likely be a peck, if he even gave her that much.

"Why're you looking so disappointed?" he asked in a teasing voice as his warm hand slid under her hair and cupped the back of her neck.

"I'm not," she lied.

He leaned down and nipped her neck. She jolted, letting out a small squeak of surprise.

He squeezed the nape of her neck. "I told you not to fake with me. Why're you disappointed? You didn't like dinner? Didn't like the movie? Or is it because we never had *dessert*?" Clear innuendo. Obviously he was teasing her.

She clamped her mouth shut.

He kept his hold on her neck and lifted his other hand, his thumb tracing her lips. A soft brush across the top lip that made her lips part, another soft brush across the bottom before he pressed on it. Her lips tingled as he slowly leaned down and touched his lips to hers, a gentle kiss that left her longing for more.

He dropped his hold on her. They stared at each other for one tense moment. She was about to spontaneously combust with all the pent-up lust.

"Hailey."

The words tumbled out. "I'm disappointed because I wanted dessert and you didn't give it to me." *Please pick up on this metaphor of sexual longing. I simply cannot put myself out there for another rejection.*

"I offered."

"I wasn't hungry then. I am now." *Metaphor, you dolt!*

He cocked his head. "So if I feed you dessert, then you'll call this a satisfying romantic date? The kind that sweeps you off your feet?"

"My feet are firmly on the ground." She lifted her chin in challenge. "I have yet to be swept off my feet."

A small smile played over his lips, his dark eyes gleaming. She held her breath as he lifted her purses from her shoulders and set them on the ground. She glanced down at Rose, who popped her head up and then settled back in her cozy dog purse.

Josh took her hand, pulling her away from the door, and finally swept her off her feet, literally, cradling her in his arms.

13

Excitement rippled through her as he carried her into his bedroom.

He set her on her feet, shutting the bedroom door behind her, his gaze dark and heated. "You trust me?"

"Uh..." She hadn't expected the question. Trust was complicated by their history.

"You feel safe with me?"

"Yes." She knew him as a protector for all of his younger siblings and more recently her, though she hadn't asked him to.

He entwined their hands together, raising her arms overhead and pressing their joined hands against the door. "Good." He spoke near her ear, his voice gravelly. "I need to be in control. No sudden moves on your part; never grab me from behind. I don't want to hurt you, understand? Those are my triggers. Are you good with those conditions?"

Her heart ached for him. She knew he'd been in combat, but she hadn't known how deeply it had scarred him. "Yes, I understand. Do you have to explain that to every woman you take to bed?"

He shifted to meet her eyes. "No. I take control and that's it, but you're different. I sense you might be more aggressive."

She shook her head. "I'm not aggressive."

"Yeah, well, I might bring that out in you." He kissed her then, not roughly, a steady pressure, a coaxing as his lips slanted over hers, his body slowly pressing against her. She melted against him, relief at finally having him on board making her fully relax. His tongue thrust inside, igniting her, and the kiss turned wild. Her heart raced, blood rushing through her veins, desire soaking her. She'd never been so turned on in her life—his hard body pinned her against the door, his hands held hers captive, and his mouth devoured her.

He lowered her hands to her sides and then placed her hands on his waist. She held on, remembering his request for no sudden moves. His mouth shifted, kissing along her neck, nipping and soothing with his tongue. She tilted her head, giving him better access; alternating electric tingles and sharp sparks of pleasure coursed through her. His hands slid up her legs, grabbing the hem of her dress and hiking it up to her waist. Next thing she knew, he'd lifted her, fitting between her legs, grinding against her as he kissed her, one hand gripping her hair, the other banded behind her back. She moaned into his mouth, gripping his shoulders, throbbing and hot. *Yes, yes, yes.* She'd needed this for so long.

He broke the kiss suddenly, eyes hot on hers as his fingers slipped between them to slide under her thong and stroke her. Her hips jerked at his firm touch.

"Shh, relax," he whispered, stroking her over and over.

She bucked wildly, and he pinned her still, one large hand on her hip, the other touching her intimately, his heated gaze locked on hers. She panted, the pressure building within her, powerful surges of pleasure rippling through her. She tried to hold back, wanting him with her. "Josh!"

"Don't fight it," he growled.

His teeth sank into her neck, and she exploded, pleasure radiating outward from her core all the way to her toes. She felt electric everywhere—her skin, her breasts, her sex. She collapsed against him, and then he was carrying her to his bed, pulling back the covers, and gently setting her down. She blinked lazily, suddenly realizing she was still dressed.

She sat up and worked her dress over her head, setting it on the nightstand.

Suddenly Josh was there, naked, kneeling next to her on the bed. She smiled goofily, feeling half-drunk. "Hello, you."

He undid her bra and slid it off her. "Hello," he returned warmly. His hands cupped her breasts, his thumbs stroking her nipples to peaks.

"I came so hard," she said breathlessly.

He groaned and grabbed her by the hips, yanking her down the mattress. He slid her thong down and off and then spread her legs wide. Then he covered her with his body, his hands on either side of her head, his erection teasing her, sliding up and down.

She slid her fingers through his hair from his temple to the back of his neck in a slow easy touch, his hair thick and soft. "Do you have protection?"

"You didn't see me put it on?"

"I was distracted by my dress. It's tough to get off with that stretchy material."

He bit her lower lip. "That dress has been tempting me all night, you witch."

She smiled, her hands sliding to his shoulders and down the muscular lines of his back. "That was my plan."

"Now we're onto my plan."

His lips met hers as he took her in one swift thrust. Her body tightened around him, still amped from before. He thrust deep, hard, fast, and her inner muscles clenched and unclenched around him. Pressure and ache and a building tension consumed her. Josh consumed her. His breath was harsh in her ear, his powerful body pounding into her, his masculine scent, his taste, all of him dominated her senses. She arched up to meet him and gasped, the pleasure intensifying. Chanting his name, her body bowed off the bed as another hard climax hit. He kept going, rocking her, and then he let go, shuddering against her, his body heavy on hers.

He held himself up over her a few moments later, held her by the jaw, and kissed her soundly. "How's that for dessert?"

She laughed. "Best dessert I ever had."

"Yeah?" He nuzzled into her neck before rolling to his back next to her. "I'm keeping you in my bed tonight."

"I'd be pissed if you kicked me out." She stared at the ceiling, floating in a happy bubble. She'd just had sex with Josh Campbell, her former nemesis. The man who fought with her, pushed all of her buttons to extreme angst levels, and now it had all changed. She felt closer to him than she'd ever thought possible. She wished she could freeze time and they'd always be just like this, relaxed and content, at peace. A small niggling of worry set in. What now? Would they stand a chance as a couple after all their fighting? Could they keep the peace long-term? And what about the fact that his dad didn't want Josh to be with her?

She didn't want to ruin the moment, so she kept her worries to herself and sat up. "I'm going to the bathroom and then I'll get Rose."

"Please tell me she doesn't sleep in your bed."

She turned to look at him and then she couldn't help but touch, her fingers roaming over his magnificent chest. She hadn't gotten the full effect before. His skin was darker than hers by a few shades, defined pecs and abs, a smattering of dark chest hair. Her gaze dropped lower. He was thick, still hard, his legs muscled like an athlete. Beautiful masculine perfection. "No scars?"

He bent his knee, showing her the back of his upper thigh. "Stab wound. My back has a few too, burn, bullet, knife slice. The few times the unexpected came up on me from behind. I learned fast."

She swallowed hard. "Are you okay?"

He straightened his leg. "I was lucky. The bullet and knife didn't hit anything critical. Burn was fallout from an explosion."

"Can I see?"

He sat up and she slowly moved behind him. The scars had healed well—a long slice by his side over his rib cage, a burn on his shoulder blade, and a puckered hole close to his other shoulder. She didn't touch, remembering his warning about not touching him from behind. Instead she shifted back to his front and kissed him gently.

"I'm sorry for what you've been through," she said.

"I'm fine."

"You're tough and strong, I know. I still wish you hadn't been hurt."

"When did you get so damn sweet?" he grumbled.

"When you finally left me satisfied." She smiled cheekily and climbed out of bed.

He flopped onto his back. "No dogs in the bed." She heard the crinkle of the condom wrapper, probably getting rid of it.

She headed for the door. "As soon as she sees me go out in the hallway, she's going to want to follow me in. Have a heart."

"Fine. Make a bed for her in the corner with a pillowcase or your purse or something. Better yet in the closet."

She turned to him, her hand on the doorknob. "She's going to beg to be picked up. Don't worry, she hardly takes up any space."

He stood, stalking toward her, looking rough and edgy and badass. A frisson of excitement shivered through her. He placed his palms on the door, caging her in with his body, his voice silky in her ear. "Let me put it this way. The second time will be slower, hotter, longer. That won't work with a dog witness. Got it?"

"Yes," she breathed.

He smiled. "Good." He backed up and opened the door for her. She headed out on shaky legs and Rose darted past her into the bedroom. Oops.

When she returned to the bedroom, it was empty. A moment later, the door quietly shut and Josh held his finger up to his lips in a shushing gesture.

"Where's Rose?" she whispered.

He tackled her, tossing her onto the bed. She squeaked in surprise and his mouth covered hers. She lost herself in his kiss as his hands roamed down her body. He shifted to her ear. "I gave Rose the steak bone. She's eating that so I can eat you."

She throbbed and let out a shuddering breath. That worked.

He smirked. "Now I know how to make you quiet."

"Beast."

He held her jaw and kissed her, deep and hot and wet. He shifted, levering himself down her body, leaving a trail of hot open-mouthed kisses, making her shiver. His tongue dipped into her navel as his big hands slid up her legs, pushing them wide apart. She stopped breathing.

A flick of his tongue and she jolted.

Then a kiss, just his lips—gentle, warm, and soft. Her lashes fluttered closed.

Another kiss with tongue. Magic. Electric. Her hips arched up to meet him. She sighed, her fingers sliding to his hair, holding him to her, floating in a warm Josh-induced haze, her body humming with pleasure, the gentleness shifting to raw and dirty in a slow slide that caught her by surprise. Breath ragged, her body wound tighter, her fingers clutching his hair, silently begging, *Don't stop, don't stop.* Sharp pleasure stole her breath as his lips and tongue and, oh God, his fingers got in on the action. She trembled, the pleasure so intense a scream caught in her throat, and then she broke violently, her body shuddering with it as he stayed with her through wave after wave of pleasure.

She collapsed, boneless, trying to catch her breath. *Fuck, holy fuck. Best orgasm of my life. I will worship his mouth forever.*

He climbed up her body and grinned. "Is that so?"

Crap. She must've said that out loud in her semi-coherent state. "Josh." She had no words. She'd said too much already.

He kissed her. "You're welcome."

Once she regained the use of her limbs, she went to check on Rose. She had to take the bone away and clean her up. Then she made a bed for her with a towel in the corner of Josh's bedroom.

She slid under the covers, and Josh hauled her against his side. She wasn't used to sleeping with anyone but Liam, who wasn't a cuddler. She rolled to her side, giving Josh her back. He tucked himself behind her, spooning her. Rose scrambled up the comforter by the foot of the bed. Hailey kept quiet about it, impressed with Rose's climbing skills.

Sleep eluded her. She shifted to her back. Then she flipped the pillow over. Then she rolled to her side, facing him. He tucked her head under his chin. A few minutes later, she rolled back to her other side and scooted a little farther from him. She shifted the pillow again.

He squeezed her shoulder. "Comfortable?"

"Almost."

"What're you doing?"

She flipped the pillow again. "Looking for the cool spot on the pillow."

"The cool spot?"

"Yes. I like the cool spot, but you heated everything up. I can't find the cool spot." This was so frustrating. All she wanted to do was go to sleep.

Josh rolled her to her back and then he was on top of her, stroking her hair back from her face. "As long as you're in my bed, princess, I'll be heating everything up."

"I noticed. Maybe I'll bring my own pillow..." She trailed off as he ground against her, waking her up again. "Oh."

"Shh...don't wake Rose."

"Careful not to kick her. She's by my feet."

"What?" Josh rose to his knees and pointed at Rose. "Back to bed."

Rose approached, tail wagging. Josh scooped her up and got out of bed with her, putting her on the towel in the corner. Then he must've thought better of it because he lifted her with the towel and left the bedroom with her.

Hailey stretched out, finally relaxing with so much space to herself. She was nearly asleep when the mattress creaked and Josh whispered, "I put the TV on so she'd hear voices and think she had company. I had to pet her for a while to settle her down. Now where were we?"

Her heart swelled with affection. Look at how well he took care of her fur baby! She opened her arms to him, and when he pressed his big hard body against her, she held on tight.

Josh sat on his bed, fully dressed in a T-shirt and jeans, waiting for Hailey to finish up with her shower. He'd showered while she'd slept, took care of Rose—taking her out and feeding her some steak he'd set aside for her for breakfast—and slipped the shoebox money into Hailey's purse. So far, everything was going according to plan. Well, he hadn't planned to sleep with her so soon, but he knew she wanted it bad, and he was done denying them both. It was worth it, oh, man, so worth it.

As soon as she was ready, he planned on making omelets with fresh herbs for breakfast. Cooking was his big selling point, the one thing most men couldn't be bothered to learn and he excelled at.

Her phone lit up with a text on the nightstand. Phillip: *How's my favorite wedding planner?* Winky-face emoticon.

Josh glared at the phone, immediately on edge. The dude used emoticons like Josh's little sister.

Another text from Phillip. *You around? Need my Hailey fix.*

He snatched the phone and turned it facedown on the nightstand. *Hailey is mine.* At least he hoped she was. *Okay, take it easy. Just because Phillip sent a stupid flirty text didn't mean Hailey reciprocated.* He stared at the phone, seriously contemplating reading through their entire text message chain. More intel might help loosen the grip of jealousy. The phone was probably locked.

He blew out a breath. He'd asked Hailey before if she trusted him, but now he had to ask himself if he trusted her. Would she go behind his back with another guy?

He glanced toward the open bedroom doorway just as Hailey approached in nothing but his navy blue towel. Forget Phillip. He was the one alone with Hailey.

God, she was beautiful, even with no makeup and only a towel. Her long hair was up in a hair band, just a little damp, tendrils falling around her rosy cheeks and neck. He fought the urge to rip the towel off her. If he kept fucking her, she wouldn't get the message that he had serious intentions.

His eyes went half-mast, hiding the lust there. "How you like the slow-burn courtship so far?" He wanted to remind her that was what he was going for.

She sat next to him, crossing her legs primly, all ladylike. "I don't think we can technically call it a slow burn now that we had sex."

"Does that bother you?"

"No."

"You like it so far?" He'd done everything he could think of for the old-fashioned romance—flowers, dinner, and a gift for Rose. Damn, he should've gotten a gift for Hailey too. Well, he had gotten her that embarrassing book. Mad had better watch her back. She was long overdue for a prank. He suddenly realized Hailey was quiet, which meant she was thinking. Had he missed a step? He didn't think she'd like candy. And he couldn't afford jewelry. What else was there?

She turned to him. "Since you asked, it would be nice to have—" her hand fluttered in the air "—a little note or something that says you're thinking of me. Something with romantic words."

He stared at her. "I text. That's the modern equivalent of a romantic note." And she was getting that from him and the playboy prince. He shouldn't have looked at her phone because now he was irritable. They'd finally connected, and he had to be careful not to screw it up. The far-reaching consequences of relationship disaster were never far from his mind, especially since he'd deliberately ignored his dad's warning to keep his distance.

She crinkled her nose. "You don't use emojis like hearts or smiles. There's never an exclamation point like you're excited about me."

"That's because I'm not a teenaged girl."

She pursed her lips. "'Sup' isn't a love note."

Love note, eh? He must be doing something right for her to say the L word. He bit back a smile. "And why not? Sup shows I'm thinking of you."

"It's just not very…"

"Princely?" *Dammit. Do not turn this into a thing.*

"Romantic."

He crossed his arms. "Why don't you spell out exactly what you want?"

She waved airily. "If I have to tell you, it doesn't count."

"I don't have a problem telling you what to do."

She slowly turned to him, heat in her eyes. "Maybe when you spend your days ordering people around like I do to pull off the perfect wedding, it makes you want a break from always being in charge."

All of him focused on her, the blood rushing through his veins. He lowered his voice, a note of steel in it. "Take off your towel and get on all fours. I'm gonna fu—make love to you so hard." See, romance wasn't dead.

She stood and let the towel drop. His heartbeat roared in his ears. He'd never get used to her stunning beauty. And then she pulled off his shirt. He stood and took the rest of his clothes off in record time. But she didn't follow orders. Instead she pushed him back to sit on the bed and straddled his lap, impaling herself on him. They both groaned.

"Fuck, Hailey."

It was fierce and hot and fast, and it was all her doing. He let her, his hands roaming her soft scented skin, his release threatening. *Hold on, hold on…fuck!* He lifted her off him, and she whimpered.

"Condom," he said gruffly, setting her on the bed. He grabbed one from the nightstand, rolled it on, and joined her, flipping her to her stomach and pulling her up by the hips. He slid home and she clasped him tightly. Hot wet heaven. He thrust deep, reaching around to stroke her at the same time. She was soaked for him. She chanted his name like he was everything. The only thing. She shuddered around him, squeezing him rhythmically, a soft cry escaping as she went off.

His release roared through him. The room went dark and

silent and then flashed back to full color and sound. Whoa. He held her hips tightly for a moment, buried deep inside, lingering for a last moment of connection before pulling out. She collapsed on her stomach.

He flopped on his side next to her. A few moments later, he looked over and pushed her damp hair out of her face. He pulled the hair band out from where it was barely hanging on and finger combed her hair. He loved her hair, so long and silky soft. He loved her. He could finally admit it. It was twisted and difficult because she was a complicated woman, but there was just no other explanation for his continued attraction to her. Even now, completely sated, he wanted her to stay all day. He knew she had to get to work. It was Tuesday morning. But he couldn't let her go until he was sure he'd locked this thing down between them.

Her eyes were closed, her lashes fanning her cheeks.

"You awake?" he whispered.

"I'm dead." She popped her head up and laughed, her pale blue eyes bright, the color high in her cheeks.

He smiled, warmth spreading through his chest, loving seeing her like this, loving that it was all because of him.

She turned to her side and propped her head on her hand, completely comfortable lying there naked with him. "I feel so good right now. Before this, I hadn't had sex in more than six months."

He knew that from her story last night, but it was nice she was sharing. "That's a long time."

"No kidding. Why you think I got so pissy when you kept turning me down?"

"I thought it was because you were desperately horny for me."

She laughed. "That too."

He took her hand and kissed the palm. "So now that you and I connected, you're not going to Villroy Island for the wedding, right? You'll cut things off with the prince." That last part was not a question. More of a demand.

She pulled her hand away. "Of course I'm still going. I was invited. I couldn't possibly turn down a royal wedding."

He took a deep calming breath. "Okay, let me ask you this, are you going as a guest of the princess or as the prince's date?"

Silence.

"His date," he ground out.

"It's not like that. He's gotten a bad rep and he just wants me to help improve his rep by being seen with me. In case you haven't noticed, I'm a classy lady." She smiled, obviously trying for a light tone.

He frowned. "So he wants to buy you a mansion, and you've agreed to be his date. Anything else I'm missing here?"

She stroked his arm, probably trying to soothe him. "I'm his date at the princess's wedding here too. That's part of improving his rep. And that's everything there is to know."

"He wants you."

Her lashes fluttered down and she dropped her hand from him. "I think he just needs my help."

He ground his teeth and sat up. "No, he wants you. No man buys a mansion and expects nothing in return."

Her eyes flashed and she sat up too. "Well, I'm naked with you not him. Besides, he didn't buy Ludbury House. I don't think the terms are reasonable."

"Hailey, this is a deal breaker. I won't share you with him. Tell him no. You won't be going as his date to these weddings."

"What's the big deal? I went with you to several weddings completely platonically."

"That's because I'm a gentleman. He's not." He at least played the part of a gentleman, even when lust was in his way.

She huffed and turned to go. He grabbed her by the arm, stilling her. "What?" she snapped.

"Him or me."

She yanked away. "Josh, you're being a ridiculously jealous possessive beast and I don't like it one bit." She got out of bed and went to his dresser, where she'd set her clothes in a neat pile. She pulled her thong on, next her bra, then her dress. Any minute she'd get the rest of her stuff and take off.

He stood firm. "I won't stand by and watch you be with another man."

She slipped a heel on. "I'm not with him!" Another heel.

He got rid of the condom, got out of bed, and pulled his boxer briefs back on. "Then I'll go as your date to those weddings."

She jammed her hands on her hips. "You weren't invited. It's not a big deal!"

"It is to me. And don't let him buy you Ludbury House. You should earn it."

She tossed her tangled hair over her shoulder. "You can order me around in bed and I may or may not comply, but I won't be ordered around on how to live my life, especially by a jealous lunatic!"

He clenched his jaw. "I'm not a jealous lunatic." *Choose me.*

"Ha! Call me when you've matured." She stalked out of the bedroom.

He followed her. "Call me when you give a crap about someone besides yourself."

She gathered Rose and her purse and headed for the door. She stopped suddenly, and in that moment hope speared through him. She'd come to her senses. She was coming back to him.

He watched as she unzipped her purse, poking around in there, muttering to herself. That was when he remembered her phone. "Your phone's on the nightstand. I'll get it."

She whirled and held up a handful of cash in one fist. "What is this?"

"Uh, money." His neck burned. He'd hoped she'd discover it much later and simply tuck it into her wallet, letting him off the hook for the previous disaster of a night when he'd tried to give her back the shoebox of cash.

She marched toward him, her gaze murderous. "You're paying me for sex?"

"No!"

She stopped in front of him. "That's what it feels like, Josh. I sleep with you and then I find a wad of cash in my purse."

He had to defuse the situation or they'd never get past this money thing. He went for a teasing tone. "I don't pay for companionship, unlike some people I know." She'd paid him to be her wedding escort, which was how he got the money in the first place.

Her jaw dropped, and he immediately regretted the words. "Hailey, I was joking because that's how I got the money."

She held up a palm, fury written all over her face. Then she stepped around him, strode to his bedroom for her phone, and returned. She pulled the wad of cash from her purse and tried to hand it to him.

He put his hands behind his back. "Just take the money. It's yours. You earned it."

Her nostrils flared, her lips in a tight line. She shoved the money in her purse, turned on her heel, and headed for the door.

"Not like a prostitute," he added belatedly.

She yanked open the door, slamming it behind her.

He punched the air. Fucking A. The woman was impossible. All he'd wanted to do was make amends and she wouldn't let him.

At least she'd kept the money. Problem solved. Sort of.

Of course, there was still the problem of the playboy prince trailing around after her while she did nothing to discourage him. Josh had told her what needed to happen—goodbye, prince.

Fuck it. If he couldn't get through to Hailey, then he'd have to get through to the prince.

14

Hailey fumed the entire walk to her office. It was bad enough Josh was acting like a jealous lunatic, but then he had to make it worse by stashing a wad of cash in her purse after she'd slept with him. Maybe he hadn't meant it in a whorish way, but it didn't exactly feel good to be paid after sex.

By the time she finished checking her email back at work, she was calm enough to have a civilized conversation with Josh. If he apologized profusely, she would make every effort to put his stupid guy move behind her. She was, above all else, a classy lady. She pulled out her phone and called.

"Morning," he said, sounding slightly out of breath.

"Are you working out?"

"I'm running, but I can talk at the same time. Sorry about this morning. I didn't like the way things ended between us."

She smoothed her hair, slightly mollified by the sincere apology. It wasn't overly elaborate, but then neither was Josh. "What part are you sorry for?"

"The truth is, I didn't think you'd take the money if I just handed it to you. I was trying to make amends. Really you should be thanking me for taking the high road."

She seethed. His apology tanked when he put it all on her. "It's so great that you're up on that high road while I'm down here getting spit on."

"I didn't spit on you. Geez, you're twisting this into something evil. For the last time just take the money. It's yours anyway. I was just temporarily holding it."

"And what about the jealous lunatic part?"

"What about you kick the prince to the curb?"

So she got a half-ass apology and another jealous lunatic jab. Was this how their relationship was going to go? Because this wasn't sitting well with her at all and he was too hard-headed to meet her halfway. Maybe this had been a mistake. She'd been worried all along about them making it work after their long history of fighting. Maybe they should cut their losses before someone really got hurt. Every time their family got together, it would reopen that wound. She broke out in a cold sweat.

"Hailey?"

"Yes," she said softly.

"All you have to do is say goodbye to the prince and things will go much better between us." She'd had a friendly text exchange with Phillip this morning. It wasn't like they were sexting.

"Why can't you get that he's important to my business? And he respects what I do. He wants to help me, and the least I can do is help him by showing up at a couple of weddings. If you trusted me…" She trailed off as it hit her that he didn't trust her, another consequence of their long contentious relationship. Her trust level in him was pretty low too. What in the world were they thinking trying to be a couple?

Josh spoke gruffly. "I want to trust you, but it's kinda hard when you plan on being another guy's date."

"It's not like that! How many times do I have to say it?"

"How many times do I have to explain myself? It's like you only hear what you want to hear."

Grrr. She wasn't hearing a single thing she wanted to hear out of his mouth. She hung up.

Her phone rang a moment later. Josh. She sighed and picked up. "What?"

"Don't hang up on me. It's a coward move, and the thing I

like most about you is your warrior spirit, so duke it out with me, but don't wimp out."

She flushed and then she found herself smiling. No one had ever called her a warrior before. That implied great strength and a badass attitude she always wished she could pull off. Most people only saw her as a perky wedding planner with excellent taste in clothes. Josh saw a warrior?

She threw her shoulders back. Yes, she could feel it now, the warrior spirit filling her chest. She stepped away from her desk and stood, legs braced apart, head held high, imagining taking on a foe and winning. She kicked at the air. Warrior Hailey kicking ass and taking names with a battle cry. *Roar!*

"Still there?" he asked.

She promptly sat down, embarrassed to be caught mid-warrior role-play, even though he couldn't see her. "I like that warrior thing."

"Good. Cuz you are and so am I. That's why we belong together."

"But maybe that's bad. We fight so much. Maybe you should be with someone who needs a warrior's protection. I don't."

"I need my equal."

She stopped breathing. All this time she'd thought he was secretly laughing at her when he actually thought she was his equal? Suddenly his complete cluelessness didn't scrape so rough. This was really good stuff he was saying. "That's really good to hear."

He grunted.

She supposed she could put up with some grunts and grumbles if he occasionally shared gems like "warrior spirit." Now she should reciprocate with something equally good. "If anyone gets in your way, let me know and I'll kick ass and take names. I'm very well connected in this town."

"I've got goose bumps."

"Really?"

"Sure."

"You're teasing again. I thought you were finally taking me seriously."

"So much frigging work," he grumbled.

"No one is forcing you to put work into me. Do what you want."

"I wish I could." He sounded morose, like she was a noose around his neck! Forget that!

She wanted to hang up on him so badly, but her warrior spirit wouldn't let her take the coward's way out. The chime rang, signaling someone was at the front door of Ludbury House. Maybe Josh had run to her. Maybe he'd be standing on the front porch with a bouquet of fresh-picked wildflowers, ready with the romantic words to make her forget how irritating he was. "I have to go. Someone's at the door."

"Later." He hung up.

She shut her office door, locking Rose in so she wouldn't distract her from Josh's romantic gesture. She took her time walking to the front door, making sure she was completely composed. One peek at the front porch through the glass panel by the door brought a shock. Prince Phillip!

She answered the door to Phillip and his two security guards. Phillip was dressed casually in a short-sleeved white cotton shirt and black athletic shorts. His guards were equally casual in black T-shirts with black pants. "Hello!" she exclaimed. "I wasn't expecting you today. Come in, come in."

The guard went first. Phillip smiled at her, his blue-green eyes sparkling. "I finally got free of meetings. I hoped you could give me a tour of Ludbury House and the town. I'm seriously considering investing in Ludbury House after our talk."

She stepped back from the doorway, reeling from this unexpected visit. She'd never gotten back to him with any kind of counteroffer and hadn't taken it too seriously.

Phillip walked past her, and then the second guard followed him in. Gosh, she didn't know what to do with him. She had work to do.

She clasped her hands together. "I, um, need to get some work done. Can you give me an hour?"

"Of course! I should've called. I was being spontaneous." He lowered his voice. "I'm impulsive that way." He glanced around. "I'll hang out in your parlor over here. I've got a book to read on my phone. Take your time."

She smiled, liking that he was a reader. She didn't know a lot of men who were. "What're you reading?"

"Political thriller."

"Cool. I won't be long." She dashed back to her office, not quite believing she was keeping a prince waiting, but work called and she had to answer.

An hour later, she emerged from her office with Rose tucked in her dog purse.

Phillip's smile flashed white against his tanned skin and dark stubble. "I found a place for lunch and booked us a private room. It's in Greenport, not far from here. We'll still have time for a tour. Lunch is at twelve."

What could she say? "That would be lovely. So, you've seen the parlor; this is my office." She gestured to her office and he poked his head in.

"Nice," he said.

She shut the door and locked it since they were going out. "This way to the dining room." She showed him the down-stairs—the long dining room, the large working kitchen, and the ballroom—before returning to the grand staircase in the front foyer. She led him up the stairs. "It's mostly empty rooms up here that I use as dressing areas for the bridal party." If Josh were here, he'd have a conniption that she was going upstairs with a man. But Phillip was merely interested in the mansion for business purposes and, as she showed him around, he admired the historic touches like the crown molding and ceiling frescoes, as well as some of the antique furniture original to the home.

From there, they took a brief walking tour of Main Street as she pointed out the different businesses, shops, and restau-rants. Josh was probably behind the bar at Garner's. Even if he didn't notice her giving the prince a tour, she was sure some of the locals would be sure to spread the word. She wasn't about to risk a confrontation at Garner's between the two men, so she didn't stop by.

"And that's basically everything," she said. "Beyond Main Street it's just houses, a few churches, and the schools."

"It's all very charming," Phillip said. "Like you."

"Oh." She laughed. "Thank you."

"My car's parked behind Ludbury House." They headed back that way. "Are you single, Hailey?"

She glanced up at him, surprised by the question. Was he interested in her? He *was* very warm and friendly. Not that long ago she would've been over the moon that her fantasy man might want her, but now she was all tangled up with Josh. Could she say Josh was her boyfriend? She wasn't sure where she stood with him. They'd had one date, sex, another fight, and a half-hearted apology, where he acted like he was in the right and she was being difficult. She mentally shook a fist at Josh. *Why are you such an impossible man?*

"I've stumped her," Phillip said with a smile.

She laughed. "It's complicated."

"Then we'll keep it simple and just enjoy each other's company. I'm done with meetings this week. I'll be staying locally so I can fully experience your charming town. I booked an entire bed and breakfast for me and the guards. It's not far from here."

She pasted on a smile, wondering what in the world she was going to do with him if he kept popping up all week. "Wow. You must really love it here."

"Truth is, I'm bored in my hotel room in the city, and you're a delight."

She flushed at the compliment. "You're good company too."

The week flew by. She only got a few texts from Josh saying, *Sup!!!* and then they abruptly stopped. He remembered to use an exclamation point—three for extra sarcasm—to indicate excitement with her. Not exactly a love sonnet. It was weird that she hadn't heard from him much this week, but she figured he was busy with the plans to take over Garner's and start construction. She was busy too. She saw Phillip every day. She'd worried at first how she was going to get any work done, but he made it easy by showing up at noon to take her to lunch at some posh restaurant or another. After lunch, they'd take a walk with Rose, and then he'd drop her off back at work. His guards went everywhere with them, blending into the background. It was all very pleasant and friendly. Today was Friday and they went together to visit Princess Silvia at Yale to firm up the wedding details. It was only a forty-minute drive from Clover Park. Now Phillip had to return to the city.

She told him goodbye as they left Yale, heading to where they'd each parked. "I hope you enjoyed your visit."

Phillip took her hand and kissed the back of it in his gallant way. "It was lovely. The fun doesn't have to end just because I'm going back to the Big Apple. I booked the private top floor of a club for Saturday night in the city. Invite your friends. It'll be a blast."

"Is it okay if they bring someone too? A lot of my friends are engaged or married now."

"Absolutely. Everyone needs a night out to let loose, even those old married fogies."

She laughed. "Okay, I'll spread the word."

He leaned down and kissed both her cheeks in his European way. "See you tomorrow. Eight o'clock for cocktails."

She bobbed her head, smiling, and went to her car, tucking Rose into her Sherpa-lined bucket seat in the back. Excitement got the better of her and she pulled out her phone for a group text to her friends inviting everyone to the club. She loved dancing. A few texts came in right away from her friends, saying they had to check with their guys and get back to her. Well, for once she was happy not to have someone to check in with whenever she wanted to go out. Except...Josh.

She shook her head at herself, got in the driver's seat, and headed for home. She hadn't heard from Josh all week besides his sarcastic *Sup!!!* He hadn't asked her out, hadn't called, hadn't bothered to walk across the street to say hi. She kept telling herself he was just busy, but it still stung. Was this how Josh treated Clarissa? *She made me a better man.* Somehow she couldn't imagine Josh ever saying something that amazing about her.

Why did she feel like she had to check in with him before joining Phillip at a club? Everyone was invited. It wasn't like Phillip had asked her on a date. The real problem was she needed more from Josh than this if what they had was a relationship. She debated calling, texting, or just showing up to clear the air with Josh. He worked weekends at Garner's. Finally she just decided to show up.

She confided in Rose as she drove. "I know, I'm a sucker being the one to go to him first, but if I don't, this is all going to turn into a big thing. I need to show him I'm a mature adult capable of having a prince for a friend. I also have to feel him out to see what the frick he's thinking." She tried never to curse in front of Rose. Dogs were sensitive to harsh language.

She sighed. Why were men so confusing? Mixed signals much?

She'd already finished at work, so she parked in the lot behind Garner's and headed inside. She spotted Josh right away behind the bar, serving up some beer with a smile playing over his lips. He turned unexpectedly, his intense gaze locking on hers, giving her a jolt. She hadn't seen him in person since they'd hooked up four days ago. She hadn't realized how much she'd missed him until she saw his familiar features—his always rumpled dark brown hair, his scruffy jaw, his old faded T-shirt that stretched across his strong chest and shoulders, his dark eyes that gleamed with knowing. She couldn't decide if she wanted to kiss him or yell at him.

She took an empty seat at the end of the bar and set a sleeping Rose by her feet. "Hi, Josh."

Josh crossed over to her. "Hailey." His tone was cool.

She leaned across the bar. "Don't even tell me you're mad at me. I'm mad at you."

He placed his palms on the bar and got in her face. "How's your prince? Everyone's talking about you spending the entire week with him. I saw you strolling down Main Street. Did you think I wouldn't find out?"

"Is that why I haven't heard from you?"

His voice dropped, low and deadly. "I was so pissed I didn't trust myself not to bash his face in or worse."

"He's a friend," she hissed. "You could've called me or asked me out or something. What the hell am I supposed to think, especially after that huge wad of cash you dropped in my purse after we fucked!"

He straightened and looked around. Several people at the bar snickered and looked over at them. Shit. She might've gotten a little loud there.

"My office," he ordered.

She silently seethed, not liking his tone or imperious command.

"Please," he said through his teeth.

"Fine." She stood and tucked her doggie purse over her shoulder. "I was going to suggest a private conversation anyway."

He rolled his eyes and pulled out his phone, probably calling for backup, because a moment later a guy stepped out of the kitchen and went to the bar. Josh gestured for her to follow him back to his office.

The moment the office door closed behind her, she said, "What the hell, Josh!" at the same time as he said, "What the hell, Hailey!"

Rose barked at Josh ferociously.

Josh retreated behind his desk, pulled a small twisted rope toy from his drawer, and offered it to Rose. The anger drained from her, watching him give her fur baby yet another gift. How could he be so thoughtful for Rose and not for her?

She set Rose on the floor to play with her new toy and took the chair across from Josh's desk. "So here we are again. Enemies."

"We're not enemies. You're so dramatic."

"What are we, then?"

A muscle ticked in his jaw. "I don't know."

She blew out a breath of frustration. "There's nothing to be jealous about. I told you Phillip is a friend."

"Is he buying you Ludbury House?"

She looked away, unsure how to answer that. She met his eyes again. "He's considering it as a business investment, but it's not a definite thing. I'm not holding my breath."

He narrowed his eyes. "Mind telling me why you spent the entire week with him?"

"He wanted a tour of Clover Park."

"For a week?"

"He was staying nearby." She went on the offensive. "You know, this jealousy thing is getting old. It's not like you and I—"

"What? We're not together? Because it sure felt like that when you were screaming my name like a fucking halleluiah."

She flushed hot. "I wasn't screaming. Don't talk about that."

His lip curled. "So you like to be dirty, but you don't want to talk about it. Spoken like such a prissy princess."

She leapt to her feet. "Don't call me that ever again!"

He slowly stood to his full six feet, glowering down at her. "If she acts like a princess and she spends all her time with a prince…"

"You never called!" she cried. "All I get is sarcastic texts. And, by the way, I counted that money and you paid me extra like some kind of fuck bonus!"

"That was interest! You're welcome."

She seethed. Once again he acted like he was in the right and she was wrong, wrong, wrong.

He walked around the desk to stand in front of her, took her hand, and placed it on his chest right over his heart. "And those texts were from the heart."

"Sup!" she spat. "You're nothing like my romantic dream of a boyfriend."

"You're nothing like my wet dream of a girlfriend."

She huffed. *Great, just great.* Why had she ever gotten

involved with him? She should've known they were a disaster waiting to happen.

His fingers slid under her hair, and her heart beat a frantic beat, knowing his move now, this was his prelude to a kiss. Her hands went to his chest, about to push him away, when he said, "You're better than any girlfriend I could dream up."

She stared at him, speechless, once again floored by the unexpected sweetness that popped out of his mouth. And then his hand curled around the back of her neck, drawing her in for a rough, demanding, all-consuming kiss. Her arms wrapped around his neck, a hot rush of desire carrying her away.

He shifted, lowering her to the desk, hiking her dress up around her waist, settling between her legs, on top of her. Oh God. They were animals. She wanted him more than her next breath. She wrapped her legs around him, her hands on his ass, pulling him closer. He rocked against her, giving her friction, but it wasn't enough.

She tore her mouth away. "Josh," she half-begged.

He shifted to her neck, nipping and sucking at the sensitive skin along the side, his hands reaching back to shift her legs off him to rest on the desk. She thought he was about to step away, but then his fingers slid her thong to the side and delved inside her. She gasped at the sudden intrusion, her hips arching up. He pushed her back down with his free hand while his fingers thrust in and out. The heel of his hand ground against her and she saw stars. Pleasure built and built and built. Fever hot. Intense.

She writhed under him mindlessly, soft moans escaping. He increased the rhythm, more pressure—too much—and everything in her coiled tight. His mouth covered hers, swallowing her sharp cry, and then she broke, her release ripping through her, on and on and on. *Fu-u-uck yes.*

He lifted his head, still holding her firmly between the legs, his heated gaze intent on hers. She panted, beyond words, staring back at him, half in shock. One minute they were fighting, the next…

A sharp knock on the door made Josh jerk away, pulling

her dress down and her up so fast she got light-headed. She sat on his desk and tried to breathe normally.

He went to the door and opened it a crack. "Yeah?"

"That special delivery came in. You asked me to tell you about it."

"Thanks. Be out in a few minutes." He shut the door and turned to her with a regretful expression, his lips pressed together. Well, he wasn't the only one with regrets. She couldn't believe she'd let him do that to her in his office. They were in the back of a busy kitchen in a busy restaurant.

She stood on quivering legs and smoothed out her dress, still not sure where she stood with him. All she knew was the sex was out of control. "We shouldn't have done that."

He banded an arm around her waist, pulling her close, and cradled her jaw with one hand, gazing into her eyes. "Probably not. But if Pete hadn't knocked on the door, I would've bent you over the desk." His teeth sank softly into her lower lip, and her stomach dipped. "And you would've chanted my name, begging for more."

She throbbed at the words as his erection pressed into her belly, making her ache for what he promised. *Focus!* "Josh, I came here—"

"You sure did." He grinned, his thumb stroking her cheek.

"To talk." She stared at his mouth. "You're very difficult to talk to."

He tipped her chin up. "Just because I'm not acting the part you expect me to play doesn't mean we don't belong together."

She swallowed hard. Maybe her expectations were skewed by her love of all things romance. She wrapped her arms around his waist and gave him a squeeze. Then she took a deep breath and met his eyes. "Okay, now don't get mad, but Phillip has invited me and my friends to a club in the city tomorrow night."

His jaw went tight, his dark eyes hard.

She shivered as shades of his warrior side emerged— strong, calculating, deadly. Not that he'd hurt her, it was

Phillip he had it in for. "I just wanted to let you know. I'm trying to head off a jealous fit."

He spoke against her lips, his hand cupping her ass possessively. "How can I be jealous when you come every time you see me?"

She was suddenly breathless. "Maybe I should see you more."

He dropped his hold on her. "I'll be there tomorrow night since your friends are invited. You could call me a friend now, right? Lover too obviously."

Her mind raced with everything that could possibly go wrong. The brawl potential. The possibility of losing the princess's stateside wedding, losing her place at the royal wedding in Villroy Island and all those connections she'd hoped to make. The fact that she and Josh had not yet gone public as a couple, and it would surely get back to their parents through Mad or any one of the many people connected to the Campbell family. Their parents didn't approve of the match. Maybe for good reason.

Josh's hand slid under her dress, cupping her between the legs. Her mind blanked. "Is it possible you didn't really want me there?" he asked in a silky voice.

Her lips parted. "Josh." She couldn't seem to form a coherent thought. Desire clouded her brain.

"So hot and wet," he growled. "It seems you want me everywhere." He gave her a swift kiss and left the office.

She just stood there in a daze for a few moments. Something rough rubbed against her ankle and she yelped, heart racing. Oh! It was just Rose with her rope toy in her mouth, wanting to play. Oh my Lord, the things Rose had just witnessed. She scooped her up and rushed out of Josh's office, avoiding eye contact with his staff, and took the back exit to avoid Josh too.

The cool night air brought her back to her senses. One thing was for certain—tomorrow night had the potential for a royal showdown. She just hoped Phillip didn't get hurt.

15

———

Josh took the time to do the deep-breathing relaxation exercise Clarissa had taught him, not once, not twice, but three whole times before his drive to the city on Saturday night. He couldn't get away from work as early as he'd hoped, so Hailey had gone ahead with her friends. A night at a club was not his idea of fun—too many people too close, fast dancing, the stupid prince—but he had to show up to let everyone, especially the prince, know that he and Hailey were now a couple. He hadn't wanted to go public so soon on account of his dad's warning to stay away, but hell, these were desperate circumstances. Somehow he hadn't gotten the couple thing across to Hailey; otherwise she wouldn't be pulling shit like this. That really burned after all the trouble he'd gone through making her dinner, kissing up to her dog, fucking her senseless. He'd even taken the time to text her using her suggested exclamation points. He took her direction to the letter and what did he get? Nothing but grief. From now on, she'd be the one taking direction from him.

He gave his name to the bouncer at the door, and a security guard escorted him inside to a bass-thumping club. The first floor was mostly a dance floor teeming with people bumping and grinding away to the beat. Strobe lights, a disco ball, and various multicolored spotlights highlighted the bodies of the beautiful, the drugged, the sexually aroused. He suppressed a shudder. He'd better not see Hailey writhing with the playboy prince. Alcoves on the sides with round tables were filled with even more people. Red velvet rope blocked access to the stairs, along with a huge bodyguard. The security guard with Josh spoke to the huge bodyguard, and the rope was removed for him.

He was left to his own devices, the velvet barrier closing behind him. *Be cool. Show your place with Hailey, and everyone else will know their place.* He scanned the room for her. The upstairs had more alcoves with tables on two sides, plenty of space to peer down at the dance floor below, and in the back, a smaller dance floor. Same music as downstairs, of course; it was so loud the floor vibrated from it.

He spotted a tall man with dark brown hair, his back to him, dancing with a bunch of women. He closed the distance, picking out the blond heads of Hailey's friends Carrie and Ally. They were dancing with Prince Phillip, naturally. The prince bent his head to say something to someone shorter, and he glimpsed her unmistakable strawberry blond hair. He moved to the side of the dance floor next to some of his friends, Zach and Ethan, who'd clearly been dragged along with their women, Carrie and Ally.

"Josh!" Ethan exclaimed. "Never thought I'd see you in a place like this."

Josh gave his cheek a light slap. "You either, man." Ethan was a tough hardass cop. "Now the professor over here is probably taking notes on the dance ritual in American culture." Zach was a professor of anthropology. His brown hair was on the longish side with a full beard that made him look half mountain man, half professor.

"Har-har," Zach said. "Dance does play a significant role in the courtship ritual. If I were you, I'd get your ass out there."

Hailey hadn't noticed him yet, still dancing in a tight circle with the prince, Carrie, and Ally. The prince's focus was completely on Hailey in a clingy black dress that ended mid-thigh, her toned legs in black stilettos. Every sweet curve from breasts to ass was highlighted in that dress, all of them burned into his brain.

Josh didn't fast dance. He could pull off a damn good waltz, but that was the extent of his skills. And even that he'd learned solely for purposes of seduction. He'd already seduced Hailey. Now he just had to make her understand the way things were. As in they were a thing. A couple. Exclusively. It was so damn obvious he couldn't believe she didn't seem to know it. Unless she was keeping her options open because the prince could offer her everything Josh couldn't. His hands formed fists.

"What's up with you two?" Ethan asked. "Ally said you made Hailey dinner. You together now?" Ally worked part-time for Hailey. It seemed Hailey had let some things slip. Fine. He'd deal with the fallout from his dad later.

"Yeah," he told Ethan.

Ethan looked over at Hailey laughing at something the prince had said. "You sure she knows that?"

He strode onto the dance floor and snagged Hailey by the wrist. She jumped and then smacked his arm. "Josh! You scared me, coming out of nowhere like that."

"Sorry." He looked over her head at Phillip looking back at him. He turned to Hailey, guiding her farther away from the interloper. "I'm here."

She laughed. "I see that. Come on, let's dance. I love this song."

"I only slow dance."

She lifted her arms in the air and danced in front of him, her hips undulating suggestively. He hauled her close by the hips and moved in a slow sway.

"Josh! I want to move not sway. Come on, let's go back and dance with the others."

"I'm here for you."

She turned and gestured to Carrie, Ally, and Phillip. Next thing he knew, they were all dancing around him. Ally kept gesturing for Ethan to join them and he shook her off. Zach jumped in enthusiastically.

Phillip squared off with Hailey, not touching her, but

moving suggestively, his hands moving up and down the space around her body.

"Hailey." Josh crooked his finger at her and made himself move. *Hip move, arm move. I am dancing, dammit.*

Hailey danced her way over to him, moving sinuously in front of him. That was more like it.

"Where's Rose?" he asked.

"Sitter! It's too loud in here for her little ears." She danced a circle around him. He turned so she wasn't at his back. She ran her fingers through her hair, lifting the strands and letting them fall.

Phillip took her hand and twirled her around. Josh tensed. Hailey spun and laughed and then took Carrie's hand and spun her around.

Phillip smirked at him.

Josh went toe-to-toe with him and stared him down. Phillip sidestepped and danced some more, his eyes on Hailey's curvy ass as she danced.

Josh shifted, blocking the view of Hailey, his back to Phillip. The hair on the back of his neck rose signaling danger, and he quickly shifted again, moving Hailey in front of him and keeping Phillip to his side. Too many people here. Too close. Every nerve ending sparked awareness. *Danger, danger, danger.* He counted backward, reminding himself where he was and why.

"Let's get a drink," he told Hailey, taking her hand and pulling her off the dance floor with him.

"Josh, I want to dance."

Phillip appeared. "She says she wants to dance. Don't drag her around against her will."

"It's not against her will," Josh spat. "Go away."

Phillip's nostrils flared. "I will not. Hailey is a good friend of mine."

"Hailey is mine," he snapped.

"Josh!" Hailey exclaimed.

"How refreshingly Neanderthal," Phillip said. "Big caveman bone for you. Come on, Hailey."

"Hailey, let's go," Josh ordered.

Hailey threw her hands up and went back to her friends.

Phillip glared at him. "Let's take this outside."

"After you."

Phillip headed for the stairs and Josh followed behind, looking forward to punching the guy right in his too pretty face. Two security guards appeared, flanking Phillip, and Josh halted. Three on one, especially when he didn't know what the guards carried in the way of weapons, was not a fair fight.

He returned to the dance floor. A few minutes later, Phillip joined him. The prince was loose, dancing like he did this all night, every night. Josh was tight, pissed off but refusing to yield the floor when his woman was dancing, being her sexy stunning self. It became like a fight all on its own.

Dance. Glare.

Hip check. Fuck you.

Dance, glower, dance.

This went on for so long Josh actually got tired from fight dancing.

That was when he realized Hailey had left. Dammit!

Hailey woke Sunday morning to the sound of Rose barking. She opened her bedroom door and Rose ran to the outside door. She must need to go out. She got the leash, clipped it to Rose's collar, and opened the door. A huge bouquet of roses lay at her feet. Oh, wow! After that crazy male posturing on the dance floor last night—she swore Josh and Phillip looked like peacocks out there doing some kind of ritualized battle— Josh came through with an apology. She'd been so over the meeting of the gonads that she'd left early with Mad, who'd agreed both men were acting ridiculous.

She scooped up the roses and walked Rose up the stairs to the backyard. Rose sniffed around, looking for the perfect spot. Hailey spotted a small card tucked into the bouquet. *Please let it say something romantic.* She really didn't want to be mad at Josh anymore. He must care about her to scare other men away; he just didn't know how to show it. Maybe he'd talked to Jake or some of his more enlightened guy friends and finally got the message.

As soon as she got Rose back inside, Hailey set the roses on the coffee table and plucked the card out of its plastic holder. Slowly, she opened the envelope, a shiver of excitement running through her.

For a lovely woman,
Sorry things got out of hand last night.
Phillip

Nothing from Josh. Her eyes got hot. She shook her head at herself, scooped up the flowers and arranged them in a vase, setting them on her small kitchen table. Phillip had never visited her home, but she had pointed it out just off Main Street on one of their walks through town. The flowers were a thoughtful gesture. She pushed Josh from her mind, got ready for her day, and went to her morning appointment at Ludbury House. She often took weekend morning appointments for potential clients.

She returned home that afternoon, made herself lunch, and ate it in front of her beautiful roses. She read the card again. *For a lovely woman.* An apology too. It only served to make her angry at Josh. Where was his apology? He acted like he owned her. He didn't even want to dance with her; he just didn't want Phillip to dance with her. Where was he? It was Sunday afternoon, so he was probably home.

She'd walk there. The twenty-minute walk would give Rose exercise and help Hailey clear her head for a rational conversation.

By the time she got there, she knew exactly what she wanted to say. She rang the bell on the outdoor intercom system. He buzzed her in a minute later.

She arrived in the foyer, and he stood casually in the open doorway of his apartment, barefoot in jeans and a black T-shirt, dark hair rumpled like he'd just rolled out of bed, stubble pronounced on his square jaw. Why she found his unkempt appearance sexy was beyond her. He didn't step back to invite her in, and she could feel the tension radiating off him despite his casual stance. His jaw was tight, his expression hard.

"Where'd you go last night?" he asked with a casualness that didn't fool her for a minute.

"I got an apology from Phillip for his behavior with you last night." *And where's your apology?*

"Good. He was an ass."

She pressed her lips tightly together, really trying to hold onto her temper. "The two of you looked like a peacock fight about to happen."

"Cock fight."

She waved that away. "Whatever." She wouldn't let him distract her with sex again. "The point is, you both behaved badly, which was why I left early with Mad. It was embarrassing." She looked at him expectantly.

His eyelids lowered, his expression neutral, which meant he was hiding something. "If you're looking for an apology, you won't find it here. I told you it was him or me. I also told you he wanted you; otherwise, why would he tangle with me? Why would he keep showing up with flimsy excuses to see you?"

She marched over to him, furious that he was acting like this was on her. Again! And he didn't even have the decency to invite her in! "You instigated that fight. You were dying to go after him."

"Not true. I protect what's mine."

She saw red. "First of all, I'm not yours. Second of all, there's nothing to protect me from. Phillip is a friend."

"Then what're we?"

"I don't know!"

"Let me know when you figure it out." He shut the door in her face.

She smacked the door. "Cad!" she hollered. Rose barked ferociously too.

She turned on her heel and left. Jealous yet he offered her nothing. Not common decency, not an apology. Nothing.

~

Josh's nothing grew to a gaping maw of nothing as Phillip sent her a huge bouquet of roses every morning for a week. No note. Just roses, roses, roses. Obviously the prince was begging her forgiveness, even though she'd already thanked him and told him everything was fine. Maybe she'd sounded so despondent he hadn't believed her. Because the truth was, even with all the lovely attention from Phillip, her heart hurt. She couldn't keep doing this thing with Josh when she got nothing in return. Maybe this was the natural end to their relationship. They'd burned bright and hot, and then they burned out.

She drooped through Friday, relieved to finally be done slogging through work. She put her laptop away and sighed. The chime for the front door of Ludbury House rang. She wasn't expecting anyone. Was it possible Josh was finally showing up with a peace offering?

She left Rose in her office and rushed to the front door. Her stomach dropped the moment she opened the door. "Mom! Is everything okay?"

Her mom was dressed in the clothes she only wore when she was ill—a ratty pink cotton shirt with gray sweatpants. A blue kerchief covered her hair, and she wore large sunglasses. "I need to get out of here," her mom said urgently. "My wedding's only two weeks away and I just can't. Tell Joe I'm visiting my sick aunt Jane or something, okay?" There was no Aunt Jane.

Her mom turned to go.

Hailey ran out on the porch. "Mom, wait!"

Her mom kept walking.

Dammit! She knew this would happen. Her mom was flaking on Joe just like Hailey had predicted all along. She raced down the steps and grabbed her mom's arm. "Cold feet are perfectly normal. It doesn't mean you're not meant to be. I know you'll have a long and happy life with Joe."

Her mom stared at the ground. "Just tell him about Aunt Jill, okay?" There was no Aunt Jill either. Her mom was an only child just like Hailey.

"It's Aunt Jane. Keep your story straight. When will you be back?"

"I don't know." She pulled out of Hailey's grasp and quickly walked toward her car parked crookedly in the driveway. It was still running, the driver's side door wide open.

"Mom, don't do this to him. Please. He's going to worry."

Her mom ignored her, got in her car, and drove away.

Hailey considered her options. She didn't want to get in the middle of this mess, and she definitely didn't want to have to face Joe and explain her mom was a flake. How could her mom not see what she had? It was so obvious Joe loved her. The look in his eyes was so warm and tender. He called her sweetheart. If Hailey had what her mom had…

She swallowed hard and went back inside. Maybe her mom would come to her senses. Or maybe Joe would go after her, except Hailey didn't know where her mom was going. She shivered. It was bad enough she'd gotten all tangled up with Josh against Joe's wishes, but if her mom didn't come back to Joe, the entire Campbell family would turn on her. She covered her mom's tracks in the only way she could think of—she texted Josh. He always worked Friday and Saturday nights. Well, except when he had to show up a prince on a dance floor.

Hailey: *Family emergency. My mom had to fly out to see my aunt Jane. Can you tell your dad? I don't want him to worry. I'll let you know as soon as I hear the latest.*

Josh: *Sure. Everything okay? Are you going too?*

Hailey: *Just her. I don't know this aunt very well. She's in California.*

· · ·

And the lies just keep coming. She hated that her mom had put her in this position. There were three dots like Josh was typing and she waited. The dots disappeared.

She put her phone down, sat at her desk, and dropped her head in her hands. She and Josh were at an impasse, it seemed. Maybe they were too alike. They were two strong-willed strategic warriors circling each other, neither willing to give an inch. But, no, that wasn't exactly right. She'd given much more than an inch. She'd tried to connect with him in every way she knew how. Why was this so difficult? Why was Josh so difficult?

Agitated, she scooped up Rose from her little bed, where she was napping, and settled back at her desk, stroking Rose gently. A few minutes later, the chime for the front door rang and her heart thumped hard in anticipation. Maybe Josh had decided to forgo texting in favor of seeing her face-to-face. She'd forgive everything if he met her halfway.

She answered the door with Rose in her arms, instantly deflating as Phillip's smiling face came into view. She opened the door. "Hi, Phillip." He was dressed formally in a black suit that looked like a custom fit with a red tie. His two guards stood unobtrusively to the side.

"Hello," he said warmly and gestured behind him.

A line of people approached from the side of Ludbury House, climbing the porch steps to her. A woman gave her a bouquet of roses, three men playing violins followed behind, and a woman with a camera joined them. Was this part of the press Phillip needed to restore his reputation?

"Hailey."

She glanced down to find Phillip on one knee, holding a huge glittering diamond solitaire ring up to her. Holy crap!

"Would you do me the honor of being my bride?"

She stared at him in shock. The violins played on, the camera clicked away, all eyes on her.

"You would make a divine princess of Villroy," Phillip said. "And you'd be integral to our new foray into tourism. In so many ways, you're exactly what Villroy needs. What I need too. Come back with me and fall in love with Villroy

Island, with who you can be there. You could be the key to revitalizing our economy, keeping the young workforce there, keeping the country alive. You could do so much not just for me but for an entire country."

Her knees went weak. *Whoa.* A princess? Helping an entire kingdom to flourish through her skills as a businesswoman? A dreamy state came over her, imagining castles and ball gowns, flower gardens, parties, weddings, economic summits.

She finally found her voice, took note of all the witnesses, and said cordially, "Phillip, this is so sudden. Can I think about it?"

He rose to his feet in one fluid motion and motioned the photographer away. "I need an answer before I return to Villroy in five days. I need to make arrangements. There's a lot of official appearances coming up, and I'd really like to have you at my side as my intended."

"Okay, thank you for understanding."

He kissed both her cheeks, smiled tenderly, turned, and left.

She rushed back inside, trembling in the aftermath of the bizarre scene. Her first-ever proposal shocked the hell out of her. She hurried to the sanctuary of her office, shut the door, and set Rose on the floor. The roses fell from her hands as she stood there, staring at nothing. She hadn't even kissed Phillip. Why had he proposed? Was he just using her for the good press? Would he lock her away in his castle while he took on a mistress?

Why were men so damn confusing?

16

———

Josh was in a foul mood. It had been almost a week since he'd told Hailey to let him know when she figured out which guy was for her—*me, dammit*—and he hadn't heard a peep out of her until today. And it was about her mom! What the hell kind of relationship was this? Was he supposed to keep dating her like everything was normal while she kept throwing the playboy prince in his face? He believed her when she said they were just friends, as in they hadn't hooked up, but he also thought the prince was turning her head with his glamorous jet-setting life. Josh didn't want to be in a competition, especially when he couldn't possibly match the lifestyle the prince could offer. He wanted her to choose him definitively once and for all. Speak of the devil.

Hailey walked into Garner's, talking to Rose earnestly, holding the dog against her chest like a baby. She looked like a crazy woman, confiding in her dog as if she might get an answer. Maybe she was crazy. That would explain a lot.

She crossed to the bar and squeezed herself through the crowd. "Josh, can you take a break?"

Maybe she was finally ready to concede she belonged with him and no one else. "Gimme a few minutes."

She nodded solemnly, her brows drawn together. Shit. Maybe it was bad news. Maybe her aunt Jane had died.

He pulled out his phone and called for someone to take his place for a half hour. Hailey might be upset enough to cry, and that could take a while. He braced himself for the excruciation of watching her suffer. He wanted to protect her at all costs, but sometimes death won. A few moments later, he gestured for her to follow him into his office. He pulled out the rope toy with beef scent he'd gotten Rose before and tossed it in the corner. Rose took off after it and chewed happily.

Hailey stood stiffly in front of his desk, eyes shiny, lips pressed in a tight line like she was trying not to cry.

His gut clenched. He walked around the desk and pulled her into his arms, hugging her. She gave him a small squeeze in return and stepped back. Her eyes watered as she looked up at him.

"What happened?" he managed over the lump in his throat. If her aunt died, he'd go to the funeral with her, even though he hated funerals.

"I just need to know where I stand…" Her voice choked and she cleared her throat. "Because Philip proposed and he wants me to help save an entire kingdom."

He went cold. "You told him no."

"He brought violinists, a photographer, all those security guards. I said I'd think about it. I couldn't humiliate him like that."

"Fuck, Hailey! I can't believe you. This is bullshit. You know what? Go to him. Have a great life."

"N-no." Her voice quavered like she was definitely going to cry. His chest clutched. Shit. He'd been too harsh.

He reached out to stroke her hair. She jerked away, her eyes flashing at him, giving him a visceral jolt of lust. He must be the crazy one, turned on by their battles. Deep down he knew the problem—their fighting was exactly what had hooked him in the first place. Here was his equal, battling with him. Who would win this war? And how could they establish peacetime?

She glared at him. "I'm here with you, Josh. Why do you think that is?"

"I don't know. All I'm hearing is prince this, prince that."

"I'm trying to figure out whatever this tangled mess is between us." She shook her head sadly, mumbling, "Maybe it's just sex."

"Just sex," he echoed.

She threw her hands up. "I don't know! With Phillip it's roses and diamonds. With you it's fights and sex!"

"Fuck Phillip! I'm working! I'm trying to build something here, something lasting."

She held up a palm. "I can't keep fighting with you. It hurts too much." She frowned and that gave him hope because she never frowned. She was being real with him in a way she wasn't with anyone else.

He took her outstretched palm and entwined his fingers with hers. "Hailey." He pulled her palm to his chest, drawing her close. She didn't pull away, just stared at his chest.

Her voice went soft. "And now this thing with my mom. I'm so worried."

He kissed her gently, trying to comfort her. She turned her head away. He cupped her cheek and turned her back, gazing into her eyes, a direct message that he cared about her.

"I can't keep doing this with you!" she cried and pulled away. She scooped up Rose.

He jammed a hand in his hair. "We do have something more than just sex. If you could just open your eyes, drop this fantasy the prince is trying to pull over on you, you'd see that."

"Nobody is pulling anything over on me, Josh," she snapped. Then she marched out the door.

He swore under his breath and went back to work behind the bar. If he knew how to fix it, he would. All he knew was that he was not going to try to top roses, diamonds, mansions, castles, and whatever the hell else the prince threw at Hailey. She had to want him for who he was or not at all.

He leaned against the bar, suddenly exhausted. Hailey was right. They had to stop battling, except he'd never known peacetime with her. How could he let his guard down when she was always ready with the next killer jab?

Hailey organized a girls' night at her place the next night. She was desperate for some perspective. She'd hardly slept at all last night, trying to figure out how to work this thing out with Josh or step away from him forever. Except their lives were way too tangled to ever completely separate. Their parents were getting married (maybe), they had a lot of the same friends, she was best friends with his sister, and they both lived in town and owned a local business. A breakup would be awkward at best, excruciatingly painful at worst.

Everyone was here, even Claire with her bodyguard, Frank, posted at the door and her driver waiting out front. Hailey's text to her friends must've sounded pathetic and desperate. *Emergency meeting to figure out my life!* had had a bigger impact than she'd realized.

She set out the chocolate chip cookies she'd baked, along with fresh veggies and dip, and a chips and salsa platter. Everyone had already passed around the bottles of wine. Claire had sparkling water on account of her pregnancy.

Hailey took the seat at the end of her floral sofa, and Sabrina promptly sat next to her, probably because she was a relationship counselor and planned to give her some advice. Clearly Hailey had relationship troubles. Mad was on Sabrina's other side, probably ready to jump in and defend her big brother's case. It occurred to her suddenly that she hadn't heard a thing from Mad about her dad being upset that she and Josh had gotten involved. Was it possible Mad had kept it to herself? Maybe she'd been too busy with school to connect with her dad. Had everyone kept it quiet? She'd thought for sure after Josh had showed up at the club, the news would spread like wildfire. Was Joe still in the dark? Maybe he'd given Josh hell and just gave Hailey the cold shoulder. She hadn't heard from Joe. And Josh might not have shared that bad stuff with her out of some protective instinct. Ugh. She much preferred to have all the facts.

She stroked Rose's little head, returning her focus to her

friends. Most of them were sitting on the floor around the coffee table. "Should I bring in the two kitchen chairs?"

Her friends declined.

"Everyone have enough to drink?" she asked. "Or eat? Maybe I could make a cheese and crackers platter. I'm pretty sure I have crackers, or I could toast up some crostini?"

"Quit stalling!" Mad barked.

Hailey smoothed her hair and took a sip of wine. Mad always saw through when Hailey was fussing to avoid hard topics.

"Is Josh being a dick?" Mad asked bluntly.

The women all looked at her expectantly.

How to answer? He wasn't doing anything bad. He just wasn't doing anything at all. Zero effort. The contrast to Phillip's romantic efforts was stark indeed.

"Men are stupid," she finally said.

Mad spoke around a cookie. "Let me just point out that all of my brothers are clueless in the romance department. They never read the manual." She swept her finger through the women who knew her brothers best. "Right, Lauren? Charlotte? Sabrina? Claire? You know it's true." Lauren and Charlotte had married her brothers Alex and Ty respectively. Sabrina was engaged to her brother Logan, but Hailey didn't think that should count since a relationship counselor was naturally good at relationships.

Hailey looked across the coffee table to Claire. This was the woman who could explain it best. She should've gone straight to Claire in the first place with this untenable situation. Claire had married Josh's identical twin, and the men were probably very similar relationship-wise, except she was sure Josh was a zillion times worse than Jake.

Lauren demurred in her sweet way, tucking her long light brown hair behind her ears. "Alex was in mourning over his fiancée. He let me know he loved me once he was ready."

"Ty was clueless," Charlotte announced, her brown eyes bright. "No question." She smiled. "But sometimes he just came out with the sweetest things that made me melt."

Josh had called Hailey a warrior once. That was almost sweet.

"I have no complaints," Sabrina said diplomatically.

"Jake was not romantic," Claire said. "He was hard-headed, arrogant, aggressive, and demanding."

Hailey sucked in air. That sounded just like Josh! Beast twins!

Claire smiled at Hailey. "Sound familiar?"

"Uh, yeah."

Claire winked. "I'm the same way."

Hailey got quiet. It seemed that wink was meant to imply Hailey might be that way too. Was she? Was that why they kept butting heads?

Claire went on. "Things didn't work so well in the beginning. It was kiss, fight, kiss, fight. Except substitute fuck for kiss."

Everyone laughed. Hailey just sat there on the edge of her seat, dying to know the answer to the impossible Josh question.

Claire shook her head, smiling. "There was just a lot of energy sparking in all different directions." She paused dramatically and the room went absolutely silent. Even Rose's ears perked up from her perch on Hailey's lap. "Until he made what we call in the movie business a grand romantic gesture."

"I thought Jake wasn't romantic," Mad said. "What'd he do?"

Claire seemed lost in memory for a moment. "It might not have been romantic in the classic sense of the word, but what he did was something that meant a lot to me. He arranged to buy out Blake's contract for the Fierce trilogy movies when Blake was giving me a hard time and, when I declined, he told me he'd invest in my movie's marketing campaign. You have to understand I was so stressed at the time, all of my money was invested in production for the first Fierce trilogy movie, and I had little left for marketing. All I had was good buzz from the press and that was turning on me. He basically played my knight in shining armor."

"Josh doesn't have that kind of money," Mad pointed out.

Claire tossed a chip at Mad. "You're as unromantic as your brothers. It was the gesture, the sacrifice he was willing to make on my behalf, not the money. I didn't accept either offer. Oh, wait! There was more. He offered to sell his company and travel to wherever I was filming just to be with me."

The women murmured in astonishment. This was news to them. Jake's company was worth billions.

"You didn't accept that either," Hailey said. "It was the gesture."

"Yup!" Claire took a sip of her sparkling water, her hazel eyes warm on Hailey's. "Josh made a gesture for you."

"No, he didn't."

"He showed up at book club."

That was true. It hadn't felt like a romantic gesture. It had all been rather awkward, a little sweet too. He did give her that accidental pregnancy romance. The only gift he'd ever given her.

"A-a-nd," Claire dragged out the word for the next supposed gesture, "he took a night off work to go to a club with you."

Hailey huffed. "That was to show up Phillip. You can't even believe what's been going on with those two cocks."

Everyone laughed. Hailey laughed too and then she told them every last detail from Josh's zero effort to their fights and hot sex. She finished with a report on Phillip's princely behavior with all the roses, his interest in investing in her, and his dreamy proposal.

"Holy shit!" Mad exclaimed.

"They're both acting like idiots," Claire pronounced.

"Maybe they're both in love with her," Sabrina suggested in her soothing counselor voice. Sabrina was very pro committed loving relationship.

That was the weird thing. She didn't think Phillip could possibly be in love with her that fast. But Josh. They'd known each other so long she supposed it was possible. But Josh hadn't expressed that. He hadn't expressed much of anything. Did she love him? She'd thought love would be this beautifully romantic thing, and that was definitely not what she had with Josh. He made her furious, made her come undone. The problem was this, no matter how mad she got, she couldn't seem to stop thinking about him, couldn't seem to keep away.

"Phillip's just using her to fix his rep," Mad said with a scowl. She always took Josh's side no matter what. Family first. Hailey hadn't told her friends about her mom flaking on Joe for just this reason. She knew Mad would take her dad's side and dump Hailey as a best friend. She needed Mad in her life. No one else cut through the BS and spoke her truth the way Mad did. It had always helped Hailey immensely, except where Josh was concerned. Her mom had better not screw this up for her. If her mom had just talked to Joe instead of running away to who-knew-where, Hailey was sure Joe would calm her down and assure her he loved her. He was just that kind of wonderful man.

"Do you love Josh?" Claire asked.

Hailey jolted. All eyes were on her. She let out a shaky breath. "I don't know. I'm so confused. He promised me a courtship, but all I got was one dinner and a lot of nothing."

"Call him on it," Claire said. "Say exactly what you want and why. Trust me, if you're not direct, he's not going to read between the lines. He might be smart, but he's up on guy speak not the subtlety of woman speak. Jake's the same way. Now me, I've learned to be direct working in the industry. You're still fairly…"

"Girly," Mad finished for her.

"Subtle." Claire smiled. "I get it. Women are raised not to make a fuss, to smooth things over, to be polite and poised. Maybe your pageant training contributed to that, but life is not a pageant, and you don't need to please him. What you need is to stand up for yourself and what you want."

Sabrina piped up. "I don't know if that's the right tactic in this particular case. It could easily escalate between her and Josh. I think she should withdraw from this weird dynamic. Let the men miss her and realize the depth of their feelings. Their actions after that will tell Hailey all she needs to know."

But what if Josh didn't do anything? What if it was just

Phillip urging her to save Villroy and his reputation and be a bona fide princess?

"You ladies gave me a lot to think about," Hailey said. "Thank you."

"We got your back, sister!" Mad said, offering her a fist bump. Hailey gave it to her. "We really will be sisters in two weeks. Awesome, right?"

Hailey's stomach rolled, nausea rising fast. She swore if she had to hunt down her mom and drag her back by the hair to marry Joe, she'd do it! Oh my! Maybe she was like Josh—aggressive and protective, not the hardheaded and arrogant part. She couldn't remember feeling that way before. Maybe Josh was rubbing off on her, or maybe it was a hidden strength emerging in difficult circumstances.

"Awesome," she told Mad, quickly handing over Rose. "I'm going to get more wine."

Mad took the distraction, Rose, and cuddled her close.

By the time her friends left around midnight, Hailey had a comfortable buzz from the wine and friendship. Her friends all thought she should step away from the crazy male situation. The theory being that the men would miss her and step up in their own way. Only Claire continued to urge her to be direct.

And only Claire remained behind to try to convince Hailey to accept a ride over to Josh's place. Claire's driver and bodyguard were waiting.

"Claire, really, it's late; I'm buzzed. I think I'm just going to go to bed."

"Then tomorrow, okay? I'm telling you, I get Josh. I know he needs it spelled out. It might be hard, but you have to just put it all out there. Do or die."

"Okay, okay," she said just to get Claire off her back.

Claire hugged her. "Call me afterward and tell me how it went."

"I will."

Claire finally left.

Hailey took out Rose for her nighttime bathroom break and then got ready for bed. By the time she finished in the bathroom, Rose was sound asleep curled up by Hailey's pillow. Maybe Claire was right and she would feel better if she just put it all out there. She was so tired of not knowing where she stood with Josh. She changed into jeans and a sweatshirt, put a sleeping Rose in her dog purse, grabbed a flashlight, and left.

Clover Park was safe for a midnight walk. The sidewalks were empty, houses dark, the only sounds the night bugs and birds. Maybe an owl? Doves? She had no clue. A rustle in the bushes had her picking up speed.

By the time she reached the old Victorian where Josh lived, she was slightly out of breath, a little spooked to be out alone, and flushed with exertion. She pressed the intercom buzzer, hoping he was up. Nothing. She texted him. No reply. Buzzed again and again. *Come on! Wake up! Damn you, Josh Campbell! I'm ready to speak my truth!*

"Hailey?"

She yelped and whirled. Josh was standing right behind her. "You scared me."

"I just got back from work."

Of course, she should've known. It was Saturday night and he worked until closing. She hadn't heard his car pull up. She'd been too busy buzzing the buzzer and silently yelling at him.

Adrenaline fueling her, she blurted out everything right away. "I want the courtship you promised me. I only got one dinner twelve days ago and I want more. We're way past slow burn, but I liked what you suggested. It felt romantic."

He stepped close, his voice a rumble in her ear. "Hailey, it's past midnight. We both know why you're here." He took her hand and guided her into the foyer and then to his apartment.

"I know, I just said why I was here," she told him as he pulled her to his bedroom.

He took her dog purse and deposited Rose outside the bedroom door, closing it quietly, and flicked on the light by the nightstand. Then he took her hand, guided her to his bed, and gave her a small shove. She landed, sitting on the mattress.

She spoke her truth in the most direct way possible. "Claire explained Jake very well, and I finally understand..." She trailed off as he joined her, his lips meeting the side of her neck, kissing his way up to her jaw while his hand slid under her sweatshirt. "Josh."

He met her eyes in question.

"I've missed you so much."

His hand tightened along her ribs. His other hand smoothed her hair back, holding it in a tight grip, the look in his eyes fierce possession before his mouth claimed hers. A spark of pure joy lit her up inside because he'd missed her too.

Josh lay on his side, taking in a relaxed and happy Hailey, naked in his bed where she belonged. He brushed her hair back from her glowing face. He hadn't held back, aggressive in his possession, and she'd matched him like he'd suspected all along she would. He hadn't reacted badly once, even with her grabbing hands all over him, climbing him, pushing him down, exploring his body. He trusted her. Or maybe he just knew he could restrain her easily and she wouldn't mind. She seemed to enjoy when he took over, flipping her to her stomach, putting her into whatever position pleased him. Ah, they were well matched in bed.

She missed me.

Thank God. He turned off the light on the nightstand. Rose was still asleep outside the bedroom door. They'd probably get an early morning wake-up call, but whatever. He didn't want the distraction of a dog begging to join them in bed.

Hailey lay on her back. He rolled to his back next to her and stared at the ceiling as he asked her something important. "I'll be the official owner of Garner's next Thursday. Banner day and a long time coming. I'll text you after it's official so you can stop by to celebrate with me."

She rolled to her side and threw an arm and a leg over him. "I'm so happy for you. Your dream is coming true."

He hoped so. The other part of his dream—the part where she came in—would happen at the same time. Probably the most important day of his life. He was putting it all on the line. His pulse kicked harder, knowing it wasn't a sure thing and could backfire so badly he'd probably never recover. He found himself holding his breath and took a deep breath. "So you'll be there?"

"Sure." She ran her hand up his arm to his shoulder. "Do you think this is love?"

He considered how to answer. Yes, on his end. But Hailey had never felt love and he wanted her to realize it on a deep level on her own. If she loved him, she should feel it. "What do you think?"

She rested her head on his chest. "I honestly don't know. Half the time you make me furious, but I can't seem to stay away."

He wrapped an arm around her shoulders, tucking her body against him. "So stick around more. Maybe you'll get used to me and stop getting so worked up over every little thing."

Her head popped up. "So it's my fault."

"See how you're starting with me again? I'm just stating facts."

She huffed.

He pushed her head back to his chest and kept his hand there, holding her in place. "You take everything to heart."

"Excuse me for having a heart. I am in the love business."

He waited in silence, letting her cool down. He didn't want to fight. He'd missed her and he felt good right now, really satisfied and hopeful things were finally going in the right direction.

"Have you ever proposed to someone?" she asked.

He wrapped her hair around his fist, loving the feel of it. "No."

"This is my first proposal."

He stilled. She had to know it was bogus, right? He'd thought she was just using that to get him to react. "He's using you. Please tell me you know that."

"Maybe."

He tugged her hair back, tipping her face up to his. "Definitely. Tell him no. Tell him you're with me."

"I'm confused," she whispered.

"There's nothing to be confused about," he growled. "You're mine."

"I'm not some possession."

"You're mine, period. Now go to sleep." He pressed her head back to his chest, tension building in him. He was in deep, invested in their future, and she was...not.

She climbed on top of him, her head hovering over his, giving him hell. "I will not go to sleep! You can't just say something like that and expect me to be okay with it. I'm a human being not a piece of property."

He bit back a smile because he enjoyed this side of her, his warrior princess. "You're grade A meat and I took a bite first." He snapped his teeth at her.

"Meat!" She tried to get off him, but he wrapped his arms around her, holding her captive. She wriggled to get away, turning him on way too much.

"Relax. I'm kidding."

She stilled. "I don't think you are kidding. You really do think because I slept with you first—"

"Did you sleep with him?"

"No."

He ground his teeth. "Did he lay a hand on you?"

"No," she said softly.

"I swear, woman." He closed his eyes, working on calm. She just had to push his buttons.

She tried to break free of his embrace, but he hung on. "I'll go."

He groaned and stroked her back. "Stay, okay?" He scowled. "Stop being so difficult."

She propped up on his chest, looking at him. "But I'm not

tired. You know us twentysomethings are just getting started at—" she peered at the digital clock on the nightstand "—one thirty. You're thirty-five, practically middle-aged—ah!"

He'd rolled her under him. "Challenge accepted." Then he showed her in explicit detail the advantages of being with an experienced man.

17

Hailey spent the whole next day with Josh. It was Sunday, she didn't have any client appointments, and he got someone to cover his morning shift. She told herself that was kind of like a romantic gesture whenever Josh chose her over work. Or maybe she just wanted to believe he was in love with her because she was beginning to think she was in love with him. It was nothing like she'd thought it would be. Not sweet or pretty, it was just there. She felt so much better with him than without him. And when they weren't fighting, things were great. She'd been a little worried after their morning round of sex they'd have nothing left to do with each other the rest of the day, but it was almost like all the sex mellowed them both out, because they had a lazy Sunday.

Josh made waffles from scratch with scrambled eggs and bacon. They ate breakfast together, went back to her place for a change of clothes, and then she taught him how to make her fudgy brownies that he'd always been crazy about. The secret ingredient was Nutella. After she agreed to let him serve them at Garner's, he smiled more that afternoon than she'd ever seen from him. He was dazzlingly gorgeous when he smiled.

Now they were back at his place, watching HGTV while he quizzed her on what houses she liked and why. It made her giddy that he cared about her opinion on houses because maybe he was imagining them having a house together. She'd never lived in a house before, always apartments, and the thought of having something so permanent gave her a deep sense of satisfaction. The only bad thing about the whole day was that Mad had texted asking if she knew where Hailey's mom was because her dad had been gone all weekend and wasn't answering his phone. Hailey suspected Joe was looking for her mom, but she didn't know where her mom was. The moment the news got out that her mom had flaked, she knew nothing would ever be the same again with her and the Campbells. They'd cool toward her. She'd always be a reminder of her mom's betrayal.

She'd turned off her phone, deciding to deal with the mom situation on Monday. Maybe her mom would be back by then. She fervently prayed she'd come to her senses.

That night after a delicious dinner of chicken francese that Josh had walked her through making, Josh got a call from Mad. He was the oldest brother, along with Jake, but he was the one in town, and she knew his younger siblings turned to him in times of crisis. They were all close to their dad, and his being gone all weekend and out of touch (probably looking for Hailey's mom) would've set off an alarm.

She stood and gathered their dishes. "I'll take care of these."

He jerked his chin at her and then said into the phone, "What do you mean he's disappeared?"

Hailey turned the water on low so she could eavesdrop as she rinsed the dishes.

"You went over there?" Josh asked. "Maybe he took an extra shift. Maybe he forgot to charge his phone." He was quiet for a moment. "Hold on." He pulled the phone away from his ear. "Hailey, Mad says my dad's been away all weekend and out of touch. Could you check in with your mom to see if he's with her?"

"Sure," she croaked.

He spoke to Mad again. "You have? I've been with her all day and her phone didn't ring. Maybe she left it at her place.

I'll let her know. Yeah, yeah, smartass. I'll be in touch. I'm sure he's fine."

Josh joined her at the sink. "Where's your phone? Mad says she's been trying to reach you all day."

She focused on the dishes. "I turned it off because I didn't want anything to distract me from our first weekend together."

"Look at me when you say that."

She met his eyes. "I didn't want any distractions."

His dark eyes burned into hers. "What aren't you telling me?"

She gulped. "Nothing."

He narrowed his eyes. "Call your mom. Mad's worried that something happened to our dad."

"Sure." She left the kitchen on shaky legs, her gut churning. This was where it all came to an end. She should've known she couldn't have something lasting with Josh. Nothing in her life had ever lasted long. Everything was always yanked out from under her—her family, her home, and now her chance at love.

She turned on her phone, registering three texts and five missed calls from Mad. She dialed her mom and it went to voicemail. She texted, but she didn't expect a response. When her mom flaked, she stopped communicating completely. Usually she went on a long drive, as if she could outrun her troubles.

Josh appeared at her side. "Well?"

"Voicemail. No response to my text yet."

"Can you call your aunt Jane's house or the hospital? Wherever she is."

She bit her lip. She didn't want to lie, but the truth was going to go over really badly.

Josh stared at her for a long moment. "It's not like my dad to go away without telling anyone where he's going or at least get in touch later. I'm sure he's with your mom. Please tell me where your aunt is."

"I'm not sure. She's moved a bunch of times. I'll try my mom again later." She brushed past him to go back to the kitchen, but he caught her around the waist, halting her progress. Her throat tightened. Josh was not going to let this go. This was the moment she'd been dreading ever since her mom and his dad met.

She turned to face him and confessed everything in a rush. "There is no Aunt Jane. My mom flaked on your dad, freaking out about getting married, which I knew she'd do, and I've just been hanging by a thread of hope that she'd return before anyone was the wiser."

He frowned. "You didn't turn your phone off because of me. You were avoiding talking to Mad. Why wouldn't you just tell her the truth so she wouldn't worry?"

She wrung her hands together. "Of course she would worry! Your dad's probably scouring the country for my mom, wasting time and money. I know your dad's been left before and this would hurt him terribly. I don't know if my mom will ever go back to him. She's always been one to flit from one relationship to another. Mad would never understand. She'd be so upset about her dad getting hurt that she'd dump me." She swallowed hard, fighting tears. "I didn't want to lose her. She made me feel like part of a family, the kind I never had and always wanted."

His voice gentled. "Mad loves you. You're the sister she always wanted. You think so little of her that you think she'd dump you for something your mom did?"

"Family first always for Mad." She rubbed her temple at the headache forming there. "I knew my mom would screw everything up."

"No one is going to put the blame on you."

"It's by association, especially because we resemble each other. I'm a constant reminder of how her dad got hurt."

"That's not how it works."

"It is! You don't understand, coming from your family. No one ever stuck for me!" Her eyes stung with unshed tears. "Nothing and no one has ever lasted!"

His arms wrapped around her. "Calm down."

She tried to jerk away, but he held tight. "Josh, let go of me. I need to fix this. I should've gotten on this earlier, but I was enjoying our time together, and I was in complete denial."

He released her. "Okay, see what you can do."

She went to check her phone and it rang in her hand. She answered it. "Hi, Mad. I'm so sorry I didn't get in touch earlier. I don't know where my mom is, but I'll call some of her friends and see if she might've left any clues."

Mad sounded frantic. "I'm afraid my dad's been in an accident. I'm this close to calling hospitals. It's not like him not to be in touch."

Hailey freaked, holding the phone in a death grip. If Joe had gotten into an accident searching for her mom, she didn't know how she'd ever face any of the Campbells ever again. She forced her voice to sound normal. "I'm sure he's fine. Probably he left his phone somewhere or turned it off. Okay? I'll be in touch as soon as I know something."

"Hailey, I'm so scared. He's always been larger than life. So strong, always there. He was both dad and mom to me." Her voice choked. "He's everything."

"I love him too. Let's just stay calm and not jump to worst-case scenarios. He's smart and savvy. I'm sure he's okay." She told her goodbye, hung up, and turned to Josh, who looked back at her with concern. "I need to go to my mom's place and find her contact info for her friends. She keeps an address book."

"You want me to go with you?"

She shook her head. "I'll take care of everything."

She left, terrified it was the last time she'd ever be on good terms with him or Mad or any of the Campbells again.

Monday morning came with little hope. Hailey had tried everyone she could think of to get a hint about where her mom had gone. She'd even called local hospitals, heart in her throat, in case something really bad had gone down. So far no news, which she'd told Mad. Joe still wasn't home.

Of course, this would have to be the day when she had

multiple client fires she had to put out. By eleven a.m. she was frazzled and exhausted. The chime on the front door of Ludbury House rang, and she raced to answer it, desperately hoping it would be her mom.

It was a man she'd never seen before, tall and bulky with muscle. Thick black hair on the longish side, piercing blue eyes, and a neatly trimmed beard. He was dressed casually in a white T-shirt, jeans, and black work boots. A tattoo peeked out of one shirtsleeve over his bulging bicep. No woman with him, so probably not a potential client. Maybe he had some kind of delivery.

"Hello, can I help you?" she asked.

He offered his hand, shaking hers in a firm grip. "Dylan Rourke." His voice was deep and grumbly. "It's about my cousin Phillip."

Omigod, Phillip. She'd completely forgotten to get back to him about his proposal three days ago. He must've sent a representative in case the news was bad.

She stepped out onto the porch with him, figuring it would be a quick conversation. Also, he was a little intimidating, and she didn't want to be alone with him inside her office. "Did he send you? I'm so sorry it took me so long to get back to him."

Dylan crossed his arms, making his biceps bulge. "You won't be accepted by the family. He needs royal lines, not an American."

She tilted her head, considering this odd bit of information. "That can't be true. What about Silvia and her American fiancé?"

He slashed a hand through the air. "It's different. She's not that close to the throne. Phillip is next in line after Gabriel."

She pasted on a smile. "Well, it really wasn't a serious consideration on my part. He doesn't love me."

Dylan's eyes widened. "Are you kidding? You're all he can talk about. He told Silvia how perfect you are, and she sent me to handle it."

Perfect? Me?

Dylan grumbled on in his growly voice. "I'm saying this

for your own good. My family is the outcast. My dad was next in line, married a girl from Brooklyn, and here we are, a whole damn royal family denied any of the wealth or privilege that comes with that."

He sounded terribly bitter.

Dylan gestured up and down her body. "I get it. You already look like a beautiful princess and you're put together. Not someone who'd fall apart under the harsh spotlight."

"Dylan!" a masculine voice shouted. "What the hell do you think you're doing?"

She sucked in air. Phillip! His two security guards hovered behind him.

The two men squared off on the front porch. Dylan had more bulky muscle on Phillip, but they had equally lethal looks on their faces. She shrank back by the door.

"Silvia said you're out of hand," Dylan growled.

"And she told me you insisted on taking care of things yourself. Go back to Brooklyn where you belong!"

Dylan jabbed Phillip in the chest. "Why don't you go back to your prissy castle you love so much."

Phillip smacked Dylan's hand away. "Don't touch me, riffraff."

"Fuck you."

"Fuck you, you interloper! Trying to hang on in any way you can, using Silvia—"

"She needed me. You're out of control."

Dylan grabbed Phillip by the front of his shirt, lifting him. Phillip's shirt ripped under the strain and he lifted a knee, aiming for the groin. Dylan deflected the blow, tossing Phillip a few feet back. The guards moved forward, anticipating a brawl.

"Both of you get out!" Hailey hollered. Geez, men were all beasts.

Phillip turned to her. "I still need an answer, Hailey. I don't know what Dylan told you—"

She spoke her truth. "I will only marry for love, so the answer is no."

"I love you," Phillip said earnestly.

Dylan grumbled, "I told you."

She stared at Phillip, speechless. How could he love her so soon? They'd met a little over three weeks ago. Very little of that time was spent face-to-face, mostly they talked by phone or text. Was his life so insular that the small amount of time they'd had together felt intimate? She couldn't say she felt the same way.

Dylan glowered as Phillip went on from the heart. "It's okay if you don't feel the same way now; with time you will. Come back with me. You're a diamond who can't shine to your full potential here. Villroy is where you belong."

Both men stared at her.

She tried to let him down easy. "I'm sorry, Phillip, the answer is no. I can't be who you want."

Phillip took her hand. "Just think about it. There's a spot on the jet for you."

Dylan shook his head, turned, and left, heading for a motorcycle he'd parked on the street. He roared off and they all watched him go.

"Riffraff," Phillip muttered under his breath before he left too.

She went inside and sat at her desk, shaken by the past few days' events. Things were weird in every part of her life.

She checked in on her mom again with no response. Now she was actually starting to worry about her mom. What if something had happened to her? She'd never left for longer than a weekend drive away.

By the time she wrapped up work for the day, all she wanted to do was return to her cozy woman cave of an apartment and watch mindless TV. When she got to her front door, a bouquet of roses was waiting. Clearly Phillip didn't take no for an answer. She grabbed the flowers, let herself in, and tossed them in the trash.

18

———

Hailey had just settled with a big bowl of buttery popcorn in front of the TV when her doorbell rang. Rose barked and ran to the door. Hailey sighed, put the popcorn on the coffee table, and went to answer it. Josh stood there, looking worried.

"Is everything okay?" she managed over the lump in her throat.

"No word from my dad," he said, stepping inside. Rose climbed his leg and he scooped her up, rubbing her behind the ear. "Any word from your mom?"

"No, not yet."

He set Rose down and made himself comfortable on her sofa. She wasn't sure how she felt about that. It seemed presumptuous, but then again, Josh had never been overly polite.

She joined him. "So you just stopped by to hang out or…"

"Do I need a reason to be with you?"

"I guess not. It's just the first time you showed up like this."

He took a piece of popcorn. "Did you get the flowers?"

She startled. "Those were from you?"

"Didn't you read the card?"

She leapt off the sofa, rushed to the kitchen, and pulled the trash can out from under the sink.

"You threw them out?" he barked from behind her.

She retrieved them, still in their nice wrapper. "It's okay. The wrap protected them."

"Why would you throw out an expensive bouquet?"

"I'm sorry! I thought they were from Phillip!" She set the roses on a kitchen chair and pulled the small card from the envelope. *Thinking of you! Love, Josh.* It was sweet both for the exclamation point, which was probably half-teasing but showed effort, and the love. Maybe Josh did love her.

He remained leaning in the doorway of the kitchen. "Why would you think the roses were from the prince? You turned him down, right? You told him you're mine."

She shook her head at his possessive side that still felt weird. If he'd said, "you're my girlfriend" or "you're my love" or even "you're my woman" she might have thought it nearly romantic. But *you're mine*? Sigh.

"Why're you shaking your head?" He closed the distance between them, his jaw clenched tight. "Tell me right now that you told him no."

She met his dark eyes burning into hers. "I did tell him no, but he's persistent. He thinks he's in love with me." *Are you?*

He glowered down at her. *Grr.* No loving sentiment would ever emerge from that mouth.

She scowled. "And stop saying 'you're mine.' I'm not yours."

"Hailey, you drive me insane," he ground out. "Literally insane. Yet I can't quit you. I need to hear your voice, even when it's irritating me, I need to see your eyes flashing at me about to rip me a new one, and I live to see you in your element taking care of business." He took both of her hands in his. "You *own* me. So it's only fair I own you too."

"Josh," she gasped out, her stomach fluttering, all of her flushed hot, "it doesn't work like that."

His arms wrapped around her waist. "That's how we work."

Her hands went to his chest. She was so flustered she

wasn't sure if she wanted to push him away or hold him close. "But it's not right."

He went nose to nose with her. "Why does a woman who's never been in love think she knows everything about right and wrong in a relationship?"

"So we have a relationship?"

"I can't even..." He nipped her lower lip.

"I need clarity—"

"Stop talking," he said, smiling against her mouth before he kissed her.

She threw her arms around his neck and kissed him back passionately. He lifted her, his mouth still sealed over hers, and walked with her to her bedroom, shutting the door with his shoulder. She was wild for him, all of her angst that had built up since she'd last seen him pouring through her. She kissed him roughly, her hands running through his hair, across his shoulders, his back, everywhere she could reach. His hands were on her ass and he guided her to the wall.

He broke the kiss and set her on her feet, turning her, unzipping her dress and sliding it over her shoulders. His hands smoothed over her skin as the dress slipped off, his warm lips trailing down her spine. She turned in his arms, yanked him up, and slammed her mouth over his. He groaned, ripped her thong off, and slid his hand between her legs.

"So wet for me," he growled. He took her hand and made her feel. "Touch yourself."

"Josh," she protested and then trailed off as he pulled a condom from his pocket, stripped, and got it on in a flash.

Then he lifted her, thrusting deep inside her, the two of them frantic for each other. She threw her head back, hips arching to meet each hard thrust. Tension spiraled through her, stealing her breath as he claimed her. *Yes, yes, yes.*

He held her jaw, drawing her gaze to him, his eyes dilated, raw and animal. His fingers slipped between them, stroking her as he gazed into her eyes, his harsh breath hot on her lips. She trembled as the deep connection overwhelmed her, a primal beat in her ears, a message that shook her to her core—she was his.

"Yes," he said, a guttural sound of approval.

She went off with a soft cry, her body clenching around him, a starburst of intense pleasure rocking her. He pressed his lips to her neck as he drove into her for his own release, bringing shockwaves of pleasure before he let go with a roar.

The world came back into focus slowly. Josh's strong arms held her, his weight partially leaning against her, his spicy male scent filling her senses. He lifted his head, pushed her hair back from her face and kissed her tenderly. She nearly cried at that tenderness.

"Don't cry," he said against her mouth.

"I'm not," she choked out.

His fingers slid down her throat, his gaze knowing. "You felt something deep."

She blinked rapidly. "I claim *you*. You're mine. I own you."

His lips curled up in a sexy smirk of a smile. "It's only fair."

She kissed him again and couldn't seem to stop, needing that connection. He was moving, walking with her still wrapped around him, still buried deep inside her. He stopped abruptly, lifted her off him, and set her on the bed. She opened her arms to him.

He leaned down and kissed her. "Give me a minute."

He left, probably for the bathroom, and Rose ran in, begging to get up on the bed. Hailey set a pillow on the floor for Rose, arranged pillows for her and Josh in bed, and got under the covers. She wanted Josh all to herself without Rose stealing his attention.

Josh strode back in, naked, looking badass and a little smug. Hmph. Did he think sex was the answer to everything? He joined her, rolling to his side to face her, wedging his leg between hers, unexpectedly applying pressure to her still tingling sex, his hand stroking down her side to her hip.

Her voice came out a little breathy. "Josh, you can't end every argument with sex."

He smiled lazily, his hand sliding down her leg. "It's

working for me."

She stilled his hand, which was creeping to the inside of her thigh. "I'm not sure if it's working for me. Things feel unresolved."

"You're mine. I'm yours. Easy."

She sighed. Maybe he was right. Maybe his phrasing wasn't romantic, but she'd felt it on a visceral level during sex, and wasn't sex when they both let down their defenses the most? Stripped bare to each other. Could it be that all that fighting was just a defense against the vulnerable feeling of belonging to each other? It was hard to feel vulnerable.

He nuzzled into her neck, tugged her earlobe between his teeth, and whispered in her ear, "Admit it, woman. Say the words for me."

She slid her hand to the nape of his neck, playing with his soft hair. "All this time I've had a plan for world domination—"

"Ha!"

"Well, of my little corner of the world, a hugely successful wedding planning business, money in the bank, and my own happy ending. I've worked so hard, you have no idea how hard—"

"I have some idea. I've seen you in action."

She dropped her hand from him and rolled to her back, throwing an arm over her eyes. "And then I had a breakdown." She inwardly cringed at the memory. "The next day, a prince falls into my lap, and I think maybe I should try less and things might work out better."

Josh pulled her arm off her eyes and propped up on one elbow. "And I had a plan to make you mine, and then a goddamn prince shows up, trying to ruin everything. You see, the problem here isn't my plan or your plan, the problem is the prince. Very inconvenient that guy showing up in the middle of our plans."

"The prince isn't our problem. We're not a normal couple."

He cradled her jaw, his thumb brushing her cheek. "Define normal."

She blew out a breath. "You know, dating, actually liking each other…forget it."

He slid his hand from her jaw, down her neck, to her shoulder, which he squeezed. "I like you okay."

"Gee, thanks. And not so much fighting. More romantic stuff, love notes, gifts of adoration, sweet words—"

"You watch too many sappy movies and read way too many love books."

She glared at him. "You said you wanted to give me a courtship. That's what it is."

"No, a courtship is when you spend time with the person because you like them and hold off on sex."

"You didn't hold off on sex."

He smirked. "That's because you couldn't stop begging for it. I put you out of your misery."

She jackknifed upright. "Josh! This is exactly the problem. We don't see eye to eye on anything."

"You like sex with me."

She blushed, which was ridiculous, sitting here naked with him. "Yes."

He sat up. "Me too. So we see eye to eye on that. And you like looking at me, touching me, talking to me, spending time with me."

"Sometimes."

He grinned. "Me too."

They laughed.

She squeezed his arm. "I'm afraid we're a pitiful excuse for a couple."

"I'm sure of it. But we're stuck with each other."

She grimaced. "Stuck with each other? I don't know. That doesn't sound quite right. I feel a little weird about it actually."

He started running his hands all over her. "You do feel a little weird."

She pushed his hands away, laughing. "Josh!"

He grinned and then he kissed her. It wasn't perfect between them, but it felt right. The kiss quickly turned carnal. Next thing she knew, he had her flat on her back. And then he was kissing his way down her body, his big hands spreading her legs. She arched her hips up in offering because his mouth was heaven.

"So weird," he said before his mouth closed over her sex.

"Shut up." White-hot pleasure surged through her. "Don't stop."

He didn't stop. Sensations flooded her, the tension building again as he used his lips and tongue in the most wicked way, his fingers thrusting inside, hitting just the right spot. Oh my God, she was going to die. Just when she was about to have the mother of all orgasms, he stopped.

"Josh!" She grabbed him by the hair, trying to bring him back. "Please!"

"Say it." He gave her a tap that made her hips jerk. "You're mine."

She met his eyes, expecting a smirk or gloating, but what she saw was a deep tenderness, love shining in those dark eyes. For her. A rush of affection stole through her and she gave back to him with all the love in her heart. "I'm yours."

He smiled, his warm brown eyes crinkling at the corners. "Very good."

He lowered his head again, giving her exactly what she needed, and she flew.

~

That night Hailey sat on the sofa with Josh, watching more of those fun home shows that they both thoroughly enjoyed, when she received an unexpected phone call. Phillip. The timing couldn't have been worse. Her apartment was too small for privacy, and Josh would not be happy with this.

"Hi, this isn't a good time," she said as soon as she answered.

"Hailey, the jet's waiting. I've been called home early. It's now or never. I won't be returning with another proposal."

She lowered her voice, though Josh was so close he could probably hear both sides of the conversation. "I'm sorry, but I gave you my answer. I should've been more up front, but my current...*thing* was so confusing. I have a boyfr—" She stopped herself because Josh was man through and through, and boyfriend sounded almost juvenile when applied to him. "A, um, someone, a man who—"

Josh grabbed her phone and barked, "I'm her lover, it's fucking serious, and, if you don't stop harassing her, I will hunt you down, rip your still-beating heart out of your chest, and eat it for a goddamn snack." He listened for a moment, nodded once in satisfaction, and disconnected. "He won't be bothering you again."

She gingerly took her phone back and set it on the coffee table. Warrior Josh was magnificent in all his fierce glory. "I don't imagine he will."

Josh grunted and hauled her into his lap, her back to his front, wrapping his arms around her waist and nuzzling her neck. "You should've explained we were serious." He nipped her neck. "He was surprised."

She tilted her head, giving him better access as he kissed and nipped his way down her neck. "I didn't know where we stood. No label seemed to apply. You have to admit we're not a typical couple."

He lifted his head. "So you finally admit we're a couple."

"It does feel that way now. Before, I was so confused."

His hands roamed over the tops of her legs. "What is this pink thing you're wearing? A pants suit?"

She stifled a laugh. "They're pajamas." It was a button-down short-sleeve shirt with elastic-waist pants.

"They're silk."

"Yeah, they were a splurge."

He spread her legs wide, sliding his hands up her inner thighs, bunching the silk material. "I like the dresses better. Easier access."

"I'd like to think I'm more than just a fuck to you."

He gripped her by the hair, turning her head to kiss her. "Love when you talk dirty." He lifted her, turning her to straddle him, his hands sliding under the waistband to cup her ass.

Her phone rang again.

He sucked on the side of her neck. "Don't answer it."

"What if it's my mom?"

He groaned and set her on the sofa next to him. She grabbed her phone. The screen showed her mom's number. "Mom! Where are you? Are you okay?"

"It's Joe. I'm with your mom. She's okay. She's just out of surgery."

"Surgery! Oh my God. What happened?"

Josh's brows drew together in concern. She mouthed *it's your dad.*

Joe went on. "She broke her leg and they had to go in to fix it so it'd set right. We'll be on our way home tomorrow. We're in Maine." That was where her mom grew up. Her mom's parents had died years ago in a car accident off a narrow winding road in Maine, both of them gone at once. She hadn't even considered her mom would return there with the reminder of her parents. It suddenly occurred to her she didn't understand her mom at all, but Joe did.

Hailey's eyes filled. What if Joe hadn't found her mom? How long was her mom all alone, suffering with a broken leg? "I'm so glad you were with her. I'm so sorry all of this happened. I was afraid to say anything about her going off on her own. I didn't want everyone to hate her. And me." She slapped a hand over her mouth, stifling a sob.

"Sweetheart, it's okay. We worked things out."

"You did?" she managed, her throat painfully tight. She wiped the tears away.

"She had some wild notion that when she got older, her looks would fade and my love would fade too. Real love isn't like that. I'm here to stay. I've waited a long time for her, and I'm not letting her go that easily."

"She's always missed her modeling days. That was the golden time in her life, and I guess she feared losing what she had then."

"Ah, Hailey, she's so much more than a beautiful woman. She's caring in all the little ways that count, and she has such a strong spirit, always with a zest for life despite all she's been through losing her parents, your dad, and doing the single-mom thing. She's been on her own for the most part since she was sixteen. I have a lot of respect for her." Her mom had started her modeling career at sixteen, travelling the world, shortly after her parents died. She hadn't known her mom was mourning Hailey's dad. She'd said very little about him.

Hailey let out a shaky breath. "I was so sure I was going to lose you guys just when I finally got a great family."

Josh rubbed her back.

"Hailey," Joe said, his voice warm, "even if something had gone haywire between me and your mom, I'd still want you in my family."

"Oh." She looked to Josh and blurted, "I'm with Josh and it's serious and I know you didn't want him to be with me—"

"Whoa, that is not true at all."

"But Josh said you told him to keep his distance."

"And I knew he'd do the exact opposite. Josh can't back down from a challenge. I knew he'd try even harder to make the relationship work if he thought I'd come down on him for disrupting family harmony. I know my boy."

She nearly collapsed with relief. She'd been so worried all this time about being on the outs with Joe and his wonderful family. It was a devious calculation he'd pulled, which reminded her of a certain someone. "You know your son because he's just like you."

Joe chuckled. "Not exactly, but pretty close. See what you're getting into with us Campbells? And once you're in, there's no getting out. Terrible *Godfather* impression there, but you get my meaning. Seriously, though, Mad brought you in way back when, and we all love you."

"I love you too," she choked out. She looked to the ceiling, trying to hold off the tears. "How did my mom break her leg?"

"She tripped in the woods on the way to her grandparents' old cabin. I only found her by asking around town about her family. I would've called sooner, but I didn't have my charger. There wasn't any cell service where she was either, so she couldn't call for help. Anyway, I got her to the hospital and she'll make a full recovery. Can you let Josh know all is well? He'll tell the others."

"Sure, he's with me now. Thanks again, Joe."

She disconnected and turned to Josh. "Your dad tracked down my mom. She broke her leg and just came out of surgery to set it."

He nodded. "My dad was a damn good cop. He can track down anyone."

"She's so lucky to have him. She has no clue."

Josh raised his brows and then pulled out his phone. "I'm texting Mad the good news and telling her to pass it on."

Hailey took a few deep breaths, calming down from her scare. Then she shared the astonishing news that his dad actually did want them to be together.

Josh shook his head and put his phone away. "I should've known." He barked out a laugh. "I was so crazy over you I didn't put it together."

She beamed, loving hearing him say he was crazy over her because she was crazy for him too.

He wrapped her hair around his fist and smirked. "So you love my dad."

She smiled a little, still warmed from the conversation. "He said you all love me, so I said it back."

He used his grip on her hair to pull her close, gazing into her eyes, asking her, no, *demanding*, she say the same love words to him.

She wrapped her hand around the back of his neck and gazed into his eyes, letting him know that she knew what he wanted, and she also knew that he knew she wanted the words from him.

His lips twitched, but his gaze never wavered. Two warriors engaged in an epic staredown. Neither of them giving an inch.

"Hailey."

"Josh."

"I love you," they said at the same time.

Then they grabbed for each other, kissing like they'd just discovered the best thing in their life. Because they had.

EPILOGUE

Three days later, Hailey got the heads-up from Josh that it was official—he was now the owner of his dream bar. She scooped up Rose, tucking her into her purse, and left work to make the short walk down the block to Garner's. He wanted to celebrate with her, and she'd cleared her afternoon schedule to be there for him.

Josh was standing outside, facing in her direction. Rose started barking excitedly. Her dog had fallen hard for Josh just like Hailey had.

"I know, Rose. He gives the best strokes, doesn't he, with those big man hands?"

Rose got even more excited, nearly jumping out of the purse. Hailey quickly clipped her leash on and set her on the sidewalk. Rose raced ahead, straining at the leash, barking the whole time. Hailey had to hurry so Rose wouldn't pull her collar tight and choke.

Finally she realized what had Rose so worked up. Josh was holding a small black dog with a round face, huge dark eyes, and pointy ears.

"Josh! You got a dog!"

He grinned. "Meet Max. He's a rescue. They think part shih tzu, part Chihuahua. I thought Rose might like a pal." He set Max down to meet Rose.

Hailey watched in delight as their leashes wound around each other while they sniffed each other like crazy. "So cute! I think they're already buddies." Both of their tails were wagging.

"Rose needed her equal," Josh said.

She smiled up at him. That was what he'd said about her. "Yes. A warrior needs her equal."

He held her by the jaw, tipping her face up, and gave her a quick kiss. "Look up."

She did. "Ah! Josh! Omigod, I can't believe it!" The sign didn't read Garner's Sports Bar & Grill anymore. He'd replaced it with a new name in deep red—Happy Endings. He'd named his dream bar after her Happy Endings Book Club, her business mission, her life's mission. He'd named his dream bar for her.

Her lower lip trembled, her eyes hot. "You...Josh...I'm so touched."

He held her by the chin. "This sign has been tucked in the basement storage for weeks while I fought to nail you down—"

"You can't nail a person down. You can love them. You can be in a relationship with them, but you can't...Josh?" She looked down at her hand, which he'd just closed around a small black box. Her heart raced, her mouth dry.

His dark eyes intent on hers, he held her hand closed around the gift. "Hailey, I wanted to show you that I had a strong foundation, owning my own business. I'll never be rich, I can't offer you a jet-setting lifestyle, but—"

"You're a wonderful man with a big heart buried deep inside. I've seen it and it's good. I don't need a glitzy lifestyle. I only think money is important so you're not destitute." She went on tiptoe to whisper in his ear, "My mom couldn't make rent when I was a kid and we ended up homeless twice. I like money for security, but it's not how I measure someone." She gazed into his eyes. "You're measured by what you do and this..." She stared at the sign again. "This is such a wonderful gesture. I'm still stunned. Your dream bar named after me."

His voice was rough and gravelly. "The dream isn't nearly

complete without you in it. Permanently. I love you and will spend the rest of my life making sure you have a happy ending with me."

She flushed and laughed a little too because he was super-romantic, but he'd also slipped a sexy innuendo in there too.

He grinned. "Marry me."

"I will!"

She threw her arms around his neck and kissed him passionately. Something hit the ground, but she ignored it as his arms wrapped around her and he kissed her breathless. They broke apart at the sound of growling.

Josh dropped to his knees, pried the ring box out of Rose's mouth, wiped it on his jeans, and opened it to her. *A proposal on both knees? Swoon!* It was a round diamond solitaire on a gold band. She adored it. He slipped it on her finger, looked up at her from his gallant kneeling position, and gave her a tender smile.

She squealed, pulled him up, and peppered him with kisses all over his scruffy face.

Josh slid his hand under her hair, cupping the back of her neck, and kissed her fiercely, possessively, like she was his. She had to return the same fierce claim.

Their dogs ran in circles around them, excited, the leashes tangling around their legs, binding them together.

Brandy and Joe's wedding was perfect. It took place only two days later, so Hailey had to work with a bride on crutches, but it only went to show how deeply Joe loved his bride. He didn't care that she moved awkwardly down the aisle on crutches or that she had to sit through most of the reception at Happy Endings bar. He doted on her, his eyes full of love, his every gesture for her comfort. And her mom positively glowed with the love she had for Joe.

Hailey let out a happy sigh, surrounded by friends and the Campbell family, which she was now a part of in so many ways they'd never be able to cut her loose. Josh was her fiancé, Mad was the sister she'd always wanted, Joe was her stepdad, and all the brothers treated her like gold. Not to mention three of her friends were married to Campbells and one friend was engaged.

Josh entwined his fingers with hers as they watched the bride and groom have their special dance, which was more like the happy couple standing still, arms wrapped around each other. Every once in a while, Joe would lift her mom in her cast and spin her in another direction.

"So cute," Hailey murmured.

"Next is the maid of honor and best man dance," Jake Campbell announced. "And let's give them a round of applause on their new engagement."

Hailey flushed with happiness as everyone cheered for them. This was the first time Hailey had seen everyone since Josh had proposed two days ago, though, of course, she'd texted and called everyone immediately.

"It was about time!" Mad hollered.

Josh pulled her to the small dance floor in front of the bar, drawing her close for a slow swaying. He looked ridiculously handsome in his tux, clean-shaven, his hair still sexily rumpled. His hair was so thick there was just no taming it, which explained why his twin kept his hair short.

"Hello, lovebirds," Joe said, dancing with her mom nearby. "You're welcome."

"Ha," Josh said. "You don't get all the credit. I got moves, old man."

Hailey blushed. "Josh."

"What?"

Her mom laughed. "Why do you think we made you maid of honor and best man in the first place? It was a last-ditch effort to get you together."

Hailey turned to Josh in surprise. He looked equally surprised. That hadn't exactly worked out like her mom and Joe might've thought. Hearing Josh tell her he'd be best man to her maid of honor had been the last straw that caused her to break down in tears. At the time, being stuck with Josh, who'd rejected her, while everyone around her was having the happy ending she'd so craved had felt like the worst thing in the world. Maybe she needed to be stuck with Josh to find the wonderful man waiting to come out and love her. Once he was done being an arrogant beast.

"Like I said, you're welcome," Joe said smugly before whisking her mom off the dance floor and back to a comfortable chair.

Josh turned to her. "What do you think? They get the credit or us?"

Hailey shook her head. "I feel like I'm supposed to say us, but…"

He laughed. "Yeah. You made things extremely difficult."

"Excuse me? If anyone made things difficult, it was you. I didn't even think you liked me."

His hand slid up her spine to cup the back of her neck. "I always liked you. Why do you think I was your paid wedding escort in the first place?"

"Because you needed money."

One corner of his mouth lifted, his dark eyes sparkling with good humor. "I thought you were asking me out, and then when you said it was part of your business plan, I pretended like I knew that all along."

"Josh! We could've been dating years ago! I could've been the first one with a happy ending!"

He hugged her. "Honestly, I don't think so. I was fighting the attraction because I thought wrongly about you."

"And now?"

He pulled back to gaze into her eyes. "Now I'm going to marry you and live happily ever after in a house in Clover Park with our two dogs and as many kids as I can get out of you."

Her jaw dropped and then she was so overwhelmed with emotion, she had to turn her head away, hiding tears. "Shut. Up."

He turned her back to him and kissed her. "You like that, huh?"

"I *love* that!"

Someone socked her arm. She turned to see Mad next to

them with her fiancé, Parker. Apparently, the dance floor had filled with the wedding party, and Hailey had been so wrapped up in Josh she hadn't even noticed. True love could do that to you.

"Hey, sis," Hailey said cheerfully. "Since we're the same age, we could even be twins. The fraternal kind."

Mad laughed. "Sure, twins. Then you'd be a great athlete."

"And you'd be great for the pageant circuit."

Mad made a weird face. "Sure, if only, right? Anyway, I figure since I'll be your maid of honor, I should probably plan an engagement party and a bachelorette party for you."

She hadn't asked Mad to be maid of honor yet, but there was no one else she'd rather have by her side. "Sounds good!"

"You guys set a date?" Mad asked.

Josh answered for them. "I'm hoping this summer once she gets a break in her wedding planner schedule. Gotta nail her down quick since she's expecting."

Hailey gasped.

"Are you serious?" Mad hollered.

"Twins," Josh said, puffing his chest out. "Hailey loved that *Accidentally Pregnant by the Cowboy* book so much I knew I had to make it real."

Hailey gaped at him. "What're you saying?"

Mad put a hand to her throat. "You knocked her up because of my book? Josh, that was just a joke. You weren't supposed to..." She turned to Hailey. "Is this what you wanted?"

Hailey rolled her eyes. "I'm not pregnant."

Mad glared at Josh. "I was actually excited."

He ruffled her hair, messing up more than an hour's worth of styling. "Gotcha. Be glad I let you off that easy for your prank."

"More to come," Mad said with an evil glint in her eye.

"Guys, come on, play nice," Hailey said.

Parker leaned close. "This is what it's like to have siblings, Hailey. Get used to it."

Hailey beamed. She had siblings now. It was fantastic to be included with such a tight-knit family.

The song ended and the four of them walked off the dance floor together.

"So the wedding is in August?" Mad asked. "That's usually a slow time for you."

"Sure," Josh said.

Hailey shook her head. "Oh, no, no, no. Are you kidding me? I need a *year* to plan our wedding. It's going to be the perfect wedding to top all weddings."

Josh let out a long low groan.

Hailey parked a hand on her hip. "I'm a wedding planner featured in *Bride Special*. I'm planning a wedding for royalty. My wedding has to be the best." Prince Phillip had called yesterday with an apology for overstepping and had even been gracious enough to invite Josh to the royal weddings for Princess Silvia in the States and on Villroy Island. Hailey had accepted both the apology and the invitation. Josh was cool with it. Not that he wanted to see Phillip again. He just wanted to be with her.

They were pretty much inseparable now, spending every night together. Tomorrow Josh and his cutie dog, Max, would be moving into her place. Their apartments were equally small, but hers was cheaper and closer to both of their jobs.

Josh took her hand from her hip and held it. "Our wedding will be the best. But won't that be expensive? I mean, trying to top a royal wedding."

She lifted her chin. "I'm very creative and have a lot of connections. I'll pull it in on time, on budget, and it'll be the event of the decade, no, the century!"

Josh stared at her for a long moment, opened his mouth, and then closed it.

"What?"

He framed her face with his hands. "You are magnificent, my warrior princess."

She wrapped her arms around his waist. "So are you, my warrior beast."

He gazed into her eyes, letting her know he wanted her

badly. She gazed back, letting him know she was on board, but shouldn't they stick around for a bit since it was their parents' wedding reception?

His hand slid under her hair, cupping her neck and pulling her close. He kissed her, smiling against her lips. Warmth stole through her.

They smiled at each other, basking in warmth, an electric attraction, and so much love, both of them knowing they were meant to be.

Dear Readers,

I couldn't resist writing the wedding planner's wedding. Catch up with Josh and Hailey and all of the Happy Endings Book Club gang one year later in *A Happy Endings Wedding*!

A Happy Endings Wedding

Hailey Adams and Josh Campbell are finally tying the knot! Not only are they launching the new destination-wedding venue on Villroy Island, two major bridal magazines are documenting every detail. Hailey, an up-and-coming wedding planner, is determined to make her wedding *the* perfect wedding right down to coordinating her canine fur-babies' outfits.

Except there seems to be a teensy problem with the wedding gown—there isn't one.

And the rings have disappeared.

And somehow the wedding venue was double-booked.

Things go horribly downhill from there. With Hailey *and* the wedding falling apart at the seams, it's up to Josh to put it all back together. What does a gruff former soldier know about weddings? Hailey is about to find out.

Sign up for my newsletter and never miss a new release! kyliegilmore.com/newsletter

ALSO BY KYLIE GILMORE

Unleashed Romance <<steamy romcoms with dogs!

Fetching (Book 1)

Dashing (Book 2)

Sporting (Book 3)

Toying (Book 4)

Blazing (Book 5)

Chasing (Book 6)

Daring (Book 7)

Leading (Book 8)

Racing (Book 9)

Loving (Book 10)

The Clover Park Series <<brothers who put family first!

The Opposite of Wild (Book 1)

Daisy Does It All (Book 2)

Bad Taste in Men (Book 3)

Kissing Santa (Book 4)

Restless Harmony (Book 5)

Not My Romeo (Book 6)

Rev Me Up (Book 7)

An Ambitious Engagement (Book 8)

Clutch Player (Book 9)

A Tempting Friendship (Book 10)

Clover Park Bride: Nico and Lily's Wedding

A Valentine's Day Gift (Book 11)

Maggie Meets Her Match (Book 12)

The Clover Park STUDS series <<hawt geeks who unleash into studs!

Almost Over It (Book 1)

Almost Married (Book 2)

Almost Fate (Book 3)

Almost in Love (Book 4)

Almost Romance (Book 5)

Almost Hitched (Book 6)

Happy Endings Book Club Series <<the Campbell family and a romance book club collide!

Hidden Hollywood (Book 1)

Inviting Trouble (Book 2)

So Revealing (Book 3)

Formal Arrangement (Book 4)

Bad Boy Done Wrong (Book 5)

Mess With Me (Book 6)

Resisting Fate (Book 7)

Chance of Romance (Book 8)

Wicked Flirt (Book 9)

An Inconvenient Plan (Book 10)

A Happy Endings Wedding (Book 11)

The Rourkes Series <<swoonworthy princes and kickass princesses!

Royal Catch (Book 1)

Royal Hottie (Book 2)

Royal Darling (Book 3)

Royal Charmer (Book 4)

Royal Player (Book 5)

Royal Shark (Book 6)

Rogue Prince (Book 7)

Rogue Gentleman (Book 8)

Rogue Rascal (Book 9)

Rogue Angel (Book 10)

Rogue Devil (Book 11)

Rogue Beast (Book 12)

Check out my website for the most up-to-date list of my books:
kyliegilmore.com/books

ABOUT THE AUTHOR

Kylie Gilmore is the *USA Today* bestselling author of the Unleashed Romance series, the Rourkes series, the Happy Endings Book Club series, the Clover Park series, and the Clover Park STUDS series. She writes humorous romance that makes you laugh, cry, and reach for a cold glass of water.

Kylie lives in New York with her family, two cats, and a nutso dog. When she's not writing, reading hot romance, or dutifully taking notes at writing conferences, you can find her flexing her muscles all the way to the high cabinet for her secret chocolate stash.

Sign up for Kylie's Newsletter and get a FREE book! kyliegilmore.com/newsletter

For text alerts on Kylie's new releases, text KYLIE to the number (888) 707-3025. (US only)

For more fun stuff check out Kylie's website https://www.kyliegilmore.com.

Thanks for reading *An Inconvenient Plan*. I hope you enjoyed it. Would you like to know about new releases? You can sign up for my new release email list at kyliegilmore.com/newsletter. I promise not to clog your inbox! Only new release info, sales, and some fun giveaways.

I love to hear from readers! You can find me at:
    kyliegilmore.com
    Instagram.com/kyliegilmore
    Facebook.com/KylieGilmoreToo
    Twitter @KylieGilmoreToo

If you liked Josh and Hailey's story, please leave a review on your favorite retailer's website or Goodreads. Thank you.

www.ingramcontent.com/pod-product-compliance
Lightning Source LLC
Chambersburg PA
CBHW071257190726
48292CB00007B/2573

Hot on the heels of one adventure comes another: Martin's sister Beth is reported as having died in Spain, so Kat and Pepper accompany Martin to the large, rambling house in which she perished.

But why is host Vincenzio behaving so strangely? What is making the unearthly screeching sounds late at night? And what is the secret of the mazed garden, complete with ancient standing stones?

As the incongruous and unfindable clock tower ticks away the seconds, Kat finds herself trapped and up against a foe who is determined to see her go the same way as Beth.

Can Kat uncover the secrets before it's too late?

A TALE OF HORROR FROM THE AUTHOR OF *ZOMBIES AT TIFFANY'S*, *KAT ON A HOT TIN AIRSHIP*, *WHAT'S DEAD PUSSYKAT* AND *KAT OF GREEN TENTACLES*.